Running from Scissors

A RUNNING STORE MYSTERY

T.C. WESCOTT

Better**Mousetrap**
— BOOKS —

Text Copyright © 2018 by T.C. Wescott
All rights reserved

Published by Better Mousetrap Books, Oklahoma

ISBN-13: 978-1-7321358-0-2

Cover design and book layout by Ebooklaunch.com

First Edition

Also by T.C. Wescott

Slay Bells:
A Christmas Village Mystery

(COMING NOVEMBER 2018)

For Ellen

ONE

Today's the day. I'm going to kill her, I think to myself as I pull my purse from under my arm.

I reach in and wiggle my fingers around until they find their target, never taking my eyes off the woman in front of me. *I could shoot her or run her down with my car. No, somebody else's car. A rental? Too obvious. Heck, I'm spoiled for choice!*

I tear my eyes away to look at the item in my hand. *Knife, hired assassin, force of nature. Sky's the limit! Whatever your pleasure, just name your poison! Ha! Hmmm… Poison. Now there's an idea.*

"Is something wrong, Lacy?" says the lady behind the register. She says it again before I snap out of my angry daydream and remember why I am here.

"Sorry, Jess, just trying to keep my head from exploding. Or somebody else's if I get my hands on them."

I still drip sweat from a three-mile run and regret not swinging by the car for a towel. I can see myself in the mirror behind the counter and realize I look more like a zombie apocalypse survivor than a relatively fit runner in her mid-forties.

It could be worse, I reassure myself. *I could look like one of the zombies.*

"Another fruitful run under the auspices of Marlene, I take it?" Jess asks with a knowing wink. She knows whenever I speak of murder, I speak of Marlene.

"Yeah, fruitful," I reply. "If I had any fruit I would have thrown it at her head."

Jess leans across the counter toward me. "No fruit on the course." She now seems more like a bartender than a sales person at a running store. "A couple of guys in the Chamber of Commerce come in here every couple of months and pay top dollar for our best shoes. I don't know what they do with them, because the old ones still look new two months later. But I'm pretty sure Marti doesn't want them stepping in tomatoes if it can be helped."

"I was thinking more of a pitted fruit. Harder impact." We laugh. The air conditioning cools my skin and Jessica's ease of manner has the same effect on my mood. I realize if she is the bartender in this scenario, I must be the angry drunk.

The purpose for my trip into Run For It is two-fold: an after-run touch of sanity and a product replacement request. A utility belt I purchased the day before has been slipping over my hips during my morning run, forcing me to remove and carry it.

A lot of runners eschew a belt to carry their water, snacks, and phone, but I like how wearing it makes me feel like a superhero. I don't feel very heroic with it bouncing around like a snake in my hand while I run, so I ask if I can trade it in for one with better adjustment capabilities.

The other running stores in Cedar Mill or in nearby Tulsa—there are four altogether—wouldn't have considered the request. But Marti and Chase, the proprietors and themselves runners, understand and sympathize with the needs of their customers.

Martina Reynolds and her husband, Chase, opened Run For It five years ago, but it wouldn't find me until last year when I moved to Cedar Mill following my divorce. Cedar Mill, Oklahoma, is a medium-size city with a small-town feel and coming from Kansas City it was just the kind of culture shock I felt I needed.

Hello, my name is Lacy Purdy: Divorced white female, frequent runner, and still a card-carrying member of the Neilsen Rating's preferred 18-49 demographic, though my card expires in four years. In my previous life I helped my husband, Curtis, run his insurance agency. By 'help' I mean I did all the administrative work that actually got us paid. But I was treated like an employee. In fact, Curtis would often refer to me as his 'secretary' when talking to clients. He said it made him sound bigger and more important and would impress a would-be insurance buyer. I wondered if it was the client or his own ego he was trying to impress.

Curtis's forty-sixth birthday came with an already burgeoned compulsion to completely change his sedentary life style. I had to admit it was a good change and I eventually followed him off the couch and to the gym. While he stretched and grunted on the equipment I made the rounds of swimming classes, Zumba, and Yoga. I even spent a few months with an enthusiastic personal trainer under whose gestapo-like regimen I developed a nasty case of Piriformis Syndrome; if I don't do regular stretches of my left leg, it will feel like there's a little gremlin in my butt pulling on my muscles and thumping my nerves.

While I took some time off from the gym to recuperate and keep Curtis's agency running, he pitched woo to a rail-thin, granola-chomping gym bunny who'd been all of twelve years old when Curtis pitched me the same woo. If I sound a tad bitter it's because I am. It wasn't a great marriage, but it was a good one, and I figured that was more than most folks get. Now, I suppose, I'm 'most folks'—single, over forty, no kids, and starting over.

Curtis and I visited Cedar Mill twice in recent years for the annual Mistletoe Marathon in December. Why a state with such unpredictable winters should risk scheduling a major marathon in December is beyond me, but I became charmed by the town the moment I breathed its air. And if there's one thing besides a lingering—though, I like to think, dissipating—bitterness I brought with me from our final years together, it was the joy I found in running.

I also possess a wealth of knowledge of the insurance industry and particular skills in administrative assisting. Skills I now put to use working for a wonderful couple operating their own private agency here in Cedar Mill. *Thanks, Curtis!*

It's hard for a runner to explain to the uninitiated why we run. You either get it or you don't. It's not necessarily for the health benefits, even if that's why some of us started out. Sure, your cardio will be great, but you'll spend a week out of each month walking like an invalid who's lost her crutches. You'll need to eat a lot of carbs to run strong, so don't expect the pounds to fall off. And you'd better be rich or prepared to live frugally, because you will spend more money on shoes than you ever considered possible.

I don't presume what motivates me is what motivates all runners, but what I feel I'm doing is chasing 'can't'.

Yes, I'm Chasing Can't.

When you begin running you'll find yourself hitting an invisible wall you can't push through. Your lungs will burn; your legs will scream. If you decide never to do something so foolish again, you're normal. If you go to bed knowing you'll get up and do it all over again just to break that wall, then congratulations— you're a runner. And the more you run, the more walls you break through. You find yourself having to run farther and push harder to find your Can't—the point where you cannot continue. The sense of personal victory that comes from proving yourself wrong becomes addictive and the better you get, the harder it is to find your Can't.

The bling doesn't hurt, either. I hang the medals I get at the end of each sponsored run on a wall in my bedroom, positioned so they're the first things I see upon waking. At the rate I'm going, I'll soon need more walls.

One of my favorite perks of running is something Oklahoma has in abundance—wind. I didn't used to think too much about wind, except what effect it might be having on my hair, but since I became a runner I can't walk outside without noticing it. A runner learns to read the wind, to use it to their advantage, or how to overcome its obstacles. Since coming to Cedar Mill I've learned you can taste the air, and the air tastes different depending on where you happen to be.

I expected to get plenty of fresh air running in Cedar Mill. What I did not expect—what no one in my running group could have expected—is that a woman would disappear into thin air before our very eyes only to reappear days later as a corpse.

But I'm getting ahead of myself.

TWO

I don't want to burden Jessica with my woes over Marlene (I have another set of ears in mind for that), so I exchange my belt for one better fitting to my fussy form and off I head into the warm July sun. I stop by my car to drop off the belt and exchange my sweaty bandana for a quick comb-through and a hair tie. I won't need my car where I am going.

A walk along Cedar Mill's Main Street is always a treat. No matter how many times you make the trek you can't help but be charmed by the vibrant storefronts, the clean-swept sidewalks decorated with chalk art, and the rows of small concrete gardens surrounded by wrought-iron benches.

The only unbecoming feature is the crosswalk squawk box ordering 'Wait!' when you press the red button. Fortunately, this is a one-squawk trip as my destination is less than a block ahead of me.

Nestled snug on one side by a bridal store that in a past life was a two-screen movie theater, and on the other side by a country and western knickknack shop that once or twice served as a bakery, sits a quaint affair the town elders might still recall as the Ben Franklin

Five & Dime of their youth. For the last generation it has served the literary needs of Cedar Mill as its most quirky and idiosyncratic independent bookseller.

The front door is adorned with a new book poster—an animated skeleton wearing a deer-stalker hat and smoking a pipe whilst battling a ferocious werewolf (or is it supposed to be a Baskerville hound?). In blood red horror font the title reads *Sherlock's Bones*. The little bell above the door jingles as I enter.

"Yo, Stax," I say loud enough to be heard but not so loud as to frighten any browsers.

"I'm sorry, but we don't allow pets here," an assertive, almost shrill voice sounds out from amidst the rows of shelves. "Is it raining outside?"

Before I finish rolling my eyes, a short, brown-skinned woman shaped like a chicken nugget emerges from behind a row titled 'Esoterica'. Her black curly hair is done up in a messy bun and her trademark Buddy Holly glasses rest precariously on the tip of her nose. That's Stax.

"Oh, Lacy, it's you," Stax says, feigning surprise. "I couldn't see you, but I could smell you, and I figured a big wet dog must have wandered in here."

Juanita 'Stax' Best is in her mid-thirties and grew up in the bookstore owned by her parents, Joseph and Patricia. Unable to have children of their own, the Bests adopted Stax when she was two. A few years later they added Larry to the family and Stax became a big sister. To look at Stax is to know she's of Hispanic heritage, but her adoptive family is not and she feels no affinity whatsoever with the customs of her heritage. She says she didn't know guacamole came from avocados until I casually mentioned it while we were dining (against her will) at an El Tequila. You can never tell with Stax.

She is a walking contradiction in more ways than one. Her parents opened their bookstore in the late eighties and adorably named it Best's Cellar. They operated it themselves until their retirement six months ago when they passed it to their children. Because Larry worked as a fry cook a few times in his career, Stax got the idea of turning a corner of the store into a small café for Larry to run while she handled the responsibilities of the bookstore. Despite protestations from her family, including Larry, that an occasional fry cook does not a head chef make, she felt certain she was on the right track.

To advertise the café, she changed the name of the store to Read It or Eat It. I thought it was a deplorable name sounding more like a command than an invite. I made the mistake only once of conveying my opinion to Stax. Her mind was made up.

The makeover, to her credit, is working. The eight tables in the café are rarely full when I come by, but they're never empty, and Stax's emphasis on carrying books one cannot get at the Barnes & Noble in Tulsa earns her a small but loyal and growing clientele. In spite of her undeniable instincts for the business, Stax claims not to have personally read a book since high school.

One would be wrong if they assumed she earned the nickname 'Stax' from having grown up among the stacks of books; or because of her rather substantial chest. I came to learn the name is a diminutive of 'Short Stack', which is what Larry called her when they were children. She was short then, and, at barely five-feet-tall on her tiptoes, she's short now. As the second child adopted into the Best family, Stax in turn christened Larry 'Second Best'.

"You were missed today, Stax," I say.

"If you came here to lie to me, Stretch, the least you can do is help me put some of these new books out." With that, she disappears again.

I occasionally help Stax out when she gets in new shipments. Although I'm only six inches taller than her, she likes to call me 'Stretch', particularly when she needs help with the top shelves.

When we first became friendly, I agreed to join her in the stacks primarily to satisfy my curiosity as to how such a brash, offensive person could at the same time be so generous. Stax was the first one to take me under her wing when I started the training classes at Run For It. Spending time with her taught me her biting rhetoric is more defensive than offensive. It also taught me she is a wonderful friend to those who are willing to make an effort with her.

"Here," she says, handing me a small but heavy box of books. The tape was cut and I spied the 'Royal Mail' insignia on one of the flaps, telling me it came from the UK. "Put these on the top shelf, lest some little old lady wanders over here from the Cozy Mystery aisle and finds herself scandalized."

I pull a couple of the books out and find myself gazing upon the images of dark, cobbled streets and a faceless man in a cloak and top hat. *Deconstructing Jack* by Simon D. Wood, *One Autumn in Whitechapel* by M.P. Priestley. All the books in the box pertain to Victorian London's real-life bogeyman, Jack the Ripper.

"You think someone who reads Madison Johns would find these offensive?" I ask.

Stax nods. "Never fails. Put a cat on the cover and they'll read bloody murder all day long. Put a picture of a real corpse in the book and they turn green and run."

"I'm not sure I can blame them." I'm a rabid consumer of mystery fiction but can't remember the last time I cast an eye to the True Crime section. "Wait, these books have pictures? Of Jack the Ripper's victims?"

Stax snatches the copy of *The Ripper Haunts* by Michael Hawley from my hands as though to protect me from it. "Yep," she says with authority. "They ain't in color, but trust me, they're pretty gruesome. Particularly the one of the last victim." At this she shivers.

"Wait, I thought you didn't read the books you sell."

"I gotta inspect the inventory, don't I?"

I try to ignore the sheepish grin she works hard to swallow, but it is contagious. "I don't know what I would do without you, Stax."

"You'd sure as hell run a lot slower. Speaking of which, how was the run today? I hate missing Saturdays, but I need these books up before tomorrow. For some reason, blood and guts is popular with the after-church crowd."

For the paltry sum of $30 twice a year, Run For It offers training programs for runners of all paces and abilities. There's the Level 1 pace group largely comprised of experienced runners who maintain an above-average pace. Most of them have numerous marathons and ultramarathons under their belt. The Level 2 group, of which I am a member, is made up of the less experienced runners. Level 3 is for individuals with a much slower pace, mostly seniors and the mildly disabled who enjoy the lifestyle and the exercise but whose bodies won't allow them to do much beyond walking.

Most of us in Level 2 are still running 5k (five-kilometer) and 10k runs as we work to master our pace and endurance. I'm currently training to run my first half-marathon in December, still six months away, while hopefully racking up a new 10k PR, or 'personal record', along the way. Tomorrow will be my first trail run and I'm hoping not to trip on a rock and twist my ankle.

Stax could run with the Level 1 group if she wanted, but she chooses to run with Level 2. She says she'd rather be the fastest runner in a slow group than the slowest runner in a fast group, but I suspect she likes to be where she's most needed.

Seeing Stax this morning so boosts my spirits that I don't want to broach the subject of Marlene, or that I am considering leaving the running group. But time and tide wait for no woman, and Stax sure as heck isn't going to wait for me to feel like talking.

So, I talk. I tell her how the run started out as normal, with Marlene and her two minions—Gretchen and Carly—at the head of the pack and me standing as far away as possible. Marlene, our group's run leader, gave her usual sermon about what she expects of us in terms of how long our running intervals would be in proportion to walking. It was only a three-mile training run but she approached it with all the drama of a competitive relay.

When Marlene speaks to a group, even a small group such as ours, she talks over everyone's head without making eye contact, as though she were a queen addressing her subjects. This led to her being dubbed 'Marlene, the Queen of Mean' in whispers well out of her hearing.

However, I'm a big girl with my big girl capris on, so if a little pomposity is all I have to deal with, I'll brush it off and enjoy my run. But after a condescending reminder to the group to remember to hydrate before, during, and after a run, she motions towards the back of the group where I stand. She points in my direction and, after pretending to struggle for my name—she whispers it enough behind my back—says it loud and clear. Now, for the first time, she makes eye contact.

I'm not one for melodrama, and goodness knows I despise a pregnant pause, but I have to stop in my rant to Stax to catch my breath before quoting—not paraphrasing, mind you, but quoting down to the last syllable—what this parking lot princess had the audacity to say to me.

"Spit it out, woman!" Stax barks, my two-second breather being a couple of seconds too long for her nerves to handle. "I don't think I could hate Marlene more than I already do, but I'm perfectly willing to be proved wrong."

I take a deep breath and dive in. "She pointed at me and said 'Um, it's Lacy right? Yes, Lacy. Listen, I've been talking to a couple of girls at Leicester's Deli where I often lunch about joining our group here at Run For It. As you know, our run takes us by their shop. I have a feeling they'll be watching us today so, *if you feel you can manage it*, please pick your feet up when you run past, m'kay? I don't want any of us to be embarrassed.'" Big exhale.

Stax stares up at me, chin on chest, eyes burning over the black rim of her glasses. I wonder if I made a mistake by telling her. I'm imaging Stax confronting Marlene and a giant mushroom cloud rising from the ground where our blighted nemesis once stood.

"She told you to pick up your feet?" Stax says, her voice a cold burn. "She called you an embarrassment?"

Screw it, I decide. *Bring on the mushroom cloud.* "Yes."

Stax removes her glasses. This means business.

"She says 'where I often lunch'? So, she doesn't *eat* lunch, she … lunches?"

"Yep, she's a luncher."

"That alone deserves a reality check."

I can see Stax is as bothered by Marlene's treatment of me as am I. For some reason it makes me emotional and I grab her in a hug. I feel her body stiffen under my arms and I worry perhaps I crossed one of her many boundaries. But she softens and returns the embrace.

"Geez, I wish some of the men around town were this easy," is her flippant response.

"I want you to know, Stax, that no matter what happens, I'm going to keep you and a couple of the other girls in my life."

I feel her hands on my shoulders, then a push. I am again staring at those big brown eyes over thick black frames.

"What is this, your Last Will and Testament?"

"No, but I am thinking about quitting the program."

"Seriously? Screw Marlene; you love running. And regardless of what she says, you're quite good at it."

"I don't plan to stop running. But I might pursue my options at one of the other stores, like Run City. Or maybe you can be my Mr. Miyagi?"

"If you quit because of that over-the-hill Mean MILF, the only thing I'll wax on and wax off will be your eyebrows. No, huh uh… we're heading over there right now."

She grabs my arm and starts to march up the aisle, but I resist.

"I don't think that's a good idea, Stax. Not while you're hot like this."

"Trust me, I'm worse if you leave me simmering."

"Look, I don't want to make waves. She's been running there a lot longer than I have and if she's who Marti and Chase want in charge, then…"

"You think Marlene acts this way around Marti and Chase? Not a chance. Around Marti she's all 'Oh, you're such a brilliant businesswoman. What an entrepreneur!' and around Chase she's all eyes and legs. Don't think I haven't had many a word with Marti about her. But look at me. I'm like the polar opposite of Marlene, so I'm sure they think I have some green

streak for her. But, now, if *you* were to say something…
well, that might make a difference."

"Me? I don't see the connection."

"Oh, please. Marlene has that whole homecoming-queen-twenty-years-later thing going on and you're like Jane Fonda when she did *9 to 5*."

"Wait, didn't she play like a church mouse in that movie?"

"Okay, when she was doing Jazzercise or whatever. Fonda in her forties. Point being, with you around, Marlene doesn't feel so Queen Bee-ey. And that's what this is all about."

"I don't know, you're probably right. But it is what it is, so maybe I should take the hint."

A little ink-smudged finger flies up in my face. "No, no hints. Instead, you're going to take her advice and you're going to pick up those feet and march with me to Run For It where we'll find Marlene. Once we do, you can watch me pick up this foot right here and shove it right up her—"

"Okay, fine," I say, exasperated. "We'll go. But no feet! I'll see if Marti has a few minutes and I'll tell her what happened. We'll go from there."

Stax drops her shoulders and appears to contemplate for a moment. "Fair enough, but no promises. I don't mind ruining a new pair of shoes for a good cause."

Larry agrees to watch the store and off we go. Short though they might be, Stax's legs are limber and toned, and I have to break into a short jog more than once just to keep up.

When the crosswalk squawk box yells at us to 'Wait!' I think to myself perhaps that isn't such bad advice.

THREE

Trudging along behind Stax I see Run For It looming large and moving closer. Normally a beacon towards which I sail, I now find myself searching for an anchor to slow my approach. It doesn't help that my run today (or maybe the stress of my confrontation with Marlene) irked the little gremlin in my butt and now my Piriformis Syndrome is sending flashes of pain undulating up and down my leg.

Marti and Chase Reynolds purchased what would become Run For It from the city for a song. When they got their hands on it, the nondescript box of a building was a derelict savings and loan bank. But there is a progressive commerce movement in the town and the Reynoldses took full advantage of it.

The running store sits behind rose bushes and a corner rock garden, surrounded by a parking lot that serves both it and the small strip mall running behind the store's building. The strip mall was constructed in soft-toned red brick to resemble Run For It's already standing façade. An ornate covered sitting area outside the side entrance relieves the building of its boxed appearance and give it an added sense of dimension. Wall-sized display windows along the street side attract foot traffic and draw attention from the drivers meandering along at the 25-mph speed limit. To see it is to want to be in it, runner or not.

Stax tromps up towards the side entrance with me lagging in tow. I've psyched myself up for a heart to heart with Marti and Chase but I cross my fingers that Marlene did not lounge around after the run.

As I come around a large family van I see the obnoxiously bright yellow Prius resting in its shadow. Only one woman in town owns a car like this. Only one *would* (it must be a custom job). Next time I'll cross my toes as well.

Stax enters the store a few yards ahead of me. I imagine her breaking into a full-throated scream upon sight of Marlene. Or worse, her stumpy little body rocketing through the store—walls of shoes and racks of headbands exploding in her wake—and slamming home into Marlene's gravity defying bosom (also a custom job?). I hope I'm not about to be an accomplice to murder.

I grip the edge of the door so hard I feel the mushy foam lining compress under my palm. I poke my head in and brace myself for whatever might be transpiring on the other side. I'm greeted by silence.

Stax stands inside the door to my left, her arms crossed in front of her and one foot tapping the cream-colored tiles. Whether by coincidence of timing or because they saw Stax I couldn't say, but Gretchen and Carly exit through the front door, *sans* Marlene. They remain outside with their backs to the display windows, talking.

Billy, a young man who works part-time at the store, explains to a hipster couple the difference between compression sleeves and compression socks. Jessica chats with a customer at the front desk.

I ponder my foolishness in allowing my imagination to run away with me. My gaze rests too long on Jessica, who, feeling the weight of it, turns and smiles at me. The customer, a small older lady with wavy grey hair, looks my way as well and says 'Afternoon, Miss Purdy.'

Her familiarity surprises me but I manage a quick 'Afternoon' in return as I try to place her in my mind. I can feel it pushing to the fore of my brain when Stax tugs at my sleeve. This is her cue to me she wants to whisper. She enjoys the thrill of a secret and likes to whisper a lot, but for all of her practice, she is terrible at it. She whispers in a low tone that carries an echo all its own, and because of our height difference, I inevitably bend down to give her my ear. Not the most inconspicuous of exchanges.

"Chase ain't here and Marlene's in the brault with Marti," she echoes as I twist myself down to her position. "She's not only psycho but psychic as well. She must have figured what your move would be."

My move? I planned to quit the program and run from another store. If Marlene is psychically linked with anyone, it's Stax. Even an imbecile would know if you treat people like garbage it's you who eventually gets taken to the curb. No doubt Marlene is trying to get ahead of the damage.

"Let's get out of here," I whisper back.

"No chance!" Stax bellows into my eardrum, dropping all pretense of a whisper. "You can play the wallflower if you want, but when I leave here, it'll be Stax: 1, Bully: 0."

She punctuates her proclamation with a defiant nod and I do my best to melt into the wallpaper.

A few eyes dart our way but everyone pretends not to hear our strange conversation. I look again to the older woman talking with Jessica. She steps back from the counter to reveal her distinctive garb—a pair of fading striped shorts reaching halfway down to her knees. I now recognize her as being a member of the Level 3 group running—or, rather, walking—from the store. They come and go at different times from us but we often pass them leaving as we're returning.

The lady and I are not acquainted but her outdated clothes make her the subject of snickers. While I would never make fun behind someone's back, I must admit I've speculated about her situation. I've wondered if perhaps she owns a retro clothing boutique. Or shops at one. Such things are trendy nowadays, albeit not in the running world. It occurs to me she is probably on a fixed income and simply doesn't possess the means to pay the high store prices for new running apparel.

I cannot see the brault from my vantage point as it is tucked into a recess on the lower level of the store. When renovating the building from bank to running store, Chase and Marti discovered if they weren't willing to take down an entire side wall and hire in serious equipment to remove the giant steel bank vault door, they'd have to find a way to embrace it. Making the most of it, they painted and papered the inside of the vault, installed two small dressing rooms in its back, and displayed the store's impressive selection of sports bras. Marti referred to it as the 'bra vault' and someone—there's no consensus as to whom—truncated it to 'Brault' and the term stuck.

The huge door always remains open, and the locking mechanism was removed in the event some wisenheimer decided to close it. It is a popular spot for quick meetings or small talk.

Two new voices join the quiet murmur of chitchat in the store. Marti and Marlene. They are moving in our direction. As they lift their feet to make the single step that separates the floor in two levels, I catch a snippet of their hushed exchange. Both women mention the word 'scissors'.

As the women come within a couple of yards from where we stand, Marlene spots Stax and myself and grinds to a halt. Marti deflates. She pushes her mouth up into a smile for our benefit, but there is a telling pause there. She looks as though Marlene has drained her tank and seeing me zaps her remaining fumes.

Stax's brown skin turns a disturbing shade of red, a teakettle left too long on the burner. My instincts tell me to take the lead here in hopes of restraining my friend, but I don't move fast enough.

Stax sucks in air and stabs the air with her finger as though in front of her hangs an invisible effigy of Marlene. "You are *not* going to call my friend an embarrassment. Do you understand me?"

Marlene, normally indomitable to the point of pretension, now stands before us a rattled mess with red eyes that speak of recent tears. She shakes her head in response to Stax's admonishment and attempts to respond, but only sputters "I didn't mean...I didn't mean to."

I want to talk it out but Stax is having none of it. "You know what you meant and you meant what you said. Thanks to you, Lacy wants to quit the program and take her business to another store. I don't think you had that in mind when you made Marlene run leader, was it?" She directs this rhetorical question at Marti.

I never said I would stop being a paying customer of Run For It, but Stax is going for full effect. I want to wiggle my nose and disappear to an island somewhere.

All life in the store stops to watch us. Billy, now showing his young couple the store's range of therapeutic shoe inserts, clears his throat as a sign for us to keep it down. Jessica gawks in rapt attention from her place behind the register. Only the older lady, perusing a rack of gluten-free energy snacks, seems not to notice the heated exchange.

Marti steps forward as though to prevent any possible escalation. "Juanita, I got this."

Everyone respects Marti greatly, including Stax. Not only is she one of the fastest female runners in the state, she has great compassion for runners of all abilities, almost to a fault. I expect Stax will cool down when Marti assures her she has the matter under control. No dice.

"You've 'got this,' do you? You mean you have *her* back, don't you?"

Now it's Marti's turn to try and keep her cool. "Marlene told me what she did today. And Lacy, I'm sorry that happened to you. I was mortified when she told me, but Marlene has taken responsibility and you'll both be happy to know she's resigned her position as run leader."

She what?

A heavy silence fogs the room. Marti looks disappointed and I want to cry. Stax's mouth hangs open and her eyes freeze big under a furrowed brow, as though the confusion overtaking her indignation forced the circuits of her brain to give up and fry out.

Marlene breaks the impasse and moves towards me. "Lacy, I'm sorry for how horrible I was to you. I know how I am and how I can be. But I was out of line this morning. I haven't been myself for the past week. The scissors and… there's just too many things wrong."

To my absolute shock she gives me a hug. And weeps in my ear. Then she is gone, out the door behind me.

Stax and I look at each other and I can tell she is as lost as I am. We turn to Marti for enlightenment.

"You know, you two could have called me, or at least held your horses until we could talk in private." Her soft voice drips with reprimand I'm ashamed to say was not out of place.

"We came here to talk to you in private," I offer meekly. "Everything else just… kind of happened."

Stax pushes air through her lips, making a 'Pfffft' sound. "How were we supposed to know she'd choose this moment to grow a soul?"

"I'll admit Marlene's a little closed off," replies Marti. "All right, she's a snob. But she's a good runner and people listen to her. Look, I don't want this to get around, but she thinks someone is stalking her. She's at her wits' end and I'm afraid you, Lacy, were the unintended victim of this. But if what Marlene says is true, *she's* also a victim."

Marti's sympathy for all sides is obvious and infectious. I feel like a total heel for my part in all of this.

"Well, crapcakes," says Stax. "Had I known all this I wouldn't have put her on blast. But that's what happens when I only get half the story."

I was about to set the record straight for Marti when a piercing cry burst our sad little bubble. It came from the parking lot.

Time stops. My breath catches in my chest. Being closest to the door I run out first, everyone else on my heels. Gretchen and Carly round the corner from their perch in front of the building. Nothing appears amiss at first glance, but a soft, whimpering sound draws our attention to the bright yellow Prius.

I run to the Prius and look through the window, expecting to find Marlene crumpled in the seat, crying over our confrontation, milking it for all it's worth. But aside from a few bags and a pair of heels, the car is empty.

"Marlene, what's wrong?" asks Marti. She stands to my right, behind the car. I join her and find Marlene, down on her knees, a simpering wreck.

Something happened to her out here. But what? Marti poses this question to her and all Marlene says in response is 'scissors'. I count this as the third time in the last twenty minutes I've heard this word. But what could scissors possibly have to do with all this drama?

"Look!" Stax cries out, right under my ear again. "In the tire!"

Sure enough. There it is, jutting from the back right tire. A shiny pair of scissors.

Marti puts her arm around Marlene and ushers her back into the store. Gretchen and Carly stare daggers at Stax and myself and follow to comfort their friend. Stax promises to call me later and pedals back to the bookstore. I find myself alone in the parking lot with a scissor-wielding who-knows-what.

"Quite the afternoon we're having, wouldn't you say, Miss Purdy?"

The older lady in the outdated running garb steps out from under the overhang and walks toward me. She must have held back when the rest of us ran out.

"I wouldn't call it uneventful," I say, extending my hand as she draws close. The firmness of her grip surprises me. "I'm sorry, but if we've been introduced before my mind must be failing me."

She smiles warmly and holds eye contact. I find myself trying not to blink.

"No, we've not been introduced. I suppose I've seen you around so much, though, I feel we've met. I must have picked your name up in harmless eavesdropping and it remained locked in the old cerebrum. So much nonsense in there fighting for space, one can know something and not know how one knows it. Do you find this is so?"

I have no idea what the woman is going on about, so I play along and try to be witty. "I suspect I still have plenty of elbow room in my brain, so an overabundance of information has never been a problem for me."

"Oh, so you're saying you're an airhead?"

I confess I didn't know how to answer her, though the answer is clearly 'no'. I look at her for a sign she is being whimsical, but she stands with her head cocked and her brow turned inquisitively inward.

"Erm…no, not exactly."

"Oh, ha! My apologies. I'm wasn't supposed to take you literally, was I? I'm such a curious creature, you must forgive me. But it's been a genuine pleasure finally making your acquaintance, Miss Purdy."

"Please, call me Lacy. I haven't been called Miss Purdy since... well, ever. And you are?"

"Me? Oh, fuddy duddy. With all this fuss, I've forgotten my manners. My name is Ruby. Ruby Maplethorpe."

"Well, it's certainly a pleasure to meet you, Miss Maplethorpe."

"I see no harm in familiarity, what with us both making spectacles of ourselves today. Please, Lacy, call me Ruby."

Did she just say I made a spectacle of myself?

"Thank you, Ruby. I see you around the store from time to time. We'll have to chat again. But right now, I really must be off."

Ruby waves a hand in front of her face as though to signal she is not offended by my abrupt termination of our strange conversation. Although she gives no indication that she, herself, considers it either strange or awkward.

The thick lenses of her glasses are wrapped in designer frames that couldn't have cost less than $700. So much for my theory of a fixed income. It is only the first time Ruby Maplethorpe will prove to me that people are often much more than they first appear.

"You go on about your day, young lady. But I would very much like it if you would come by my house this evening. Would eight-o'clock be all right with you?"

"I'm sorry, did you say you want me to come to your house tonight?"

"Yes, that's what I said."

"Might I ask what for?"

"I believe I have the solution to your problem."

"My problem?"

"Yes, indeed."

"Well, maybe some other time. Tonight, I plan to rest."

"Oh, for the trail run tomorrow? I'll be there as well. That's why it must be tonight. Oh, look at the time. I must be off. I'll see you at eight, Lacy. Ta Ta!"

Off she goes. I watch her get into a little Taurus about fifteen years old with paint as clean and shiny as the day it rolled off the assembly line.

In hopes of putting this strange day in the rearview mirror, I plan to spend the evening enjoying a pick-me-up cocktail of *House Hunters* reruns, a heaping bowl of Fettuccine Alfredo (with mushrooms. Yum!), and a nightcap of Lorna Barrett. All the murders in her fictional Book Town notwithstanding, I like to imagine I live in a place where I'm surrounded on all sides by books. Stax doesn't know how lucky she's got it.

My evening promises more weirdness than my already weird day as I am obliged to spend part of it in the home of a woman I don't know who thinks I'm an airhead and promises to solve a problem I'm not sure I have.

As I head to my car it occurs to me I have no idea where Ruby Maplethorpe lives.

No. I'm not an airhead. Not at all.

FOUR

It's the noon hour as I watch Ruby Maplethorpe putter away in her car. My Saturday morning run proved physically underwhelming and emotionally exhausting, but the day is beautiful and I have it all to myself, so I decide to take in some of the quirkier shops on Main Street.

There is Past Presents, an indoor collective of garage sales absolutely brimming with toys and pop culture mementos from earlier generations. Whatever might have been under your Christmas tree when you were five or ten or seventeen would likely be found among the tables and shelves and piles lining the mall's busy aisles.

Farther down the lane is Denim If You Got'em, an all-denim store with a surprisingly full range of products for men and women alike (I confess I picked up a halter top here once and am still awaiting the proper occasion to wear it).

1912, named for the year of the town's founding, is one of my regular stops, not only for the variety of 'you can't find it anywhere else' items, but also to visit the joyful proprietor, Veronica, who is quickly becoming someone I consider a friend.

For a cool snack on a warm afternoon you can't do better than Brrrr-ito, a Mexican-themed dessert shop tucked into the back of an out of the way cul-de-sac.

But there'll be no enjoying a choco-taco today. Marlene's insults this morning, followed by her breakdown and the presumed threat of the scissor blades in the car tire, have blocked the sun on a cloudless day. I know it is all in my head, but melancholy is like a spoiled child—sometimes the only way to get it to go away is to humor it a while.

I settle my thoughts on a quiet evening at home. I picture myself on the couch atop a cool pillow and under a warm cat (Meatball, my Russian Blue, is an avid chest-napper), solving a TV mystery with Angela Lansbury; or maybe, if I find the energy, I'll turn up the tunes and do some cleaning. Given my present mood, I suspect I'll end up spinning Sarah McLachlan and mopping up my own tears.

Nope. It's a true crime night. Whenever you think you've got it bad, flip it over to ID Discovery and you'll learn some people have it a whole lot worse than you do. I don't like to read true crime but a TV binge of murder would go down smooth with a heaping plate of Italian comfort—pasta. Since I'm a runner, I'm not binging on comfort food, I'm 'carbing up'. See, things are already going my way.

Oh crud. While planning my homey little evening it totally skipped my mind that I have plans at eight o'clock with a woman I don't know at a house goodness-knows-where to do goodness-knows-what. Exit Angela Lansbury, enter Ruby Maplethorpe.

My two-bedroom rental rests smack dab in the midst of a neighborhood constructed in the post-World War II housing boom. It's safe to say about any two-bedroom house still standing in this area went up around the same time, when rapid housing construction was needed to facilitate the many young families at the start of what would eventually be called the 'baby boom'.

I've not done much with the outside, other than mow the grass and trim the small bushes. But inside this little house is my sanctuary. Nothing fancy, but some throw pillows here, throw blankets there, and pieces from local artists put up in just the right places, and I'm in my zone. I selected my furniture for comfort, not style, and for some reason I find strength in that. They are the first significant items I purchased following my divorce and I knew Curtis would hate them because they didn't catch the light and shine like china. My couch and not-quite-matching love seat are bland, light blue, billowy, fluffy, heavenly clouds. I'm more than okay with this.

No extravagant pasta for me tonight. I want to be on my butt as much as possible, so just marinara and noodles, with four strips of bacon chopped for protein. I refuse to allow myself to be bothered for standing Ruby up. How am I supposed to know where to find her? I get clever for a moment and try looking on Facebook, but no dice. I'm not broken up about it and am just settling in next to a grooming Meatball when I hear my screen door squeak open and the rap of knuckles on my sturdy old door.

Gretchen Herring's cute, freckled face smiles at me through the screen. Gretchen is one-third of what Stax likes to call the 'sneering squad', with Marlene anointed head sneerleader.

"Hi Lacy, I hope I'm not interrupting something," Gretchen says. Her eyes are pleading and her skin pale, even for a natural redhead.

I greet her warmly and welcome her in. Truth be told, I like Gretchen. She works part-time for Marlene at her travel agency and I suspect she feels some sort of obligation to her employer to team with her at the running store. Gretchen mentioned to me when I had her over for tea one afternoon (before I suddenly found myself cast as Hatfield to Marlene's McCoy) that Marlene introduced her to running. I suspect the much younger Gretchen (I put her in her early twenties) is a bit under the spell of her confident, successful, and (I'm not too catty to admit it) attractive boss. In return, and to my lasting chagrin, Gretchen confessed it was she who introduced Marlene to Carly. Oh well, nobody's perfect.

Gretchen's relationship with Marlene didn't prevent her from sending me whispers here and there when Marlene inexplicably started to sour towards me. I didn't like what I heard, but I appreciated Gretchen putting her neck out for me.

I don't want to stand awkwardly in the middle of the room with this young woman, so I offer her the love seat and I take the edge of the couch.

"I am so sorry about Marlene and how she acted this morning, Lacy," she effuses. "I could have died when she said what she did about your running."

"Did you tell her that?" I ask, a little more viciously than I would prefer.

"It isn't easy, telling her things." She drops her head to watch her hand fiddle with the cover of the armrest. "I want to open my own business one day. I'm not going to learn the ins and outs of running a business working for my father's construction company, and Marlene said she could help me. So, I took the job at her agency. The pay isn't much, not good at all, but she's been true to her word and is letting me learn from her. Besides, if I ever want to get a loan, I'll need her and Anderson as references, so…"

She doesn't need to finish her sentence. She's between a rock and a hard place and I understand where she's coming from. But what she says next surprises me.

"I just want to be happy and I don't want to depend on a man to live. I'm not like Marlene at all. If I do get married one day, it's going to be for love."

I'm not sure if that is too much information about Marlene's personal life or too little. But it makes for an uncomfortable silence. I decide to change the topic.

"So, what was all that about scissors this morning?"

Gretchen's eyes widen and color rushes back to her face. "Oh, it's so creepy. It's not the first one, you know. There was a pair in her mailbox one morning and another waiting for her when she came out of the grocery store. She acts tough, but I can tell she's terrified. She won't leave the office and walk to her car by herself and she won't let me leave by myself, either. She thinks someone's trying to kill her."

"Has she called the police?"

"I don't think she wants them to know."

I find that hard to fathom. "Why not? Some nut is stalking her and leaving scissors, of all things. Doesn't she want to know who it is?"

"I think she knows. But she won't say. I probably shouldn't tell you this, but…"

"You don't have to tell me anything you don't want to," I say, but I'm crossing fingers she will.

Gretchen closes her eyes and sucks air in through her nose. I hold my breath.

"She hasn't told me anything, but it's a small office, and I hear her and Anderson talking. A long time ago, I guess when she was about my age, she owned a hair salon in Tulsa. This was before she married, but one night in her salon a girl who worked for her was murdered. Stabbed to death with a pair of barber's scissors. I don't think Anderson knew about any of this before the scissors started showing up."

"That's terrible. Did they catch the guy?"

Gretchen shakes her head. "Apparently not. I think Marlene herself was a suspect. Maybe that's why she's not too crazy about calling the cops about her stalker. She doesn't want to dig all that up. She has a new career now, a new name, and is well known around here."

That much is true. You can't go anywhere in Cedar Mill without seeing Marlene's face on a billboard or a bus stop bench advertising her travel agency. Whenever she's in charge of selecting our run routes we somehow manage to run past one of her advertisements.

"You said Marlene thinks she knows who's stalking her with the scissors. Does she think it's the person who killed that girl?"

Gretchen's mouth turns up and pushes to one side, her eyes doing a little circle dance. "That's what she says. I wonder, though."

I know I am being nosier than I have a right to be, but I am engrossed by what this girl is telling me. I get the impression she wants to unload and I excuse my curiosity by telling myself if it isn't me, she'll be telling this to someone who might not be so willing to keep her confidence.

"You wonder?" I ask. "You mean you don't believe her?"

The question exasperates her and I promptly regret it. "I don't know, I really don't. I work with her during the week and then I'm at my dad's construction sites all weekend. What little time I have to myself I want to spend running. No stress, no drama. Now Marlene has made it her mission to beat my time. Swears she's going to smoke me at Chicken Hill tomorrow. I don't know, maybe I should just let her so she'll shut up."

She appears to be melting into the soft cushions of the chair. "Sometimes when I'm running I think about not stopping. Just keep going and get away from all this. It's too much."

I rise from the couch and give her a hug. I remember my twenties all too well and how every little drama was a world-ending disaster. But I never had to work in close quarters with Marlene Petrick while a scissor-wielding maniac lurked in the shadows. A hug is the least I can do.

I lighten the mood with some small talk and by the time Gretchen leaves her spirits are lifted somewhat. I promise to cheer her on during the run tomorrow morning and encourage her to give it her all, Marlene be damned.

I no sooner pluck Meatball up from his spot on the kitchen counter and settle back onto the couch when my phone rings.

"Hey skinny girl," barks Stax's familiar rasp. As usual, she has me on speaker phone. "How do you feel about putting some meat on those bones? I found a BOGO to Smokey Joe's Barbecue, so it's my treat this time."

I look at the clock and see it is already half-past-six in the evening. Where'd the day go?

"Sorry, Stax, you're a little late. I already filled up on pasta."

"Rats. You're going to make me waste my BOGO on Larry, aren't you?"

A thought comes to me. "Hey, Stax, you know the older lady who walks with the Level 3 group? She was at the store this morning when we spoke to Marlene."

"You mean when Marlene went all Joan Crawford in the parking lot? Yeah, I know who you're talking about. Her name's Ruby. She's one of my best customers. She brings me more books than she buys, and she buys a ton. Why?"

"You wouldn't happen to know her phone number, would you?"

"I said I sell the lady books. I'm not trying to date her. No, I haven't asked for her phone number, you perv. What's all this about?"

"She wants me to come by her house tonight but she didn't tell me where she lives."

Stax is silent for a moment and I swear I can hear gears turning.

"She's like crazy old, right?" Stax asks.

"She's an older woman, yes."

"Well, you're no spring chicken yourself," she blurts, as though I'm the one calling names. "You're plenty old enough to remember the world before the Internet. Don't you remember telling someone your name and saying 'call me' and you knew they knew it meant you were in the phone book? Well, I bet Ruby thought you were smart enough to figure that out. Clearly, she doesn't know you."

"Of course! She'd be listed and her address would be there as well."

"Hey, glad I could help. God gave you looks and He gave me a bust and brains. It's a shame He didn't see fit to put it all in in one person. But then, I ain't met a man yet who'd deserve such a creature."

I get off the phone with a promise to see Stax tomorrow morning at the run and dust off a copy of the Greater Tulsa phone book encompassing Cedar Mill. Flipping to the M's I find her right away. Not more than three miles from my own house.

"Welp," I say to myself, "you know what you're doing this evening."

But, really, I had no clue.

FIVE

I arrive at Ruby's house five minutes early. Her yard is a sizeable corner lot blessed with the most lustrous collective of blossoms and blooms I have ever seen outside of the gardens in Cedar Mill's park district. I don't know enough about flowers or gardens to tell you the reasoning behind Ruby's choice of flowers. or why she planted what where, but even this novice can see there is a hidden pattern to this beauty. I would come to learn that, through the eyes of Ruby Maplethorpe, there are patterns to everything.

Ruby's house is larger than mine but not so big it doesn't appear quaint. Instead of your normal everyday slat siding, her house is fortified with stonework, giving the impression of a centuries-old cottage in the English countryside. Albeit one with state-of-the-art storm windows.

I park on the curb alongside a cobbled pathway guiding me up to a porch where light from a bronze wall sconce glows warm beside a door that opens before I can make use of the rustic knocker.

Ruby is wearing a green day dress. Although the style predates her running garb by decades, the classic make of the dress is far more stylish than I imagined Ruby in her everyday life. I am flattered she touched herself up with a light application of rouge, as I assume she troubled herself on my account.

She welcomes me into her living room and what I see makes me dizzy. It's like I stepped into a time portal and emerged into a drawing room from another era. Running along the walls of the spacious room is a banquet of antique furniture, hand-carved in lacquered woods and fitted out in soft fabrics that, through the greatest of care, do not appear to have aged.

Past the window on the outer wall and covering almost every inch of the far wall are painted portraits and old photographs. I know a thing or two about picture frames from working summers in an art gallery during my college years, and I can see all the frames on display are Edwardian and Art Deco. One oval frame is a Tiffany Sterling Silver that would pay my rent for a year. Whatever Ruby Maplethorpe is, she's not destitute.

Ruby notices me ogling her wares and blushes, muttering 'Oh, I never throw anything out' as an explanation for her paradise of old world charm. She offers me a seat and disappears around the corner, emerging a moment later with a silver tea tray.

"Thank you," I say, "but I can't take caffeine after two or I'll be up all night."

An exaggerated look of pity comes across my hostess's face as she turns to set down the tray.

"Yes, dear, I suppose you are a mite skittish, aren't you?"

What does that mean?

"As it would happen," she continues, "this is a sweet rose tea from India. It's for relaxation. Perfect for you. No caffeine at all."

Perfect for me?

She pours the golden liquid into two china cups embossed with pink roses. I accept mine as she rushes to the side of my chair to place an embroidered cozy on the small side table, next to a lead lamp with a stained-glass shade. Poised under the lamp is a fading color photograph of two women in a small, modest prop-up frame. I think I recognize one of the women. I am certain I recognize the other.

"Is that you, Ruby?"

"Yes, it is."

"And is that…"

Ruby takes a seat on the divan. "Agatha Christie? Yes, dear, it is she."

I am shocked. How ancient is this woman?

"But didn't she die like a long, long time ago?"

Ruby laughed. It was pleasant, like a song.

"She passed, I believe, in 1976. If I'm not mistaken about your age, you would have shared the earth with her for quite some years."

Five, to be exact.

"The photograph was taken in 1968," recalls Ruby. "I was in London and had been invited to visit the Detection Club. As an American I could not become a member, you see, but they were splendidly cordial. To be invited for even a visit was such an honor."

"I'm familiar with the Detection Club. Wasn't that a group for authors?"

"Yes, mystery writers."

"Wait...so you're a mystery writer?"

"Have you ever heard of the Inspector Butterwell books?"

"Yes, I think I've read them all. Pearl Oakley, right? What about them?"

Ruby leans back into the divan and takes another sip of tea. I can see her blue eyes twinkle over the lip of the cup. Could it be?

"Are you saying you're Pearl Oakley?"

She lowers her cup to reveal the grin I imagined her wearing. "Ruby. Pearl. A simple swap of precious stones. Oh, and trees. Maple to oak. Seems rather silly now but I thought myself immensely clever at the time."

I am flabbergasted by the revelation. As a young woman I discovered my love of mystery fiction. The challenge by author to reader to solve the puzzle before the fictional sleuth reveals all at the end. At least, that's how they used to write them. After I read Agatha Christie and Dorothy Sayers I went looking for other authors and discovered Pearl Oakley's charming tales of intrigue set in the fictional English village of Holms St. Courtenay. The bumbling but preternaturally wise Inspector Edmund Butterwell reminded me of my late grandfather, so there will always be Oakley books on my shelf, though the last of the series was published more than twenty years ago.

Now, here I am, sitting in Pearl Oakley's living room. Only her name is Ruby Maplethorpe and she's a retired walker in old shorts.

I shamelessly go fangirl on Ruby and start asking questions. She pretends to be put off by it but gives in so quickly I conclude she is flattered that someone of a younger generation is a fan of her work.

She explains her late husband Edwyn was in a line of business that provided more than enough money to support the two of them. However, not being one to sit idle, she took up the pen and gave voice to her inner sleuth. Her first book became a modest bestseller and for the next twenty-five years she published her mysteries. When Edwyn passed away, twenty-two years ago now, she lost her ability to find any charm in death and hasn't written a word since.

The light in the room hasn't changed or shifted since we sat down, but I see a shadow fall over Ruby as she speaks of Edwyn's loss. She smiles and the shadow runs away.

"But I didn't ask you over to bore you with tales of past glory."

I assure her I find her anything but boring. But I am curious about the real reason I am here.

"You mentioned you thought you could fix my problem?"

She sets her teacup aside and stands, brushing out the folds in her dress.

"I don't 'think', dear, I know. Something is set up for you in the spare room. Would you care to come this way?"

I follow Ruby down a dim hall, past three doors, to a fourth room. After the wonders I witnessed in her living room I let my imagination run wild with what might lay beyond this door. Treasures from the Orient? A sarcophagus from Egypt? The Ark of the Covenant?

When the door opens and the light comes on I see an empty room. Empty except for a white massage table set up in the center of the room.

Ruby extends a hand to usher me in. "Having your bum rubbed by an old woman you just met wouldn't cause you any discomfiture, would it?"

My imagination never prepared me for this moment. "No more than any other person," I reply, which is the politest way I can think of to indicate that yes, it most certainly would cause me 'discomfiture.'

"Wonderful, then plant yourself face down and we'll get started."

"Are you serious?"

"My dear, I see how you walk sometimes, the way you reach your hand down to massage yourself. You're probably not aware you're doing it any more. It's Piriformis Syndrome and it's quite curable."

I confess I feel a bit violated. Not because she wants to rub my bum, but because she knows things about me a stranger should not be expected to know. "I do stretches," is my feeble reply.

"Stretches only relieve the problem temporarily. To loosen the muscles permanently requires a specific type of deep tissue massage. Now, lay down and I'll show you something I learned in Shanghai. I can't promise it won't hurt a bit. But, as the saying goes, you'll thank me in the morning."

I feel as helpless as a baby under her will. This woman oozes confidence. Not arrogance or anything palpable, but a quiet confidence that she has seen things you haven't and knows things you don't. So, I lay down on the table.

"In the 1970s I was quite an avid jogger," she says as she starts in on me. "It was thought of as a fad at the time, but it was quite popular. Oh, I'm aware 'jogger' is a dirty word nowadays. Everyone's a 'runner' now. But that's what we called it back then."

Ruby explains that with the exception of writing and Edwyn, she's never been able to stay too long with any one pursuit. Too much out there to see and try, she thought. So, in the early eighties, she packed away her running gear, but never threw it out. Subconsciously, she believed, she would return to it one day. I now understand the significance of her retro running clothes and feel a pang of guilt for the silent judgment I passed on her. Maybe I deserve the torture she is now inflicting.

"All right, Lacy, I believe we're done. Sometimes it takes more than one treatment, but it shouldn't be any more than three. Let's make a date for Monday evening, shall we? And remember, this is a fix, but it's not a vaccine. If you don't want to contract another case I suggest you begin running like an adult and not an angry first grader."

Where does this stuff come from?

I stand from the table, happy my leg doesn't collapse under me. But my left butt cheek hurts like the dickens. I hope it won't affect me too much on the hill tomorrow. But hey, I figure I became something like friends with Pearl Oakley tonight. That alone is worth a kick in the keister.

The night is running long and we both need to rise early, so Ruby escorts me to the porch and makes me promise I'll let her know if the pain doesn't dissipate.

Truth be told, I would pass the night in her living room if she asked me to. But Meatball will be waiting for his mommy on the blanket by the door, so I say good night and turn to walk away.

I feel a little tug at my elbow.

"I did have one quick question for you, if you don't mind. About this morning, with Marlene—"

"I'm so sorry you had to witness that. For some reason Marlene dislikes me and—"

"No, dear, I don't wish to know about your personal drama. I may be an old woman but I still have a life to live and such petty squabbles only steal away from it."

Ouch.

"What I wanted to ask about, dear Lacy, is the curious pair of scissors protruding from Marlene's tire. Those were barber scissors, were they not?"

"Yes, I believe so."

Ruby nods as though she already knew as much. So why ask?

"Do you know why barber scissors would hold significance to Marlene? If the many photos of her around town are to be believed, she works as a travel agent."

I recall what Gretchen told me and fight the urge to spill the beans to Ruby. As curious as I am to learn what Ruby would make of it all, I am not about to betray a confidence.

"Yes, she's a travel agent," I reply. "As for the scissors, I have no clue."

Do I look as unconvincing as I feel? Ruby's face gives nothing away.

"Hmmm, well, all right then. My memory isn't what it used to be, but it's not altogether gone, and as a writer of crime you tend to pay notice to wrongdoings when they have that special thing which sets them apart from others. When I saw those scissors, I recalled a murder as yet unsolved that occurred not far from here some fifteen or more years ago. It involved a pair of scissors and I'm certain a woman named Marlene was mentioned in it. Does any of this ring a bell with you?"

"No, I'm afraid it doesn't. But I only moved here a year ago."

Ruby nods, her mind elsewhere, perhaps in a hair salon more than a decade ago. "If I'm correct and there's a connection between what happened then and what's happening to Marlene now, I think it's likely something terrible might be on the horizon."

"Really? But fifteen years is a long time."

Ruby grins and touches my wrist. I feel a chill. Not from Ruby, but from the realization that there might be a dangerous person in our midst.

"The past is a funny thing," she says with the lightheartedness that comes from personal assurance. "We might leave it behind, but that doesn't mean it's finished with us. The past is often to be found just over the hill or around the corner."

SIX

I arrive at Chicken Hill a little earlier than necessary. This because I found myself crawling out of bed thirty minutes before my alarm would say I needed to. I slept a full eight hours, but if the condition of my sheets is to be believed, I spent at least a portion of the night tossing and turning. I don't recall any dreams but I can't escape the sense there had been scissors—long and shiny and sharp.

It is my ritual to enjoy LIT, a vitamin-enriched powdered caffeine drink, before each morning run, but this is the first time I can recall needing the caffeine just to make it *to* the run. But it does its job and by the time I park my car in the half-filled lot I feel mostly human. I head past the visitor's center and join the gaggle of runners milling around near the start line.

Run For It sponsors small to medium-sized runs in Cedar Mill and surrounding towns, and if history is any guide, I won't be able to get a moment alone with Marti until the run is completed.

I learned from watching Marti that sponsoring a run is no easy thing. To start with, the location must make sense and be practical. Often this means coordinating with the local police to help block off streets and provide protection to the runners. Then comes course design, which requires certification. You can't have a twenty-five-mile course and call it a marathon, which is twenty-six-point-two miles.

Let's not forget the numbered bibs with tracking mechanisms, and the all-important 'bling', which is the award one receives for completing the run. Additional medals are awarded those who finish first in their given category—something I need not concern myself with as, at least so far, I am strictly a middle-of-the-pack runner. Marti sees to these details as well as the various odds and ends that I, as a mere participant, would have no clue about.

Chase is good for a few phone calls and a meeting here and there, but Marti is the oil in their engine. Chase isn't lazy; his strengths simply lay in different directions, such as the store side and contacting other local business owners to contribute sponsorship in exchange for advertising in the packets handed out to participants. He is also a great idea man. But Marti is the muscle and it's fair to say she will clock more steps today than all the rest of us even though she will not herself be participating in the run.

I want to talk to Marti to gauge what if any fallout there might be following the embarrassing episode at her store the day before. But that isn't going to happen anytime soon, so I decide Chase will be my best bet.

I don't need to look far to find him. He is standing away from the rest of the pack, sipping on a Gatorade in the shade, but he's not by himself. There is Marlene, all white teeth and batting eyelids, laughing at whatever he is saying. Instead of speaking to Chase I try hard to make myself invisible and slip by them. It doesn't work and he calls out a hello to me and wishes me a good run. I smile and say 'Thanks' and hurry on by. Marlene lets her blue eyes wander anywhere but on me during the brief exchange.

If nothing else, I'm relieved to see Marlene alive and in one piece. I wasn't aware until now that I was in fear for her safety, but I suspect it's been in the back of my mind since Ruby's haunting premonition the night before.

If any trouble is going to befall Marlene it will have to wait, for today the sun is shining and the people are out.

Seeing that Marlene is okay hit a button in me, and whatever baggage I carried fell right off my shoulders. I am ready to run! I draw closer to the start line and spot Carly and Gretchen near the front. Being two of the fastest runners outside of a handful of near professionals from Tulsa, the front of the line is where you expect to find them.

Carly wears a visor that reads 'RUN HAPPY', though her brown waves are no less lustrous from being pulled back into a pony tail and tucked under it. She pretends not to see me. I find her visor ironic because I can't recall ever having seen the woman happy. I've seen her smirk a number of times while whispering under her breath, but that's a very different thing.

I catch Gretchen's eye and flash her a smile. She returns it with a friendly wave and that makes me feel good.

There are many other familiar faces on display, some without names and only familiar from having seen them at other runs. But I am pleased to see many people from the Run For It running groups, such as Amy, who is also Meatball's groomer; and Sue, whose little shop off a hidden turn along Main Street makes the best sushi I ever tasted.

"Hey, Newbie!" shouts a voice every bit as loud and obnoxious as friendly. Stax is standing under a leafy tree, feeling no rush to take her position in line.

As per usual, the faster runners take to the front of the line, the walkers are in the back, and the normal everyday runners make up the larger chunk in the middle. You'll find me there. Stax always starts the run at my side but finishes well ahead. It's fine with me because when you run it's just you and your two legs. And that's the cake. The bling, the social circle, the parties, are all just icing.

In a normal run, Ruby would be too far back in the crowd for me to see her, but the numbers today are smaller and I can spot her with other walkers from her group. She appears to be enjoying herself. I plan to stick around after I finish to cheer her on through the finish line. That's the best way to let a runner know you like them. Stick around and cheer for them. Stax did that for me at my first 5k with the store and I've made a point of paying it forward ever since.

The whistle sounds. Slowly, the people in front of me start stepping forward, and I follow suit. We move forward a little faster, a little faster, then a lot faster. As soon as my foot hits the white line, I'm off.

The run is every bit as grueling as I expected. The first couple of miles are more of a climb than a run as we trek over jagged, rock-strewn cliffs that level out for a while, then tease you with a downhill stroll before sucking you into another exhausting incline. A few miles in, my calves are screaming and my toes are buckling. When I hit my next walk interval I employ a trick I learned when I first started 10k training. I eat a pickle. Or, in this case, I drink pickle juice. It works. The high salt content of the juice replenishes lost sodium, iron, and potassium. I can stop cursing Marti's name now, at least for a few minutes.

After the first few miles we come to a walking trail. From the heavy exhales and cheers around me I understand this to be the 'easy' part of the run. It certainly is scenic. A flattened dirt walking path wrapping around an expansive wooded area to my right and overlooks a deep crevice to my left. Locals call this crevice the canyon, but it is too small to qualify for such a distinction. Nevertheless, a wooden fence of sorts runs along its length to ward off the overly curious, as a fall over the side would prove injurious and possibly fatal.

I stick to the right side of the trail and enjoy my view into the shaded woods. With the sun beating down overhead I could use the shade, but this is my chance to make up the time I lost pulling myself up hill. Because I am at an elevation, my trek to the finish line will include a lot of downhill running and to that I very much look forward.

Along the way I see aid stations for the first time in my brief running career. For your normal street run you'll pass a number of water stops, where you'll find volunteers (wonderful people, all of them) pouring and handing out water. Nature runs, fraught with dangers not inherent on flat concrete, require extra precautions. These come in the form of aid stations replete with tents for shade as well as chairs and first aid for anyone who might overexert or otherwise injure herself. Although impressed with the level of thought and detail Marti put into them, I am delighted to see the tents I passed thus far are void of runners in need.

The remainder of the trail is uneventful, though beautiful and aromatic. Stax long ago pulled ahead of me so I am running this part alone. Around mile nine I make the personal decision to start spending more time in nature. But next time I'll come alone and take it slow. Running along the winding trail, with its many twists and turns, makes me a bit dizzy at points. I know that might also be the first pangs of dehydration and I kick myself for not taking more water breaks along the way. I foolishly thought I might be able to PR. But nobody gets a personal record on a trail run, unless they're comparing it to the times of previous runs on the same trail.

In spite of my foolish bravado I complete the run intact, albeit sweat-soaked and starving.

I find Stax sprawled in the grass, panting like a dog and pouring a bottle of water over her face. Rarely at a loss for words, Stax, in her present condition, is able to say only one word, which she repeats over and over between huffs and grunts—Pancakes.

Mmmm, pancakes. I won't argue. I used to wonder why so many of the girls would gather for pancakes after a tough run, but now I think I get it.

As I sit in the grass recuperating with two water bottles I notice Carly and Gretchen milling about, looking like lost children in search of a parent. Carly breaks away and runs towards the parking lot where a news crew is packing up. I guess they got whatever footage they needed before I finished. Oh well, my fifteen minutes of fame will have to wait.

Gretchen runs to Marti who is talking with the finish line photographer. Whatever Gretchen tells Marti causes her face to turn from surprise to concern, and she begins making phone calls.

"Something's wrong," I say.

Stax's frantic panting softens to a lewd heavy breathing. "Yeah, there's not a fat, syrupy pancake hanging out of my face."

"No, with Marti. Gretchen and Carly are acting all worried and now so is she."

"What, did they misplace their Queen Bee? Maybe she decided to go solo. Let's hope she takes her new show on the road. Far, far away from us."

Stax can joke but I don't find it so funny. She doesn't know that whoever is messing with Marlene now might be a murderer from eighteen years ago. But I know. And I have to do something.

I stand from the grass and start to make my way over to Marti as Carly returns from the parking lot. I hold back as I watch Carly say something to Marti and Gretchen. Gretchen becomes excited and from my distance some yards away it appears that Marti is attempting to calm her down. She steps forward and raises her arms.

"Excuse me, everyone," Marti says in her loudest voice this side of a scream. "I'm going to need everybody's attention. If anybody has a few minutes to spare, we'd appreciate your help in locating someone who was running today. Her name is Marlene Petrick. Her bib number is 538 and she's 5'9", with long, blonde hair in a bun. She's wearing a pink Run For It shirt and green shorts. I already called all the aid stations and they've not seen her. If you should locate her, please make sure I'm notified as soon as possible. Carly is calling the police now in case...something happened. Thank you, everyone."

I look toward the forest, beyond the trail, past the trees, and imagine I see someone. Not Marlene, but a distorted figure, without a face. It holds a long pair of scissors.

And it stares back.

SEVEN

I tear my eyes away from the tree line and shake the daydream out of my head. There's a sinking sensation in my gut I haven't felt since Curtis told me he wanted a divorce. That might seem odd since I don't like Marlene, but frankly speaking, I didn't care a whole lot for Curtis by the time our marriage ended. When something bad happens to someone you know, it doesn't matter if you like them or not, you still feel it.

Stax is up from the grass now and we both run over to where Marti is standing. A gaggle of runners collects around her and, speaking all at once, say they saw Marlene running on the track earlier but lost sight of her, or they came in from the back and are sure they would have noticed someone in distress. In short, nobody can explain her disappearance.

I overhear Carly speaking on the phone to the police. The officer asks if Marlene might have finished the run and left without being noticed. Carly observes that Marlene's car is still in the parking lot with her purse visible inside.

If Marlene slipped and sprained an ankle she could still make her way to an aid station or at least ask a passing runner for help. If she fell and hit her head on the path she'd have been discovered and an alarm raised. Something is terribly wrong.

A small group of runners splits up to search the trail, with some entering from the finish line and others from the start line, the plan being to meet in the middle and hopefully discover Marlene along the way. Gretchen heads one group and Carly another. These runners are all much faster than myself so I stay behind. Besides, when the police officer comes I think I should be there to tell him what Gretchen shared with me in the event she is not willing to speak up.

Stax thinks it is all a bunch of drama by and for a drama queen and while I hold hope she might be right, I'm not willing to bank on it. It doesn't take long for a police cruiser to arrive. It carries only one officer.

The badge on the outside of the blue shirt reads Diebold and the chest on the inside of the shirt says VIP gym membership. When Officer Diebold—first name Trent, I came to learn—notices the majority of the people present are women, his big chest gets a little bigger and his back a little straighter.

His actual opening line: "I understand you've got a little problem, ladies."

Marti, technically the person in charge, did the talking. Chase came along but was not yet up to speed. She explains a runner—who witnesses will swear was on the trail with them—did not arrive at the other end; her car is still in the parking lot, and it is unlikely she could fall down or pass out and not be seen by passing runners.

Officer Diebold is not impressed and makes no attempt to disguise his irritation when he learns we dispatched hunting parties and didn't bother to wait until they returned to call the police. That a crime may have been committed is beyond his comprehension. To be fair, it is beyond the comprehension of most present. But not Gretchen. Carly is cool as a cucumber, sipping her water and fiddling with her hair, but Gretchen's eyes are like saucers flying over cheeks as red as her own hair.

"Officer Diebold," I say, stepping forward. If Gretchen won't speak up, then, by goodness, I will. "There's reason to believe Marlene Petrick is in danger."

Diebold turns his big meaty crew cut in my direction. "You mean besides the fact you can't find her?"

I don't appreciate the condescension, but I am prepared to ignore it if it means there is a chance we can bring Marlene to safety. "Yes," I say more assertively than intended. "I believe someone is after her because—"

"Officer, you'll have to excuse us," interrupted a woman behind me. "We've all just completed a grueling run and I suppose we've got too much blood in our heads at the moment."

I turn to tell this woman how the cow ate the cabbage and see it is Ruby. As a walker, she's one of the last off the trail and has no doubt been brought up to speed about Marlene by the search parties.

Ruby is smiling grandmotherly at the officer, but for a moment she moves her eyes to meet mine. The skin around her eyes flexes and undulates. I'm not fluent in eyeball Morse code and I doubt such a thing exists, but there was a message in her look and I received it loud and clear—Shut Up.

I don't understand why Ruby doesn't want me to talk to the police, but for some strange reason I trust this woman I barely know. It's not because she turned out to be an author I admire. Stephen King could walk out of the woods and tell me to stifle it and I would tell him to go play in the street. It is something more personal with Ruby. I trust her. And she apparently trusts me enough to *expect* me to trust her. This encouraging thought would occur to me only later.

"Is that right, ma'am?" says Officer Diebold. Since he is a young man of maybe twenty-five I forgive the 'ma'am'. "Or do you really have something to tell me?"

I already had my response. "No, she's right. I think I just need some water and an air conditioner."

Lying to the police was not an item on my bucket list, but I suppose I should pencil it in so I can strike it off.

Marti's phone rings. It is someone from one of the search parties stating the two groups met and neither were successful in finding a trace of Marlene. Marti relays this information to Officer Diebold along with the chilling observation that the fence separating the trail from the drop off into the canyon is still intact, which means it wasn't broken through by someone tripping and falling into it. Nevertheless, Marlene could just as easily have fallen *over* it.

The canyon!

I can't believe it hadn't occurred to me. The wooden fence is only three or four feet high and serves better as a warning than as actual protection. Marlene could have fallen over the side on a tight turn and hit her head. It's difficult to imagine an experienced runner doing such a thing, but it's still possible. She might be lying at the bottom unconscious but otherwise all right.

I see concern cross Officer Diebold's stiff brow for the first time. Knowing a woman may be injured is something he must take seriously. And this he does. He asks a few of the runners familiar with the off-trail walking of Chicken Hill to show him how he can get down to the bottom of the canyon. I hear a male runner mention it will take only ten minutes or so to walk to the bottom and if Marlene is there they won't be able to miss her. Diebold calls for an ambulance as a precaution and heads off.

I allow my hopes to rise as I watch the deputy head off down the trail. Stax still can't believe all this fuss is over Marlene and suggests we should be looking for her under a steaming pile of flapjacks. Ruby, on the other hand, shares neither my naïve optimism nor Stax's blissful ignorance. To her, waiting for Diebold's return is a mere formality. She knew they wouldn't find Marlene at the bottom of the 'canyon'.

Officer Diebold returns and releases the awaiting EMTs. He tells us he found no evidence of an injured runner or anything to suggest a crime had taken place. He did notice the large patch of wilderness dead center of the circling trail and said he thinks a search is in order. He felt it should take no more than twenty minutes to find Marlene if she is in there. But he didn't want anyone outside of police personnel stepping foot in the woods until he 'released the scene'.

Diebold stands at the edge of the parking lot, staring down the car entrance as though through sheer force of will he can summon of his comrades. When they show up we watch in rapt attention as the three men separate and search the woods on foot, in quadrants.

It's only a matter of time now, I think. I might have said it out loud, as anxious as I am. If I did, Stax and Ruby chose not to comment. Stax is beginning to comprehend the gravity of the situation. Marlene must be somewhere and the only place left is a place she wouldn't be if everything were okay. I fear any minute now the ambulance will return and a somber Officer Diebold will begin to clear the scene and take statements.

It takes a full half hour before the three officers find their way out of the dense foliage and back to the green. The news they failed to find Marlene is met with surprise and disbelief. The news they found no sign of foul play at all is met with indignation.

"Officer Diebold, you need to get back in there," Marti says with more force than I imagined her capable of. "Get more men out here or something. A woman can't just disappear into thin air. She's got to be in there somewhere."

Diebold makes the 'settle down' gesture with his hands and steps forward like a jungle lion anxious to exert his authority.

"All right, listen everybody. You reported a woman missing, so I came out here. You thought she might be in that ditch you call a canyon, so I looked. Wasn't there. You said the only place left she could be is in the woods. I call my buddies in, we look. Not there.

There's no torn clothes, none of you heard a scream, nobody saw a struggle, there's no blood … I'm sorry, but I think I've spent my morning investigating a crime that never happened."

"How can you say that?" replies Marti. "You couldn't have searched that forest too closely in the time you were in there. You can't say there's not a crime scene, can you?"

"Did we pick up every leaf and look up every tree? No. But the woods aren't so thick we couldn't see a woman in there, whether standing up or … lying down. Nothing but greens and browns in there, folks. You know, in my line of work, *not* finding a body is good news. I'm starting to wonder if some of you don't *want* this woman to be dead."

He said it half-jokingly, but he still said it. *Dead.* And the suggestion was there, however facetious, that one of us might be the culprit.

"Okay, I confess," Stax says. "I wanted Marlene dead. But that was yesterday. Today, I just want some frickin' pancakes."

I thought I might have a heart attack. You never say 'I confess' to a cop. But Diebold's pursed paper-thin lips begin to stretch into a smile. Stax's ability to defuse the friction in any situation borders on the magical. Provided, that is, she isn't the cause of the friction.

"All right, ladies," Diebold says, backing away. "I'm out of here."

"What do you suggest we do now?' asks Marti.

"I suggest you take the advice of this little lady here and go get some grub. If your friend is still missing come this time tomorrow, file a missing person's report.

Until then, I suggest you not step another foot in there (points in general direction of the trails) if you don't want to leave something behind we might end up finding."

And with a stern look and a fast swivel, Officer Diebold is gone.

The little group surrounding us breaks up into smaller groups of two or three and moves toward their cars, their gossiping murmurs fading with their feet.

I remain behind with Stax and Ruby. My stomach pleads for food and my brain aches for answers.

"So, what now?" asks Stax.

The noonday sun beat the cool from the air and my exposed shoulders begin to sting. Poor Ruby, whose age can only be guessed at but who is far older than myself, reaches into her ancient fanny pack and withdraws a handkerchief with which she gently swabs the beads of sweat from her forehead. I notice the handkerchief is monogrammed 'E.M.' for Edwyn Maplethorpe.

"We need to get out of the sun," I say. "Ruby here hasn't even had a chance to sit down since the run."

"There is much to discuss," is all Ruby says.

"You two can talk your heads off, if you like, so long as it's at the Pancake House," offers Stax. I know that look. She is minutes away from eating her own shirt.

"I don't think Pancake House is very private," I say. "How about we go home, take a shower, and rendezvous later."

"That'll work. Larry's closing up the bookstore at noon, so let's say we hook up there in an hour? Or 'rendezvous', if you're little Miss Fancy Pants over here. I'll fix us something in the café. Does that work for you, Ruby?"

Stax's light chastising of me and my sigh in response pleases Ruby. "Sounds splendid. I tend to think better after a good bath, and you know how fond I am of your store, Miss Best. It reminds me of the quaint old bookstores of my youth."

"That's because it *is* one of the quaint old bookstores of your youth, Ruby. I'm too cheap to update. And please, don't call me Miss Best. It makes me sound like a female version of Mr. Right."

"Oh? You prefer Juanita?"

"Not exactly. Call me Stax."

"Why ever should I call you that?"

"It's sort of what I go by."

"Oh, I see. Must be a defense mechanism of sorts. Makes you feel taller, does it? Tougher perhaps? Hmmm. Very well. Stax it is, then. I'll see you ladies at two!"

Ruby probably had no idea she just gob smacked Stax, nor would she be capable of appreciating how difficult that is to pull off. I needed the laugh, but a thought occurs to me that pushes away any humor. I have a question to ask Ruby and it can't wait until this afternoon.

"Ruby," I call out. Her tired legs haven't carried her too far away.

I look around to confirm there is no one else in earshot. "Why did you stop me from telling the officer about Marlene's scissor stalker?"

"He'll be hearing about that soon enough. He doesn't need to hear it from you."

"But why not?" I ask.

"I'm sorry to say, but I don't believe Marlene is going to come popping her pretty little head into Run For It tomorrow like nothing happened. In twenty-four hours' time, she'll be the subject of a missing person investigation. But what's missing is apt to be found when looked for and I fear when Marlene is found, the case will then be one of homicide."

I no longer feel hungry. Has writing mysteries for so many years turned this sweet woman morbid? Or has it honed her instincts for the criminal element to such an extent that she possesses almost preternatural powers of observation? I have no way of knowing, not yet. What I do know is she hasn't answered my question.

"But what does that have to do with me and why should it prevent me from telling the police what I know?"

"My dear, don't you see? Once they find Marlene, they'll no longer be looking for her, they'll be looking for her murderer."

"I should hope so."

"They'll ask questions."

"Yes?"

"They'll ask if Marlene made any enemies. If anyone made threats against her. If she's had a fight with anyone recently."

"Oh."

"You see now? Yes, I suppose you do. They'll think themselves on the trail of a killer and that trail will lead right to your door."

63

EIGHT

I shower as fast as I can, anxious to get the sweat and grime off my skin and out of my hair. I normally don't mind wearing the fruits of my exertion as a badge of honor, but something wrong happened on that trail and I don't want any part of it to remain on me.

I keep myself moving so I won't obsess over Ruby's idea that I am destined to become a murder suspect. If something bad happened to Marlene, then I suppose there'd be no way to avoid it. After all, I fought with her in front of witnesses the day before. And more than once I've made flippant comments about murdering her. The actual commission of murder is so far outside my character that I never saw the harm in such ranting. It's just a way for me to decelerate when Marlene had my engine running hot. In hindsight, it is a terrible coping mechanism that might soon land me in a small room under a hot light.

Meatball is waiting for me in the hall, warbling his request and staring up at me with his beautiful lemon-yellow eyes. I pluck him from the carpet and hold him close, squeezing his soft little body a little tighter than usual. I bury my face into his blue-gray coat and just stand there in the hall, wrapped in my towel, enjoying the comfort that only a trusted pet can provide.

But Meatball has other plans. He tires of my squeezes and jumps from my arms, urging me into the kitchen. It must be treatsie time. I fetch one of his grain-free fish-flavored dental crunch treats and set it on the tiles before him. I can scarcely afford the food and treats I special order for him from the Internet, but there are a few areas in my life on which I refuse to skimp: who I spend my time with, what I feed my cat, and running shoes.

I couldn't find a parking space outside Read it or Eat It so I stole one from Ye Olde Chocolate Shoppe. On a whim I decide a little dessert might not be out of step in the rather heavy pow wow we are about to have. I open the door, causing the little bell to ring, and prompting a call of 'Right with you!' from somewhere in the bowels of Hilda's chocolate factory. The familiar sing-song voice brings a much-needed smile to my face.

I'd wager not many towns in America have their own chocolatier. That's a shame. Like so much on Main Street, to see it from the pavement is to step back in time. The frosted window behind which waist-high displays tease with gourmet chocolates stacked top to bottom, the Victorian décor, the period stenciling. I'm convinced I'll never taste their kind again outside of this shop, unless I should happen to find myself in Europe.

I step into the shop's quaint parlor and am consumed by the aromas of sugar and lavender and boiling jams. There must be a hundred other scents mingled with these, but my nose is trained by my taste buds to search for these specific aromatics each time I come in.

Amidst the myriad of unique flavor combinations offered in the store, my favorites are dark chocolate filled with a luscious raspberry jam, and a milk chocolate bite infused with more than a mere hint of Lavender. I am also an avid consumer of the marshmallow pops. Two for a buck! I grab six, making sure two are covered in sprinkles. Stax's preference. Not sure of Ruby's tastes, I grab two in milk chocolate and two in dark.

Hilda Carnegie emerges from the back, wiping her hands on a towel. She welcomes me in her usual delightful manner by calling out my name with such operatic exuberance one can feel her voice as much as hear it. If not for the candy counter separating us I would have hugged her.

I order some of my personal favorites and suggest Hilda select others to add to the bag, informing her I am headed to a get together with a couple of friends from my running group.

"Oh, were you at the run today?" she asks as she wraps a couple of long stem chocolate-dipped strawberries for me.

"Yes, I was. My first trail run." I cut it off there, not wanting to wade into the quagmire of Marlene's disappearance.

"Quite strange about Mrs. Petrick, isn't it? A couple of runners came in a while ago and told me she went missing during the run. Is that right? I can't conceive of such a thing. Do your friends like nuts? Caramel?"

"Yes, that'd be great. And yes, it's true. I saw her there myself. She started the run but never crossed the finish line."

Hilda shakes her head as she deposits the chocolates into tissue wrapping and then into a small, clear bag. "It sounds like black magic to me. Mrs. Petrick was a beautiful woman, but I don't at all care for how she carries herself."

I am intrigued. "So, you knew her?"

"Mmph, well enough. She'd come in here from time to time. Not always alone, mind you. Why, she was here just two days ago. Sat with a man right over there."

There are a few small tables in the shop where patrons can sit and enjoy their chocolates or scones with a warm tea, coffee, or cold drink. She motions to a particular table positioned in the corner under a replica of a Victorian gas lamp.

"Her husband?" I ask.

She shakes her head emphatically now, her eyes wide with scandal. "No, I know Anderson well and it was not him. You must know the fellow I'm talking about, because he's a runner. He and his wife own that store down the street."

"Run For it?"

"Yes, that's the one."

I'm now the one with Scandal Eyes. "Are you talking about Chase Reynolds?"

"That sounds right. I only met him once when he and his wife first went into business. They came in to introduce themselves. His wife took a liking to my sweets and comes in on occasion, but I've only seen him—Chase, is it?—in passing until two days ago when he came in with Mrs. Petrick."

"Did you happen to hear what they talked about?"

"Oh no, I'm deaf to such things. But I did notice she was awfully cozy towards him."

That sounds like Marlene.

I pay for my chocolates and thank Hilda for her time and effort. I have too many other things with which to concern myself, such as a meeting I'm in danger of being late for.

I hustle across the street to the bookstore and find Stax's 'Closed' sign turned out and the window blinds pulled. Ruby's car is parked in a space in front of the store. The door is locked so I knock. The blinds over the big window shuffle a moment before the door opens and Stax peeks out.

"You're taking this cloak and dagger business pretty seriously," I say.

"Darn right. If anyone's going to make me disappear it's going to be David Blaine. Provided he makes his clothing disappear as well."

I come in to find Ruby seated at the far corner booth where Stax has three places set with sandwiches and chips.

I didn't walk fast enough to the table to suit Stax so she got behind me and pushed at my back.

"I'm trying to be a good hostess and not eat until everybody's here, but you're making it hard."

"Hey, I was getting us dessert."

I hold up my bag of goodies and Stax salivates. Once at the table I scoot in next to Ruby.

"You saw Hilda, I see," Ruby says.

"You like chocolates?"

"Love them, when they're made right. She imports her chocolates from Belgium, did you know that? Absolutely exquisite. It is thoughtful of you to think of us like this."

I beam and set marshmallow pops and long-stem strawberries next to everyone's plate. Now it was time to drop my bombshell. "While there I happened to pick up a piece of news about Marlene."

"No, huh uh," argues Stax. "Not a word about this Marlene business until that sandwich is in my belly."

"Yes, quite right," agrees Ruby. "Discussing stressful matters while eating is terrible for digestion."

We enjoy our cold sandwiches (Larry is generous with the good stuff) and chips and nibble at our chocolates while making small talk about our personal performances at Chicken Hill. When Ruby pulls out a legal note pad and two sharpened pencils, I know it is time for discussion.

"If you two would be so kind as to humor an old lady," began Ruby as though delivering a prepared speech, "I would like to officiate the proceedings and I suggest to be most efficient with our time, we should stick to schedule as closely as possible."

"Schedule?" I ask, unaware we have such a thing.

"Yes, I've prepared a simple schedule. It's to this effect—First, we discuss the What (that is to say what we believe may have happened), then the How (how we believe it happened), and finally, if we're so bold, we tackle the Who (the person or persons responsible). Is this agreeable?"

It is hard to argue with Ruby, not only because she makes sense, but because she is so cute. Each time she defines a point she is making, she'll grip her glasses by one arm, lower them down her nose, and look up at you.

"Very agreeable, Ruby. Stax?"

"Yeah, sure."

"Splendid," says Ruby, pleased by the lack of objection. "Miss Stax, would you please start us off by telling us what you believe happened."

Stax looks stunned, as though selected from a crowd of a thousand and not a ragtag group of three. "What I believe?"

"Yes, dear. I'm sure you've given it some thought."

"Well, yeah. I have as a matter of fact. What I figure happened is Marlene started the run like the rest of us, but instead of finishing it like the rest of us did she disappeared—POOF!—off the face of the earth."

"Really? That's what you've come up with?" I ask.

"Well, yeah! You got something better?"

She has me there.

Ruby rested her pencil. I guess she didn't think Stax's scenario worth recording.

"Stax is not wrong, but I think what she offered could best be described as an oversimplification of the facts."

I am surprised. "Are you saying you agree with Stax? You think Marlene simply disappeared?'

"Not simply, my dear. There is nothing simple about what happened to Marlene. And she didn't disappear, she couldn't have. A person can't just disappear. But they can cease to appear, and that's what I believe happened to Marlene. She ceased to appear."

Stax takes her Buddy Holly glasses off and waves them over her head. "Let the record show I do not disagree with what you just said, Miss Ruby."

"I'm gratified to hear that, Miss Stax."

"Let the record also reflect I cannot disagree or agree with what you said because I didn't understand a single world of it."

On that Stax and I agree.

"In simpler terms," continued Ruby, "Marlene did not disappear. She was physically there, or somewhere, but when people looked for her, they were not able to see her. That's what I meant by ceased to appear."

Interesting. "Do you mean she was hiding?"

Ruby wobbles her head back and forth as though considering the suggestion. However, I suspect this is more for my benefit than anything. She no doubt considered the idea and discarded it while we were still standing on the park green.

"I don't think so, dear. People who want to disappear tend to look for the least conspicuous time and means to do so, not the most conspicuous. We must assume whatever happened to Marlene was not of her own making."

"Okay, I think I'm getting it," Stax says. "You think she was abducted, right? Someone grabbed her off the trail and pulled her out of the park, right?"

I held my soda to my lips but don't drink. "But how easy would that be? He couldn't take her out the main way because Marti and at least a half a dozen people were out there at all times. Not to mention the news cameras."

"We're getting ahead of schedule," cautioned Ruby. "We're only discussing the What. 'How' will have to wait. So, to frame the question properly, what Stax suggested is Marlene might have been escorted out of the park by her abductor. Is that correct?"

"That's right. Why not?"

"Let's explore the possibility," Ruby says while scribbling something on her notepad. "Lacy already observed Marlene could not have left the park in the traditional way or else she'd have been seen. I'm not familiar with Chicken Hill but I did pay attention on my walk today and the highest points provided a good view of the surrounding terrain. Did you two notice this?"

We both nod 'yes' but to tell the truth my eyes were on my feet the entire time I traveled uphill. However, the nod satisfies Ruby, who continues describing the terrain.

"The main entrance and parking lot are to the south. To the north and the west one would have to traverse the canyon and then climb the rocky hills on its other side, which would leave them visible for some minutes to all the passing runners. So that must be counted out. To the east there's a wire fence, much taller than the more decorative wooden fence along the trail. This end of the park is not open to the public, but I suppose if someone were agile enough he might be able to traverse it. However, when you add a second body to the mix—Marlene's—it rather does up the ante, don't you think?"

Stax shakes her head. "No, that couldn't be it. I've seen that side of the hill from down below. There used to be a fruit stand on that dirt road my parents liked to go to. That fence is there because when you get past it there's a sheer drop of at least a dozen feet."

Ruby clicks her tongue. "Oh my, that wouldn't do at all."

"Unless he rappelled," I offer weakly.

Ruby and Stax seem to actually ponder the idea, so I say "Guys, I'm joking."

"It's no joke, Lacy," Ruby says. "In a situation like this no idea is too incredible to at least consider. However, I agree that attempting to rappel with a hostage, conscious or otherwise, seems a little farfetched."

Stax scratches at her forehead. "So where does that leave us?'

Ruby finishes her notes, lays down her pencil, and looks back and forth between Stax and myself. "The question is 'Where does that leave Marlene'?"

Her tone gives me chills, but I forge ahead. "And where might that be?"

"Isn't it clear? Why, she's still there."

"Where?'

"Somewhere on Chicken Hill."

NINE

I about jump from the table. "What, you think she's still on the hill? We've got to get out there and look for her!"

"We'll do no such thing." Ruby doesn't raise her voice, but there is a finality to her words. Nevertheless, I need a darn good reason to abandon a person in need, so I persist.

"If you believe Marlene is trapped there on the hill then why are we not there right now? Why didn't you speak up when the cops were there?"

"Because, my dear, Marlene is dead. That much is clear."

"Wait," Stax says, "how do you know? I mean, you're obviously smart and all, but how could you know if she's dead or alive?"

"If she were alive she'd have walked off the hill by now."

"Not if she is hurt."

"Then she would have called for help."

"What if she's not conscious?"

"The search parties would have found her. Wherever she is, she's not visible, which means she's been hidden.

Accident has been ruled out, and a moment ago we were able to rule out abduction. What's left for options but foul play?"

"Ummmmm," stammered Stax as she searched for another alternative. "Suicide!"

"In which case, she'd still be dead."

"Okay, so she's dead," I say, exhausted from the exchange. "She still deserves to be found. And we have a couple hours of daylight left."

"I'm an old lady, dear, and on a bad day a stiff wind can blow me over. But, on a strong day, I assure you I am quite formidable when of a mind. Today's a strong day and I'm of a mind to keep you as far as possible from that hill."

Stax touches my arm. "Yeah, Stretch, I kind of agree with her."

"I can't believe this!"

"Listen, Wonder Woman," continues Stax, "you heard what the cop said. Stay out of the woods or else risk leaving something behind they can find and use against us. Now, I ain't worried about myself. Okay, I'm a little worried about myself. But mainly, I'm thinking of you. You had to go and pick a fight with Marlene yesterday, so now you're going to be a suspect when they do find her. All the worse if you're the one who finds her."

"What about you, Stax? You got louder with her than I did."

"Yeah, but I do that with everybody. And besides, you've made a lot of comments here and there about killing her and stuff. Not that I think you would! But still, you said it."

"You have, too!"

"Yeah, but duh, I say that stuff all the time. It's not out of character for me. It kind of is for you."

I want to argue that death threats are not at all out of character for me, but it occurs to me I'll be arguing at cross purposes.

Ruby scoots herself out from behind the booth and stands beside me. "I say we take a break. We've covered a lot of ground, but there's still much more to cover. We would be best served tackling it with clear heads. So, let's stretch our legs and get a little fresh air and reconvene here in about fifteen minutes."

"Huh uh, no thanks," says Stax. "I stretched my legs and got loads of fresh air this morning and look what it got me. I think I'll stick with the moldy old paper particles floating around in my store, where so far nobody has managed to go missing."

Stax melts into the shadows of her deserted bookstore. Ruby lightly grips my arm, her hand both soft and firm.

"Lacy, I understand how you feel. You don't just like to help people, you feel you need to. And I want you to appreciate this is what we are doing. Look at it this way—we both know you had nothing to do with whatever happened to Marlene, but the police don't know that. So, let's not give them another reason to spend any more time looking at you than they need to. The best way we can help Marlene now is to help the police find her killer. And hopefully to prevent anyone else from being hurt."

"Do you think someone else will be hurt?"

I'm not ashamed to say I am afraid. Afraid for Marlene and afraid for myself and my friends. But when I look to Ruby and see that grin of hers, so full of fire and surety, I let go of the fear and grab hold of her strength. I can see what she is thinking even before she says it.

"Not if I have anything to say about it."

I join Ruby for a short walk around the block. The mid-day sun beats down on us with all its summer force and I find invigoration in the warmth. The sight of all the people out enjoying a normal day helps me forget, albeit for only a moment, that my day is anything but normal.

When we again take our spots at the booth, our cups refilled with soda from Larry's fountain, we pick up where we left off in discussing what might have befallen Marlene this morning.

No metaphorical stone is left unturned. Stax suggests that perhaps it is all a cruel put-on by Marlene who stashed a disguise in the trees the night before and slipped out unrecognized to escape in a waiting rental car. Theoretically, it's a feasible theory, but Ruby points out it lacks the crucial element of plausibility—if she wanted to disappear, why not slip out in the middle of the night? And why not take her own purse?

We also agree that even if a man with a gun likewise stashed a disguise and forced her into it, they would be highly conspicuous walking out together as a couple without participating in the run. And Marlene is not so meek as to allow herself to be taken captive without risking at least a scream.

We were getting into Twilight Zone territory with our theorizing and had to admit to ourselves we don't have enough information to determine what happened to Marlene, other than at some point during her run she miraculously 'ceased to appear', as Ruby prefers it. Our major breakthrough is concluding Marlene could not have left Chicken Hill. Whatever happened must have happened under the noses of a hundred runners and three police officers and yet generated not a single known witness.

"So, we're done with the 'What'," I say. "Do we dare attempt to try and figure out *how* Marlene was subdued and hidden in plain sight?"

"Yeah, Oh Mystic Eye of Mystery," Stax says playfully to Ruby, "please enlighten us."

"I haven't the foggiest idea of how this was done, ladies. If we knew that, we would likely know who killed her. But I believe I can tell you what kind of creature we're up against."

As we push forward over the table to listen I glance across the brightly lit café to the darkened bookstore beyond and imagine I see the shadows move.

"I dare say we're up against that rarest and most challenging of puzzles—the Howdunit."

"I've heard of 'whodunit," observes Stax, "but…"

"Whodunits are commonplace. Some are trickier than others, but usually it's a simple matter of following the evidence back to the culprit. The Howdunit, however, is a far more unpredictable animal. You see, when investigating a Whodunit, you learn to trust the evidence and your instincts about what the evidence tells you. That's how you catch your man. But when you find yourself up against a Howdunit, the evidence will lie to you and lead you down dead-end alleys. Or, even worse."

Stax leans in, peering over her frames. "Worse? How worse?"

"It's hard to say as so much depends on what the villain is trying to accomplish. But one must go to great lengths to orchestrate an impossible murder, and for that, they must have a good reason. Most often, that reason is to conceal their own culpability. Sometimes, it's also to manufacture evidence against someone else."

My head hits the table. "Oh my, and all this right after Marlene and I had a fight. Do you think I'm being fit up for this?"

Ruby places her elbows on the table and folds her fingers together. If you entered the room at this moment you might think she's leading us in prayer.

"Hmmm, I don't think so, Lacy. Whatever happened must have been in the planning for some time. It's impossible to say who, if anybody, the killer is planning to frame. It might be he—or she—is hoping to create a mystery that's impossible to solve. If it can't be solved, they can't be implicated."

"So, here's the sixty-four-thousand-dollar question," Stax says with a mouthful of ice. "How do we solve a crime that's impossible to solve?"

"By reminding ourselves that nothing is impossible and no crime is perfect."

"That we can do," I say. "What else?"

"We'll need to start gathering some information. And we must do it quickly because we can't be sure what might happen after the police get involved. Any ideas?'

"I say we talk to everyone who was there, see if their stories match up," offers Stax.

"My apologies, I should have specified good ideas. Do you ladies have any *good* ideas?"

"What! Hey, what's wrong with my idea?"

I clear my throat and answer, in my most measured tone. "Stax, darling bestie of mine, there's only three of us. We have maybe twenty-four hours. And there were over a hundred people on the trail this morning. How are we supposed to talk to all of them at once?"

"I don't know, Skype? And watch who you call 'bestie'. Do you have any bright ideas?"

As a matter of fact. "I do have one. If we can get the bib times from Marti we might see something that stands out."

"That sounds promising," Ruby replies. "Such as what?"

"For starters, we could see each runner's finish time. Pretty much everyone there today are people I've seen at other runs. My thought is we could compare their finish times today with their average times across numerous runs, all of which are available on the Internet. That way, we can see if somebody took longer than usual to finish the run. Whoever hurt Marlene must have lost some time doing it."

Ruby purses her lips and makes a 'hmmm' sound. "Anything else?"

Isn't that good enough?

"Well, I don't know, that's what came to mind."

"I know!" shouted Stax, jumping off her seat like a spring popped under her.

Ruby and I wait for the punchline.

"You see, the way I figure it is this," begins Stax, one eye cocked over her black frames. "Marlene is one of the faster runners, right? At least out of our store. Forget about those guys who run like The Flash, because they don't count. But we know Marlene was towards the front of the pack until whatever happened to her happened, up there with Gretchen and Carly and those other chicks with windmills for legs. So, if anybody witnessed anything, it would be one—or more!—of the first ten or so people who finished."

Stax leans back in her seat and waits for a reaction. As for me, I think it makes perfect sense. Stax effectively took a list of over a hundred names and shortened it to ten or less.

"Bloody brilliant, Stax!" effuses Ruby with far more enthusiasm than my original idea apparently afforded.

"Brilliant, ey? Maybe I'm the Sherlock and you're the Watson, Ruby."

"What does that make me?" I ask.

"Mrs. Hudson. Speaking of which, my cup is empty."

Ruby tsk-tsk'd. "Now, now, you two. It's not play time yet."

I'm reminded of elementary school when I'd been caught cutting up and tried to play innocent. I wipe the smile from my face and give Ruby my rapt attention.

"I'm going to call Marti and see if I can get that list today. You two are more familiar to her, but I want your names to pop up as few times as possible in the police inquiry. We won't know how Marlene was murdered until her body is discovered, but this information might prove invaluable by the time this is over."

"You really think it'll point us towards a witness?" asks Stax.

"It might at that, it might at that. But there's something else I'm hoping to see at the front of the list."

Stax and I crowd around the little old lady. The gleam in her eye makes me wish I were already poring over those names and times.

"My brave fellow adventurers," Ruby says in measured beats, followed by the most pregnant of pauses. "I expect in this list of ten we'll find the name of Marlene's murderer."

TEN

"Just send the Hobbses in when they get here, Lacy. I'll be ready for them. Can I get you any tea while I'm up?"

Caroline has been waiting on me all day like a mother home from work with her sick child. Only she isn't my mother. And we are at work.

"No thanks, Caroline. I'm well-hydrated."

I smile and tap my giant sixty-four-ounce cup of water. Her mind at ease, she disappears into her office to await our next clients.

Caroline and Bill Lefferty own their own independent insurance agency in a sleepy turning off Main Street. They were a Godsend when I arrived in Cedar Mill with no job prospects and a dwindling savings account. It was a quirk of timing that brought us together, as their previous administrative assistant got married and then pregnant and decided to head off for greener pastures behind a white picket fence. As I am on the opposite end of the marital spectrum and already well-versed in the duties of running an insurance office, it was a perfect match.

You can't pick your parents but you can pick your employers and I don't think I could have picked a happier, more stable couple to work for than the Leffertys. Married forty years and still in their honeymoon throes, I envy their chemistry. Curtis and I would justify our fighting by blaming it on the business we shared and the amount of time we had to spend together crunching numbers, going over files, and balancing budgets. But the Leffertys thrive off the shared time and responsibilities to the extent that whenever Bill has to be out of the office, Caroline becomes progressively more fidgety.

Today is one of those days. Bill is running some in-home appointments in a neighboring town and won't be back until after lunch. Caroline heard that a runner went missing during the Chicken Hill run and has been treating me like a trauma victim all morning, concluding on her own that it could just as well have been me as Marlene. Explaining that I saw nothing and had not myself experienced any wrongdoing calms her only slightly.

I would have accepted the offer of tea except the Leffertys only brew decaf. But I'd had two sleepless nights in a row and am starting to feel its effects. I scrounge in my pen drawer for an abandoned packet of LIT (my pre-run energy drink of choice, now good for any time of day) when the phone rings.

It's Stax.

"Why didn't you call my cell?" I ask. She never calls the office line.

"Ruby thinks it's smarter if we minimize contact. You know, if the cops start digging."

"They'll still figure out you were calling me when they see this number."

"No plan is perfect. Anyway, it's time you get the heck out of there."

"Excuse me?"

"Skip school, play hooky, puke on your desk and take a sick day. Just try to get out early."

"What's going on?"

"There have been developments."

"Developments? Who do you think we are, Scotland Yard?"

"Marti called Anderson Petrick this morning about Marlene. He's refusing to file a missing person's report on her, so Marti's headed over to the police station now to do it herself. That means our clock is ticking."

Yes, I'd say that is a development. It's only a matter of time before the cops come calling, and when they do, I'd prefer it not be at the agency. The Leffertys are good people and I don't want their name mixed up in this.

"Okay, I can't leave now. Bill should be here in a while and then I'm sure they'll let me take off. So, you talked to Marti? What did she say about us getting the finishing times?"

"Ruby's the one who talked to her. Marti was so mad about Anderson that she agreed to e-mail Ruby all the data."

"Ruby uses e-mail?"

"That's what I said. Ruby told me 'I'm old, I'm not a Neanderthal.' You know, I'm really beginning to like that chick."

"What's she doing now?"

"She's running my store."

"And what are you doing?"

"I've been pulling data all morning. I'm pretty good at spreadsheets so I agreed to compile the finish times from all the runs around here the past six months. Once they're all on the sheet I can make it populate an average pace time for each runner."

"Sounds complicated."

"It is if you're computer illiterate. But I'm not, so—"

"Yeah, yeah, yeah. What do you need me for then?"

"Gumshoeing. I should be done with this spreadsheet by noon and I plan to do some digging around town. You know, find out about Marlene's nightlife. Four gummy shoes are better than two, ergo the pukey desk."

"I'm not going to puke on my desk."

"Just get to the bookstore ay-sap. So you're not eating my dust I'll leave a list of places for you to hit. See Ruby for it. We're only hitting places that are open after dark, so, this being Cedar Mill, it won't be a long list."

I notice a car pull up and park outside my window. I don't recognize the man and woman in the car and decide they must be the Hobbses, Caroline's eleven o'clock appointment.

"Hey, I gotta run. I'll be there after lunch."

I hang up the receiver and get my smile ready for the Hobbses. I never stand until after the people enter, because in my own mind I look creepy just standing and smiling at someone as they walk into the room.

As I sit waiting for the door to open my mind wanders back to Marlene. I realize that in all the excitement yesterday I forgot to tell Stax and Ruby about my conversation with Hilda the chocolatier. Maybe I didn't want to remember that she served chocolates and drinks to Chase and Marlene just two days before the run. Stax wants me to dig up dirt on Marlene and I already hold a soiled shovel.

Bill returns to the office shortly after noon and he and Caroline are gracious enough to give me the rest of the day off. I confirm the remainder of their appointments and set out the folders for each prospective client so I don't have to worry about leaving them in a fix. If anyone will soon be in a fix, it's me.

I arrive at Read It or Eat It to find Ruby manning the counter, and to all appearances, loving it. A patron asks about a particular series of romance novels and Ruby regales her with tales of having dined with the author some years before. I peek in on the café and find Larry busy with three tables' worth of hungry diners. The mingling aromas of old books and fresh spices are not as incongruous as one might think.

Once I am able to get a minute alone with Ruby, she informs me that Marti called to let her know that the police are organizing a far more thorough search of Chicken Hill and will immediately begin making inquiries into Marlene's disappearance. I am relieved by the news but also feel my pulse quicken. They're going to find Marlene, and when they do, they're going to come looking for me.

The best I can do is what I am doing—looking for answers. Ruby fetches the list Stax left for me and I am not at all surprised to see that it is a list of dive bars. You know the kind of place—tucked far back into the bowels of a strip mall long past its prime; small, smoky, everything is brown except the fading green of the lone pool table. To Stax's credit, the bars are all on the same side of town, from which I surmise our respective lists were compiled based on geography and not best/worst.

Ruby stops me on my way out the door. There is something else Stax wanted her to give me—a photo collage replete with images of Marlene dolled up from her travel agency advertising and her more natural appearance in a visor and singlet from the Run For It website. It makes sense that if I am to be inquiring about her I should be able to communicate who it is I am inquiring about. Good thing Stax and Ruby have their heads screwed on straight because mine feels like it is held on by duct tape and rubber bands.

The inquiries don't take as long as I expect and are far less fruitful than I'd hoped. Although most of the publicans, bar maids, and patrons went out of their way to look at the photos and offer their condolences, none of them recognized Marlene as having come into their bar. There were glimmers of hope as a few individuals felt certain she looked familiar, but it was her image on the billboard advertising they recalled.

I feel deflated as I turn onto Main Street and head back towards the bookstore. Out of my windows I watch the carefree buzz and motion of my fellow Cedar Mill residents and for the first time I feel separate from them. There is a dark cloud in the sky that only I can see.

I don't relish the thought of arriving back at Read It or Eat It empty-handed and decide to put off the shaming for a few minutes with a visit to Run For It. There are only a few vehicles in the lot, but one of them is Chase Reynolds's RAV4. A little sunlight shone through the clouds. I do have one lead to my credit and now is my chance to act on it.

Jess is helping a lady choose the right pair of shoes and doesn't see me enter. Chase is on bended knee over a box of knickknacks for counter display.

"Are those whistles?" I ask. I know the answer, but it's as good an icebreaker as any.

Chase is startled by my voice but relaxes when he sees me. "Yes, they are. And mace key chains. I ordered this protective gear last month as new impulse buys but the wrist jewelry was still selling so well that I didn't bother to put them out. I can't help but wonder now—"

"If it would have made a difference? If maybe Marlene had had a whistle or mace she might not be missing?"

"It occurred to me."

He sounds winded, not from exertion but worry.

"Marlene was a big girl and an experienced runner. I'm sure your counter stock didn't play a part in whatever happened yesterday."

"Was?"

"I'm sorry?"

Chase swivels around on his knee to face me. "You said she *was* a big girl. Do you assume she's dead?'

Oops.

"I'm not assuming anything," I stammer. "I guess I meant 'was' as in she's not here now, for whatever reason."

"Yeah, you're right. I suppose we'll know soon enough."

He stands straight, towering over me, and looks me in the eye. I surprise myself by freezing. It is a moment before the spell breaks and I speak again.

"Soon enough?"

He nods. "Marti is out there now, on Chicken Hill, watching the search. She called a little while ago, said there's a small army looking for … anything. So, I suppose we'll know something soon enough."

I was about to ask a more pointed question when Jess and her customer moved into hearing range. I inquire for a more private place to talk. I expect him to escort me to the brault, but instead I find myself following him through a door into the back rooms of the building, an area I've heard them refer to as the 'catacombs'.

This is my first time seeing the catacombs and hints of its history as a bank are visible in the tanned wood doors with frosted glass windows and rustic brass knobs.

We end up in a spacious room that I assume once belonged to a bank manager. It now seems to double as the store's head office and paper repository. It's hard to see how this cluttered and disorganized mess is the engine behind Run For It as not a shred of the store proper's Feng Shui is on display here.

I take my seat in a plastic chair in front of a chipped and stained desk piled high with papers, folders, and notebooks. Chase sits behind the desk facing me.

"What's on your mind, Lacy?"

Where to start? "I suppose this business about Marlene has my head spinning. I was curious if you had any insight."

My question appears to confuse Chase. His brown eyebrows arch and crinkle and for the first time I notice the start of crow's feet at the corners of his eyes. "How could I have any insight?"

"Not about her disappearance, of course. I mean about her as a person. You know, her life. Did you know her socially at all?"

"No. Neither did Marti, as far as I know."

"You never ran into her around town and grabbed lunch with her? Something like that?"

"Why would you ask that?"

"Well, she's been running from this store a long time, so I just thought—"

"A lot of people run from this store, Lacy. As much time as this store takes from me, I'm afraid there's little time left for entertaining."

"So other than here and at runs, you didn't know Marlene?"

Chase pushes his chair back from the desk, abandoning his relaxed posture. "These questions are beginning to make me feel a little uncomfortable. Is there an accusation somewhere in there?"

My interrogation skills apparently need a lot of work. But there is no going back now. "No, Chase, really. No accusations," I lie, feigning shamed embarrassment. "I'm a little turned around by Marlene's disappearance and I'm trying to get a handle on who she was."

Chase stands from his chair, straightens the wrinkles in his yellow shirt, and sighs. My little act has not placated him.

"I need to get back to the store. As for Marlene, I'd let the cops ask the questions. That's their job. If someone did do something to her, then there's a bad guy out there. He may not take too kindly to you going around town asking questions."

He steps in front of the door and my skin goes electric. It is a sense of panic, that I am no longer safe. I realize how helpless I am in this chair, in this room far away from civilization, with this tall, strong man who just lied to me about not seeing Marlene socially. Who told me that there might be a 'bad guy' out there who wouldn't like me asking questions.

What if the bad guy isn't 'out there' but in here, right now, with me?

ELEVEN

C hase opens the door.
"Are you coming?"

I practically jump from the chair. Once in the hall and moving towards the exit, I didn't feel out of the woods just yet, so I say, "I'm sorry I upset you, Chase."

His hand grips my shoulder. He's strong. He breathes hard out his nose. "I was already upset, Lacy. I'm upset about Marlene. I'm upset Marti's involved in this. That the store's involved in this. No matter how it turns out, I don't see a good side."

He sounds sincere enough, but is it an act? I decide I can ponder such questions once I am out of this creepy back hall. I will myself to walk casually but my feet don't obey and my pace quickens as I move.

Chase notices my urgency and moves to get ahead of me as we reach the door. He grabs the handle but doesn't turn it to open.

"Lacy, I'm sorry if I made you nervous. That wasn't my intention. To be honest, you were making me a bit nervous back there."

You're still making me nervous, I think. But he doesn't seem so threatening now.

He opens the door and I slip out into the brightness of the store proper. Jess looks at us with a curious expression, no doubt wondering what we'd been talking about in private. Run For It is one of my favorite places in the world, but right now I can't get out of here fast enough.

"Thanks for the talk, Chase. I need to get going." I felt I had to say something. The lingering threat of danger and murder is no excuse for rudeness.

"Hey, Lacy," Chase calls out behind me. I wait until I reach the side exit door before I turn to face him.

"Remember what I said," he continues speaking once I make eye contact. "Sometimes, when you have an idea, it's better to keep it to yourself."

I wait until I'm halfway across the parking lot before I break into a run.

I stop outside the door of Read It or Eat It to take some deep breaths and calm my nerves. I catch myself looking over my shoulder. Do I really think Chase would follow me? I have to confront the possibility that this man I've known since I came to Cedar Mill could be dangerous.

Stax is busy at the register with a short line of customers, so I wander into the café to find Larry cleaning some utensils behind the counter. A young couple sips frothy drinks at a small table, but otherwise the café is unoccupied. I let my eyes wander over to the empty booth in the corner where last night so much had been discussed. It seems like a lifetime ago.

"Hey, Lacy, you're getting to be a regular sight around here."

Larry's food is good, but I suspect it is his warmth and sincere enjoyment of people that keep his customers coming back.

"Hiya, Larry. Yes, I suppose my circle of friends is rather small."

"You don't see me complaining."

There is no getting around Larry's smile. He is more than a few years younger than myself, though not so many as to raise eyebrows; he is also more laid back and soft-spoken than the men of my past, which perhaps isn't so bad a thing. The men of my past are in the past for a reason. But I never entertain the idea of getting to know Larry in any way other than as Stax's brother. *Because* he's Stax's brother.

"I'm waiting for Stax to free up," I say. "Figured I'd put a little money in your pocket."

"Oh yeah? What's your poison?"

"Water, please, of the bottled variety."

He waves away the dollar I hold out.

"No good here, Lacy."

"Thanks, Larry. So, if I want to throw a party I can count on you to cater free of charge?"

"I'm generous, not stupid."

We enjoy a laugh. Not a big one, but a good one. The kind you always need more of.

"Ixnay on the chuckles, you two. I make the funnies around here." Stax enters the café carrying an armful of books.

"Just the lady I came to see," I say. "Well, one of them anyways."

"Ruby ain't here."

That surprises me. I thought we were due for another of our meeting of the minds when the store closed. "Everything okay?"

Stax shrugs. "Depends on how good of a cook she is."

"Hey, I do the cooking around here," Larry says.

Stax rolls her eyes.

"See, now you've got my brother stealing my lines. So lame. Ruby invited us over to her place tonight. Six o'clock. Be there or be square. Or, in your case, be there *and* be square, since you can't help it."

I bid adieu to the Bests and head home to clean up and spend a little QT with Meatball. The poor little guy is out of sorts with mommy gone so much lately. I find the paper towels on the kitchen floor and the toilet paper clawed off its roll. I feel guilty, but I can only be in so many places at once. I assuage my guilt by plying him with extra treats.

I put a load of laundry in and manage to grab a little 'me' time on the couch, cleaning out the rapidly-filling DVR. I didn't realize how much time I waste in front of the tube until I spent a few minutes calculating the hours of vapid entertainment I had programmed.

Ruby once again dresses for the occasion: nothing too flashy, just a summer dress and a little rouge. But this time she adds jewelry of the variety you wouldn't wear in just any neighborhood. And there is some sort of splendor circulating in the air around her. I step one foot into the house and the most wonderful aroma takes charge of my senses and pulls me over the threshold.

"Good evening, Lacy. What you're smelling is beef stroganoff. An old Russian woman traded me the recipe for a signed copy of *The Case of the Corpulent Corpse* quite some years ago."

"If it tastes anything like it smells, I'd say it was a good trade for both parties." I mean it. *Corpulent Corpse* is one of my favorite Inspector Butterwell stories.

Ruby gushes appreciation for my kind words and disappears toward the kitchen with apologies. I follow her as far as the living room where once again I find myself entranced by the quaint opulence of her old-world décor. For all there is to look at, something I expect to see is missing.

"Where's Stax?"

Rudy pokes her head around the corner from the kitchen. "She's in the study, dear. Give me just a moment and I'll take you to her. One must be careful not to burn one's cream sauce."

A moment later Ruby is at my elbow and ushering me past the divan and into the hall towards a door.

"You'll find your friend in here."

She opens the door to reveal the most remarkable room I've ever laid eyes on. It puts even her immaculate living room to shame. The plaster and wallpaper evident elsewhere in the house are here replaced with what appears to be oak wood and, over that, red velvet. The ceiling is oak as well, and from its center hangs a Victorian lamp with its glass shade stained soft amber. Similar standing lamps are scattered around the room atop tables and desks. On the far wall is a functional fireplace of the type one might imagine warmed the study of Charles Dickens. In the far-right corner something like a portrait painting on an easel is covered with a dark green sheet.

The walls are lined with floor-to-ceiling shelves weeping under the weight of first editions. Upon closer examination I realize I am gazing upon a treasure trove of classic mystery fiction. Dorothy Sayers, Margery Allingham, some chap named Carr, and a couple dozen more names, familiar and not so (and, of course, Queen Agatha); all first edition hard covers still in their dust jackets.

Oh, and Stax is here as promised. She has tears in her eyes and I'm about to rush to her side to offer comfort when she says "Look at these, books, Lace. Don't touch them! But look at them. My word, if these were mine you'd be looking at my pension."

I forgot for a moment that she is a bookseller, and to such a person this room is akin to Fort Knox.

It occurs to me that this study must originally have been the master bedroom of the house. I find myself wondering where Ruby sleeps—or, for that matter, if she sleeps—when in she walks with heaping bowls of beef stroganoff.

For the next few minutes all thoughts escape me except how much of this rich, creamy pasta I can fit into my body before I become dyspeptic. Following the example set at the café, and in what is becoming a tradition, we do not discuss the gruesome business of murder while eating. Instead, we partake of small talk, such as Ruby asking how my hind section feels since her massage, necessitating that I provide an explanation to Stax, who I'm certain will never let me hear the end of it.

It was an exceptional meal, but no meal can last forever. As the dishes are carried off and the evening tea is served, the air grows still and the atmosphere heavy with anticipation.

"Time to get down to work, ladies," says Ruby, moving near the rectangular object hidden by the green sheet. Stax, behaving like an apt pupil, takes a seat facing Ruby. I haven't budged from my chair since my gluttonous feast and don't intend to do so for a while.

Ruby surprises us by jumping up from her chair with a startled 'Oh!' "I suppose one should prepare first, and I've set this up for our purpose."

She removes the dark green sheet and reveals not a portrait but a shiny white board.

"A dry erase board?' asks Stax.

"Precisely," replies Ruby, pleased with herself. "In my writing days, I had a chalk board for the purpose of plotting out the intricacies of my murders—my *fictional* murders, that is—and also to help me keep my characters straight. One must be careful not to have two men named Bill if it's not integral to the plot, or— Heaven forfend—give the damsel in distress blue eyes in the first act when you've jeweled her with orbs of emerald in Act Three. No, one must be organized. However, I was fussing endlessly over all the chalk dust settling on my knicks and knacks and mucking up my oriental rug. Insufferable! Edwyn, dear heart that he was, surprised me with a dry erase board one day and it is on this that I created my last five masterpieces—if you'll allow a retired writer her delusions of grandeur."

Ruby pauses a moment, her eyes settling fondly on the old board as though in it she could see her late husband. "It's been in storage all these long years, but it's time the old boy is called back into service."

"So, we tell you things, and you'll write 'em up there?" asks Stax, as though the concept requires explanation.

"More or less. We'll track our leads on this side (points to the upper left) and our suspects over here (points to upper right). When we exhaust a lead or clear a suspect, they'll be erased with this (holds up eraser) and a new one added to take their place. Our challenge will be not to collect so many names that we run out of board."

"And how do we do that?" I ask.

"Investigation. Good old fashioned knockin' and talkin' as the hardboiled boys used to say. Too many suspects means you're not doing your job as a sleuth. In a typical whodunit, you have five to seven suspects, and certainly no more than nine—"

"But we're in a Howdunit, aren't we? Is that different?"

Ruby's shoulder bounces a little at that. She nods grimly.

"Yes, yes, it is. Very different."

"How many suspects are there in a Howdunit?"

Ruby throws up her hands.

"One can never say, Miss Stax. If it's a murder in an isolated location, such as a mansion that's been snowed in, what you have is essentially a Whodunit with an impossible murder."

"Why is that?" I inquire.

"Because you'll have a limited pool of suspects."

"Our pool is more like an ocean."

"Exactly, but I don't think it's quite that bad."

"How do you figure?"

"I'd say whoever is behind it must have been at the run."

"One of the runners?"

"Most probably, but not necessarily."

Stax runs a finger along the rim of her bowl, sopping up the delicious cream sauce. "The scissor killer from Marlene's salon?"

Ruby nods.

Stax fidgets in her seat as though a ghost is playing with her hair. "Do we want to talk about that first, or talk about what I found out today?"

Ruby laughs. It is hearty and real, like her cooking. "Stax, you lovely creature, you're nothing if not adorable. I know you're itching to talk about your discovery. I've managed to drum up what little information there is about the salon killer. But what you have might prove more pertinent. So, without further ado…"

She motions for Stax to take the spotlight and returns to her chair.

Stax clears her throat. "Well, I was working my list today, showing Marlene's picture around, and I wasn't having any luck until I got to the Jazz Palace. You ever heard of the place?"

Ruby and I signal that we had not.

Stax sighs. "Me either. If Bon Jovi and Hank Jr. aren't on the juke, then they ain't getting my beer money. Anyway, this place is pretty fancy, like they are angling for a more highfalutin crowd. I thought to myself, 'If I were a snob like Marlene, this is just the kind of joint I'd hang out in', and so I showed her picture around."

I am on the edge of my seat. "And?"

"Nope, she never went in there."

"I believe that's what you call an anti-climax," I say.

Stax crinkles her nose and looks me in the eye. "Chill out, will you? I'm about to climax."

An intense moment follows where I'm not sure if Stax and I will erupt into fits of laughter. A perplexed look from an oblivious Ruby defuses the urge.

"I mean, I'm getting to the point. It so happens that the lady who runs the Jazz Palace once used the Petrick Travel Agency to book a series of Caribbean cruises and so knows both Marlene and Anderson. She made a comment that Marlene's ex-husband came every now and then and that caught my ear.

"I ask if she meant Anderson and she says yes, even described him, so there's no doubt who we're talking about. Of course, Anderson and Marlene are very currently married. Ain't no 'ex' about it! I ask if he came in alone and she says 'No, he always comes in with the same woman,' and described this mystery chick as younger than Marlene (surprise, surprise, the dog), wears a lot of make-up, but more classy than trashy, and—get this she's redheaded."

Ruby's lips purse and she taps at them with her forefinger as though to make them behave. Stax's little tidbit obviously holds a significance that evades me.

"You know what this means, right?" asks an animated Stax.

"What it *might* mean, dear," counters Ruby.

They look to me for accord and are rewarded with a blank stare. Stax lays her best 'are you an idiot?' look on me.

"Maybe I missed something," I say, "but whatever you think this means or might mean is lost on me. Anderson is stepping out with a redhead? That's unfortunate, but not what I'd call shocking."

Stax throws her arms up. "Oh, come on, Lacy! How many good looking redheaded women do you think there are in Cedar Mill?"

"I wouldn't have the slightest …"

Then it hits me. "You don't really think—?"

Ruby uncaps her black marker and reaches up to the white space just under the word 'Suspects.'.

"We'd be remiss to ignore it, dear," Ruby says as a name begins to emerge under that flawless hand of hers.

I think to myself that it can't be. There is no way. But I know I am fooling myself. I've read enough murder mysteries to know that it all too often turns out to be the last person you expect.

"Well, we're off and running," chirps a chipper Ruby. "We've got our first suspect."

And that suspect is Gretchen Herring.

TWELVE

I argue for Gretchen's innocence and virtue like a good friend should. But I had to concede certain salient points: Gretchen works with Anderson at the agency and the boss having an affair with the help is the oldest cliché in the book; Gretchen knows Marlene, is familiar with Chicken Hill, and was on the scene at the time of her disappearance. Oh, and she is definitely redheaded. There must be other redheads in Cedar Mill. Hundreds of them, no doubt. But I can't think of a single one other than Gretchen who might fit the description provided by Stax's source.

I've never seen Gretchen with make-up on or wearing anything fancier than a singlet and shorts, but that's how we all look when we run. Who at Run For It would ever guess I am the owner of a dark blue denim halter top? In an effort to persuade my partners of Gretchen's good will I mention how she came to my house on the evening before the run to apologize for Marlene's behavior. My good intentions quickly backfire.

Stax slaps her thigh. "That settles it! She's guilty as sin."

"How do you figure?"

"What's the best way to avoid suspicion?"

"Don't commit a crime."

"Okay, but suppose you've committed one?'

"Why don't you tell me."

"You pretend to be the victim's friend!"

"So that's what you've got? She's friends with Marlene so we assume it's all an act just to get close to her and kill her?'

"Why not? It made sense to Perry Mason."

"Ruby, what do you make of all this?"

Ruby lowers herself onto the edge of an antique settee and exhales. "I'm not yet ready to put a noose around the girl's neck."

"Thank you!"

"As you say, she may only have been a friend to Marlene and not a diabolical villain hiding in plain sight."

The image of little Gretchen as an evil crime genius raises a laugh in me that I make no attempt to squelch.

"However," continues Ruby, "there are some unflattering facts to consider."

Stax rubs her stubby little hands together excitedly. "Uh huh. Here comes the gospel."

"No gospel, Miss Stax. As I'm sure you're aware, gospel means 'good news', and I'm afraid there's no good news to be had in this mess. No, our mission is the truth, only the truth. In the case of Miss Gretchen, she worked in close quarters with Mr. Petrick, did she not?"

I jump in. "Yes, and also Marlene."

"True, but it is Anderson and not Marlene who was seen with this redhead at a nighttime hot spot."

I concede the point.

"Gretchen is a young woman," continues Ruby, "and it's not unheard of for such a creature to fall under the spell of a handsome older man. And suppose such a woman, while in the clutches of what she believes is true love, makes moves to rid the board of other pawns blocking her ascension."

"You tell 'em, sister!" cheers Stax.

I narrow my eyes at Stax. "Do you really think Gretchen did it?"

"Oh, I don't have the foggiest. But I do like that it's my clue that put her name on the board."

I am white-knuckled and ready to scream. If we are going to treat this like a game, then it is time I play my hand.

"You know, Anderson wasn't the only one 'stepping out.'"

"What do you mean, dear?" inquires Ruby in her usual soft-spoken fashion, in contrast to my frustrated barking.

"Yesterday, before our meeting at the café, you'll recall I stopped in to get some chocolates from Hilda? Well, she heard of Marlene's disappearance and shared a little piece of gossip I didn't think too much of at the time. But in light of all this suspicion facing Gretchen, I feel I should say something."

Stax holds her arms out expectantly, as though waiting for me to throw her a pass. Ruby remains her usual prim self but I can feel the weight of her eyes on me.

"A few days ago, only two days before Marlene disappeared, Hilda said Marlene was in her store sitting for some time with Chase Reynolds. I have no idea what it means, but there it is."

Stax slaps my knee. "Chase Reynolds? As in *our* Chase Reynolds?"

"Yes, the same. Hilda said they shared a table and looked rather cozy."

"This does complicate things," observes Ruby.

"How so?"

"Well, we seem to have both Mister and Missus Petrick enjoying clandestine rendezvous. Whether it is with or without the knowledge of the other remains unclear. It may or may not have anything to do with what happened to Marlene, but the little feather in my brain tells me not to ignore it."

"Feather in your brain?" I ask.

"Yes, you might call it instinct. It's a little tickling of the senses I learned long ago to ignore only at my own peril."

"And it's telling you what, exactly?"

"I make no claims of telepathy, mind you. I just can't help but feel that somewhere in these private and sordid relationships is the answer to our questions."

"Wait, are you saying you think Chase might have killed Marlene?" Stax spoke as though the idea only just occurred to her.

Ruby stands from the settee, tapping the air with the capped end of her marker.

"Not necessarily. However, Chase is also a married man. Married to our beloved Marti. Purely hypothetical, as is everything we're discussing, but what if …"

Ruby paces, eyes down, as though working up the courage to say the words I am thinking. She pauses, turns towards us, and takes a deep breath before continuing. "What if Marti found out about Chase's indiscretions and decided she should take it upon herself to trim the weeds, so to speak?"

A lively discussion follows as Stax puts up a defense of Marti Reynolds much stronger than my efforts on behalf of Gretchen. I agree Marti is no more likely than any of the three of us to be the murderer, but I hold back in my defense of Chase. I recall the way I felt when I was in that little office with him in the bowels of Run For It; how I couldn't get out of there fast enough. Trapped is the only way I can describe it. And that's how I verbalize the episode to Stax and Ruby.

It might all be in my head. Goodness knows I'd been a blender bottle of emotions all day and the salacious tidbit Hilda gave me about Chase and Marlene must have colored my judgment about him to some extent. There is nothing about our exchange I can point to as being evidence of guilt, but there is something he said as I left that stood my hairs on end.

"Sometimes, when you have an idea, it's better to keep it to yourself." I repeated Chase's words verbatim to Ruby and Stax.

"That sounds like a threat to me," Stax says. "Did it sound like a threat to you?"

"Well, it is a heck of a way to say 'good afternoon'," I reply. Truth be told, it's more the words than the tone I found menacing. But is that genuine menace or just my frazzled nerves?

In the end we chose objectivity over sisterhood. After all, this is a hunt for a potential murderer and not a popularity contest. If Chase is indeed carrying on with Marlene, it raises the specter of motive for both himself and Marti (assuming she knew) to want Marlene removed from the equation. Both were not only at Chicken Hill but organized the run and had ample opportunity to set up some sort of trap.

But what of the scissors? Marlene was being stalked by someone planting scissors where she was sure to find them. This means whatever happened to her was not a crime of impulse or passion but was an act both cold and calculated. Very cold, in fact, as it hearkens back to an almost-forgotten murder from eighteen years ago. Gretchen would have been but a small child herself at that time.

Ruby assures us that in the beginning stages of an investigation it is healthy to have more questions than answers, but I am finding it all quite frustrating. For good measure, and because he's the spouse, Anderson Petrick is added to the growing list. We now have four suspects on the board but not a shred of evidence to support an argument against any one of them.

"It's time we start gathering evidence," I say.

Ruby moves across the room towards a large mahogany desk. "That's very astute of you, Lacy. Yes, we now must work to prove or disprove our various theories."

"What if instead of that we find evidence that makes someone else look suspicious?" asks Stax.

"Then we add them to the list and keep moving forward."

It is one thing to talk of gathering evidence, but how does one go about it? We're not the cops, or private investigators.

"So, where do we start?" I ask.

"We start right here and now," Ruby says, returning to her spot on the settee, but now with a small laptop computer. Who knew she was so techy?

"Lacy, you'll recall Stax was creating a spreadsheet for all the runners who were towards the head of the run at Chicken Hill. It is to trace similar runs they participated in over the last six months or so to see if there is any noticeable deviation in their times yesterday. A significant break in stride could be quite telling."

"And what did you learn?"

Stax shrugs her shoulders. "Don't know. Ruby got me the times from yesterday about ten minutes before I had to head over here. I entered the data and saved it but haven't had time to look it over."

Ruby opens the laptop and logs on. "Stax was good enough to e-mail it over to me so she didn't have to bring her hardware. But I'll let her have the honors. Besides, reading spreadsheets was not one of my majors."

Ruby hands the computer over to Stax who spends a solid minute perusing the screen like a doctor reading charts. As I wait for Stax to interpret the data for us a telephone in another room rings out and Ruby excuses herself to answer it.

"Whoa, I didn't see that coming," says Stax, reacting to whatever she sees on her screen. I am about to inquire when Ruby reenters.

"That was Marti," she says, and from her somber expression I didn't expect any good news. "She's just returned from Chicken Hill. The police have completed their search."

"Still no Marlene?"

Ruby shakes her head. "Marti says they had a dozen or more people searching the hill and the area around it. They were out there for hours so they must have been over every inch of ground a few times. I dare say I have new respect for the Cedar Mill Police Department as that was a more thorough search than I expected."

"For all the good it did," I say, sounding too much like a sulking child. "Did they find anything at all?"

"Nothing they thought relevant. Marti mentioned a patch of material they found, not so much because they found it suspicious as they aren't sure what it is."

"And what is it?"

"Marti couldn't say, but she had the presence of mind to retrieve a piece they discarded. Smart girl."

"So, back to square one—a runner who disappears into thin air, a murder no one else thinks has been committed, and four suspects, none of whom are particularly suspicious."

"Uh, make that five suspects," Stax says, wearing the smirk she affects whenever she thinks she's being clever. One cheek pushes up and makes her glasses crooked. It's funny the things you notice about a person once you get to know them.

Ruby rushes over to sit next to Stax. "Oh, you've got something?"

"I just might. Most of the runners were right on track with their accumulated averages. But one was either not having an easy go of the hill or else was up to no good."

"Was it Gretchen?" I surprise myself by arriving so quickly at her name.

Stax shakes her head. "Close, but no dice."

Close? "You don't mean Carly, do you?"

It was a shot in the dark, but when Stax puts a stubby finger to her nose to signify 'Bingo', I knew I'd hit home.

It's not that I thought Carly incapable of murder—if personalities were admissible as evidence then any case against her would be a slam dunk—but it doesn't fit in this case. Why would she want to hurt Marlene? She is no less pretty, a good ten years younger, and to all appearances quite harmonious with her.

"How much time are we talking about?" I ask. Maybe it was too marginal to matter.

Stax runs her finger across and along the screen. "It looks like over the past three trail runs she's been pretty consistent, even PRing each time, though only by seconds. Then we get to Chicken Hill and she's a full eight minutes past her last time. I'd say that's pretty substantial. It's like she lost eight minutes somewhere on the trail."

"Eight minutes is a long time," Ruby says. "But of course, we can't jump to conclusions. There might be a perfectly innocent explanation."

"Maybe, but how would we find out what that is?" I ask.

Ruby stares at me for a moment. It is as though time froze or someone hit pause on the room. "Oh, that was a serious question! I thought perhaps you were setting me up for another one of your private laughs with Miss Stax. But you really mean it when you ask how we might find out why Carly lost so much time in her run."

"Err, yes," was my meek reply.

"I thought all of us learned in kindergarten that the best way to get a question answered is to ask it. My, how your teachers have failed you."

Gulp.

Stax places the laptop on the hand-carved eagle table in front of her and retrieves her cell phone, brandishing it in the air like an icon. "You need someone to make calls? I'm your girl. I got most of their numbers already, and if I don't have it, I can get it."

"Very good, Stax," Ruby says with exaggerated approval. "That's precisely the kind of gumption we need if we're going to get Lacy off the hook."

"What!" I don't bother to hide my consternation. "I'm loaded with gumption! I've got gumption up to my eyeballs!"

"That ain't gumption, honey, that's cleavage. And it looks like I've got you beat on both counts."

Shut up, Stax.

"I'm glad to hear that, dear," Ruby says as she buzzes her way back over to the dry erase board, "because I've saved the dirtier work for the two of us. Now, Stax, be sure to call Carly first and get her explanation. Maybe disguise your intention by offering your condolences on the confusing disappearance of her friend. It might have been pretend, but she did seem rather flustered yesterday after the run—"

I was dying to jump in and find out what this 'dirty work' is that Ruby signed me up for. But she was on a roll. As she spoke, she wrote Carly's name on the board.

"Now, make careful note of what she says, down to the syllable. After this, call the other runners who started behind her but finished ahead of her. They must have passed her on the trail, so it's important to find out if they saw Carly, and if so, what they saw. Oh, and ask if anybody else was with her. We'd be remiss to assume we're only looking for one culprit. With that in mind I should add one more entity to our rogue's gallery."

She stops for a breath and to write the word 'Unknown' under Carly's name on the board. I assume this refers to the yet-to-be-captured salon slayer from Marlene's past. The idea that this ghoul could be traveling in our circle gives me chills. But I am not about to let it distract me from my goal of finding out just how much dirt is going to be under my nails.

"Ruby, about this 'dirty work' you mentioned …"

"Yes, dear?"

"What do you have in mind?"

"I thought we might pay a visit to the Petrick Travel Agency. As it's the den not only of our victim but two of our suspects, it could prove a boon to our investigation."

That didn't sound too dirty to me. "I'm not sure how much Anderson would want to tell us and I bet Gretchen would feel a bit ganged upon with the two of us throwing questions at her. But, if you think it could be worthwhile, I'm more than game. I'll take my lunch early tomorrow so we don't miss them, assuming they break at noon."

Ruby places the marker in its tray and turns to face me. "Oh no, tomorrow's no good. We're going tonight."

I wonder if perhaps the old gal isn't going a bit senile. "But it's after six. They'll be closed."

"Yes, that's the idea. But right now's no good. There will still be too many people about. The agency's next to a sleepy little neighborhood where people will be walking their dogs and children will be playing until dark. How does a midnight ramble grab you, Lacy?"

What I am hearing isn't senility, it is insanity. "I don't think I like where this is going at all."

"You're not the superstitious type, are you? I should think you'd know by now that ghouls are as likely to strike in the cold light of day as in the lonely moonlight of the witching hour."

"Maybe I'm losing my mind, but what you're talking about sounds an awful lot like breaking and entering."

Ruby erupts into laughter, loud and hearty, with a hand held to her stomach as though her spleen might slip out her navel. "No, no, dear. We're not going to break anything. What are we, savages? We're just going to enter!"

THIRTEEN

When a cat looks at a clock they see only a big hunk of plastic, and yet, somehow, they know when it's treatsie time or time for you to wake up. And, as I discovered on this night, they also know when you're up way past your bedtime.

Normally on a work night I'm in bed with a book by nine-thirty and lights out an hour later. Since runners are the only idiots who get up earlier on their days off, my weekend routine begins a half hour earlier. Meatball plans his own schedule around mine so he's ready to settle in next to me and watch me read until finally nodding off.

Here I am at eleven-thirty, sitting on my couch, fully dressed. Meatball sits on the love seat alternating between the grooming tasks that consume much of his time and staring blankly at me like I am a crazy lady. I consider the task to which I set myself tonight and decide 'crazy' isn't far from the mark.

At a quarter to midnight I make my way out into the black of night. I don't recall having seen my street at this hour so I take a moment to look around. There is one night-owl still burning lights half a dozen houses up the road, but otherwise, the homes rest in slumber.

I no sooner put my car into park along Ruby's curb than I see her little figure come down the cobbled walk towards me. She insisted I dress in dark clothes, so I chose a dark blue blouse and a pair of purple yoga pants that somehow evaded numerous donation purges. Ruby resembles her own shadow, clad as she is head to toe in solid black. I thought there was a difference between dressing dark and looking like you plan to commit a burglary, but to Ruby there is no such distinction.

"Isn't this exciting?" she asks as she settles in the seat and closes the car door. Her expression is one of a child on her way to the fair.

"Is it supposed to be?"

She slaps her leg, feigning indignation. "Well, yes! Here we are, two amateur sleuths on a dead-of-night mission, going where we're not supposed to go to find what we're not intended to find. How could one not be thrilled?"

"I suppose. On the bright side, it's a first offense. And we might get time off for good behavior. Does your lock picking work on prison cells by any chance?"

"Lock picking? Goodness, no, there'll be none of that. We'll just open the door and take a look around. Nothing too serious."

I pull out of Ruby's neighborhood and onto a larger street. The moon is high and sits burnt orange in a blue night sky. I keep my window cracked but it is cool enough to let the AC rest. In spite of the darkness, I feel vulnerable. The more so because my 'partner' thinks Anderson Petrick would be so considerate as to leave the door unlatched for us.

"Just open the door, huh? And how do we manage that?"

She looks at me as though my nose is falling off.

"It's a normal round door knob, dear. All you have to do is turn—oh!—silly me, I suppose I didn't tell you how I spent part of my day. No wonder you're confused. I took my lunch at the little sandwich parlor tucked between the hardware store and the women's gym. You know the one?"

"You mean the Subway?"

"Yes, that's the one. I was eating my salad—thick bread is murder on my digestion—and pondering how we might get a peek at the inner workings of the travel agency, when it occurred to me it's a public place and so why not just pop over there. After all, I'm not entirely a stranger. So, that's what I did."

As Ruby talks I hang a left onto Main. Here the street widens out and I notice I am the only car on the road. Except, that is, for the police cruiser gaining behind me. I have to remind myself my tags are up to date and I've done nothing wrong ... not yet.

"I just sauntered in there like never-you-mind," continues Ruby, "and there was Gretchen at her little desk up front. She was surprised to see me but quite pleasant about it. I told her I'd come to offer Anderson my condolences for his missing wife. I wasn't surprised to find he had taken the day off. Perhaps he's distraught over Marlene, but if not, one must put on pretenses. So, I instead offered my condolences to Gretchen, and again she was most gracious. I started her reminiscing about her missing boss and let her go on long enough so that when I excused myself to use the restroom, it didn't seem out of place."

"I assume you didn't actually need to use the restroom?"

"I most certainly did! I treated myself to a soda with my salad and it went right through me. But I was on a mission and, I'm proud to say, I succeeded. Little buildings like this always have a back door that opens up to the alley. With only three people, none of them smokers, I figured this door was only used to take the trash out to the dumpsters. Well, I learned from my new friend at the sandwich parlor that trash days in that district are on Mondays and Thursday, so I thought there was a fair chance it wouldn't get used today. I simply unlocked the door, said my farewells to Gretchen, and off I went."

"So that's what you mean by we'll just walk in?"

She nods in a manner that says she's very proud of herself.

"Did it occur to you they might have an alarm system?"

"It did. And they don't."

I relax a little. I weigh the risks and decide our purpose is worth it. Somebody in my circle did something terrible. I want to know who and why.

"Lacy, where are you're going?" asks Ruby.

"Err … the travel agency."

"Poor dear, your eyes are open but your brain's asleep," she says, clicking her tongue. "All this cloak and dagger won't amount to much if we leave your car in front of the place for all to see. We must park elsewhere and walk."

She is right, of course, both about my sleepy brain and about parking and walking. I decide to park behind Stax's bookstore. It isn't particularly close, but it's a familiar place, and right now familiar feels good.

It's my first time walking the back streets and alleys of Cedar Mill in the dark of night. It's not likely to become a habit, but I can't deny there is something beautiful about a good town when you catch it sleeping.

As Ruby and I walk side by side past the generators, dumpsters, and cast-outs along the back side of Main Street's storefronts, the crunch of gravel under our feet echoes like a roar in the still night. I decide to speak.

"We got so distracted discussing how Marlene might have disappeared that you never got around to telling us what you learned about the salon murder."

Ruby nods and takes a deep breath. As much as she might enjoy the hunt, it is clear she has no relish for the loss of life. It is something she takes very seriously.

"It was in the summer of 2000, so eighteen years ago almost to the day. I don't believe she'd met Anderson yet. Marlene was young and somehow found the capital to open her own salon in one of those small strip malls you see all around Tulsa. You know, the ones that lost their anchor store years ago and now look like they don't know what to do with themselves. From what I understand, Marlene's salon was nothing special, yet it was successful. Remarkably successful according to my source, himself a retired investigator. Word got around that Marlene's girls were offering more than pedicures and perms."

"You mean drugs?"

"No, dear. Marlene dabbled in, shall we say, a profession much older than either narcotics or acrylics."

I wouldn't put much past Marlene, but brothel Madame wasn't even a blip on my radar.

"But the problem with such endeavors is they inevitably take place in private," observes Ruby, "and that makes it hard for the authorities to build a case. They tried for months and had all but given up when a young woman stepped forth. She was an employee of the salon, fresh out of cosmetology school. She says Marlene paid better than the other salons and she was grateful for the opportunity. But she always felt there was something a bit off about the place. That was the scheme—hire the girls in when they're desperate, get them used to a certain income and then spring on them the 'extracurricular activities' expected of them.

"Marlene wouldn't make the approach but have one of her girls do it. Devilishly clever of her to consider that if the new girl didn't respond well to the idea and quit or was summarily dismissed, she'd have nothing but her word to take to investigators and nothing at all to say against Marlene herself."

"So why did the police put any stock in this girl when she stepped forward?"

"Because she hadn't said no."

Oh.

"She was seduced by the money at first, and by the pressure of her older, more experienced peers. Eventually, she came to regret her decision, but by then Marlene had sunk her teeth into the poor girl and she felt obligated to continue her sinful work. However, her better angels grabbed her and carried her out of there and into the arms of the police."

"Who sent her right back in."

Ruby nods and I clench my hands into fists, wondering how much consideration was given to the young woman's safety by the men she trusted but who, it seems, were hell bent only on making a big bust.

"The police sent her back in wired. They still used wires then, you know, so one would have to be very careful. But before she could get anything incriminating, she was murdered. The investigation was exposed at that point and Marlene closed her salon, her fellow conspirators scattering to the four winds. No arrest was ever made."

"And no clue to the killer's identity?"

"There was a clue. You'll recall I said she was wired."

We step out of the alley and onto a back road leading to a smattering of small offices and garages. A warm breeze whips around the corner and tickles my goosebumps.

"You mean her murder was recorded?"

"Every last breath, I'm afraid. My source offered me a copy but I settled for a transcript. The killer never spoke, but the young lady—her name was Kayleigh Cook—spoke as though she knew the person and expected to see them in the salon. While the police couldn't rule out a familiar client, they felt it was most likely an inside job and narrowed their list of suspects down to four—all of them women."

"And one of them was Marlene."

"Indeed."

"Although I suppose she's now in the clear if she's also been murdered."

"That presupposes the two cases are connected."

"Wasn't this young woman, Kayleigh, murdered with a pair of scissors?"

"Yes, she was. In fact, I saw a photo of the murder weapon. It's identical in every respect to the pair of scissors left in Marlene's tire the other afternoon."

"Well, there you go. It must be the same killer."

"Must it? We don't know Marlene was killed with scissors."

"True, but you're convinced she's been murdered. And there's scissors everywhere. What else could it be?"

"Revenge, perhaps? If someone close to Kayleigh holds Marlene responsible, they could be inflicting their own brand of justice."

That makes perfect sense and I find myself frustrated by it. We need fewer possibilities, not more.

"Do you know what became of the other three suspects in the murder?"

"My friend says two were quite easy to locate—one straightened her life out and is raising a family in Massachusetts. Another sadly walked a different path and is serving a sentence on drug charges."

"And the third?"

"She's been harder to locate through normal channels, but he's good at what he does. She'll turn up. Oh! Time we get into stealth mode."

"Are we there?"

"That we are."

It's funny to think I could be lost. Walking through a town at night by its alleys instead of its street is rather like trying to recognize a person by looking at their X-ray.

The Petrick Travel Agency is a stand-alone wooden box with picture-windows in the front that look out over a rustic wooden porch, finished in a way that makes it appear fashionably unfinished. Not so much care was taken with the back of the building—a flat sheet of brown wood with an ugly green steel-reinforced door. It is at this ugly door that I commit my first crime.

The door opens as Ruby predicted. Enshrouded in darkness, the hall ahead of us looks like a black tunnel that goes on forever. Ruby removes a small pen light from her pocket and leads the way in. Why didn't I think of bringing a flashlight? Oh, yeah, because I'm not a crook. But I did bring my cell phone and I remember it has a flashlight app. That should work fine as anything brighter would be visible to outside passers-by.

We first come to a room on our left. A quick look reveals it to be a large office smelling vaguely of leather. The dominant color is brown and the walls are decorated with posters of exotic destinations. We decide this must be Anderson's office and Ruby calls dibs, suggesting I continue on to find Marlene's. 'What are we looking for?' I ask. 'We'll know it when we see it' was the response.

After first poking my head into the restroom and a supply closet, I find my target. Marlene's office looks like what you might expect a narcissistic, unimaginative ex-cheerleader's office would look like, complete with portrait photography of herself and Anderson (but mostly herself), a tin mural of 'LIVE, LAUGH, LOVE' consuming half a wall, some Dora the Explorer figures to tie it all in with travel, and the obligatory romantic getaway promotionals. Under the 'LOVE' tin are two chest-high filing cabinets. I consider pilfering those first but her personal space calls to me, so I tiptoe my way behind her desk.

The window behind me is conveniently covered with Venetian blinds twisted open just enough to allow the moonlight to bathe her desk and render my flashlight app moot, at least for the moment. Her desktop is spotless, which doesn't surprise me. I suspected her desk, much like herself, would be kept and orderly on the outside and a complete mess on the inside. I slide open the top right drawer and give myself a figurative pat on the back. The drawer is like a dry cesspool full of crinkled gum wrappers (some with gum still in them), paper clips, uncapped pens, loose change, and the largest collection of old condiment packets I've ever seen. I notice a few sweet and sour packets from a Chinese restaurant long out of business and surmise that what they contain must now be more sour than sweet. I don't want to dig through this drawer, but I am a woman on a mission, and thank goodness I brought gloves!

I find nothing of interest in the desk drawers, save for a couple pairs of women's frilly undergarments that—even with gloves on—I refuse to touch. I think of Chase when I see them and feel a passing pang of guilt for making the connection. He'd never cheat on Marti. Not with the likes of Marlene.

Movement in the hall catches my eye and I freeze like a deer, but it is only Ruby's light bouncing off the walls as she moves around. I breathe a sigh of relief and tell myself not to be so paranoid. *Yes, there's a killer out there, but they're not coming after you.*

Then comes the unmistakable sound of shattering glass. Perhaps Ruby knocked something over. I wait for her to call out an 'oh, criminy!' or something of the like but nothing comes. Her bouncing light is gone as well. Has she hurt herself somehow? I imagine Ruby lying helpless on the floor of Anderson's dank office and am about to run to her aid when I hear the sound of more glass falling. It isn't a lamp that broke but a window. The sound is coming from the front office, where we haven't yet looked. Where someone may have been waiting the entire time, watching us, or biding his time until we showed ourselves.

I don't move a muscle. I just stare at the shadows in the office doorway and pray they don't start moving. Then it comes, a new sound. A dead bolt is turning. *Is he leaving?* I ask myself. I remember how the front of the building is laid out, with large windows on either side of the door. What I am hearing is the sound of someone breaking *in* by reaching through the broken window and unlatching the door.

I hope there's another lock to the door, one requiring a key. Maybe the intruder is just a burglar with terrible timing and he'll get frustrated and go away.

Instead, the door opens. The crickets are loud now, like they're in the room with me. I hear glass shards crunching under rubber soles as the front door is closed. The crickets are still where they were, but the feet have moved to the top of the hall.

It is bad enough to know I'm sharing my quiet town with a maniac.

I didn't count on sharing a room with one.

FOURTEEN

I drop down and slide under the desk. It is all I can think to do. I should be okay If the intruder only peeks into the room, but if they want in the desk, I'm screwed. All I can do is hold my breath and watch from my spot on the carpet. There is just enough room where I can look out and see all the way to the door.

Marlene must carry her own iPad or Notebook, because there is no computer in her office. There is sure to be one at the reception desk, so if the intruder is indeed a burglar, perhaps he'll be satisfied with that and scram.

No such luck. I can hear them coming before I see them, and now here they are: two feet. Dark shoes. I can't see well enough to tell if they are men's or women's, but whoever they belong to is now in Marlene's office and walking towards me.

My heart stops when the feet halt in the center of the room. Do they know I'm in here? Could they? Yes, if they saw us enter. But if they saw us enter they would have come in the same way, through the open back door, instead of breaking a window. Well, there is one thing we have going for us.

The feet are moving again. Are they coming around the desk? No, they're headed to the far side of the room.

I hear a noise like old metal. A click, a squeal, and the hard howl of an ungreased pulley. The dark stranger is opening one of the filing cabinets. Based on the position of the feet, I figure it is the one closest to me. Papers rustle as fingers flip through thick folders. Another quick squeal and a slam as the drawer closes. Whatever they wanted, they knew where to find it.

I see the feet turn around. The tips are pointed right at me. I imagine I next see bent knees and a face peering under the desk. And groping, evil hands. The events of the last few days, in particular the last few minutes, have given my mind leave to run with wild abandon, and I have to work hard to keep from panicking. But as fevered as my imagination is, it has not prepared me for what will happen next.

Something hard and metallic hits the floor in front of me. In spite of the carpet it comes down with a 'clang'. A light beam hits the floor and I realize the burglar/killer/whatever has a flashlight. Not good for me. In the light I see the glint of stainless steel. As the beam settles on the object I can see quite clearly that it is a pair of barber scissors.

In that moment, any hope I was witnessing a standard, every day, random burglary, went out the window. I am trapped in a room with a killer. Possibly a multiple murderer. My body withdraws from the edge of the desk, as far away from the scissors as I can get. The next thing I know I am rendered blind by an orange light.

I have been discovered.

I am about to release a gut-wrenching scream of operatic proportions when the light goes away. Through my muddled vision I can see the scissors are now gone. The beam of his light must have blinded me as he bent down to retrieve the dropped scissors. The black shoes retreat from the room. A moment later the front door opens and closes again.

I refuse to take a breath for the next hour. Well, it was probably only twenty seconds, but it feels longer when you're depriving yourself of oxygen. The small office building is quiet again though the outside noises are still audible on account of the broken window. I crawl to the door and peek up the hall, then down the hall. I brace myself for dark shoes and scissors, but there's only darkness. I stay still for a moment longer before calling out to Ruby.

"Right here, dear," came the soft voice from another room. "Is the coast clear?"

"Seems to be," I whisper.

Ruby steps out into the hallway, running her hands down her dark clothes as though concerned about dust and wrinkles.

"I suppose we'll find out soon enough, what with all our chitchat. Come, Lacy, get off the floor unless you mean to sleep there."

Ruby is remarkably calm given our experience. She didn't have sharp scissors dropped in front of her face. I tell her about them and the pilfering of the file drawer.

"I must see that drawer," she says, rushing past me to the filing cabinets. Ruby jerks open the top drawer and bounces the end of her penlight over its contents.

After only a moment's inspection she slams it closed. When she opens the second drawer I hear her make a quiet, joyful sound.

"Find something?" I ask.

"No, but I believe our phantom friend did. Look at this."

I peer over her shoulder and see a manila file open with some loose papers inside.

"What am I supposed to be looking at?"

Ruby points out the open file in the middle of the row of folders, all of which are pushed to the front and back to leave ample room for this file to be open. Like so many things with Ruby, it was glaringly obvious once pointed out to me.

"Did the killer put something in the file?" I ask.

"It doesn't appear so." She thumbs through the small stack of papers from the folder. "All these are what you might expect to find in an employee's file in her manager's office. That means the killer—or whoever was just in here—took something out."

"Employee?"

"Yes, didn't you notice the name on the front of the folder?"

I had not, but I look now. It reads 'G. Herring'. Gretchen.

"What was in Gretchen's file that someone would break in to take?" I ask.

Ruby closed the drawer and turned off her light. Either she hadn't heard my question or she didn't find it worth answering because she went to the door and peered out into the hall.

"We're going to need to take a look around the front office," she says, still whispering.

I was not at all fine with this. Believing the person with the scissors is gone and knowing it are not at all the same thing.

We keep our lights off and perform a quick inspection of the front office, looking in every dark corner, behind every piece of furniture, and in every crevice for a crouching bogeyman. Ruby peeks out the window as I hold an ear up to the broken pane lest we see a figure dashing behind a tree or hear the crunch of leaves under feet. We don't, so we set about the business of seeing what the front office can tell us.

As with many small offices in Oklahoma (my own included), a guest enters into a sitting area to the right, decorated to resemble an average mid-American home, and greeted on the left by a friendly receptionist. There is little about the sitting area to appeal to our sleuthing senses, so we gravitate to the reception desk.

Gretchen keeps her drawers much neater than did her employer. Not a big surprise there. She seems like a young woman who—if a bit insecure—has it together. What stands out to me is an award proudly displayed on one corner of her desk. The hard-plastic base has a small gold-coated plaque on the front of it bearing Gretchen's name, last year's date, the name of the organization (Sew What?) and Gretchen's achievement of 'Best Burlap Technique'. The award atop the base is a bronze rendition of a woman's hand holding a sewing needle.

I try to picture Gretchen spending hours in a chair patiently sewing and mastering her technique and find I can't conjure the image. It doesn't add up with the somewhat scattered but athletic young woman who is so motivated to enter the business world. Perhaps I don't know her as well as I think.

I see the curtain in front of the broken window move out of the corner of my eye. Ruby yelps. It is just the wind moving the curtains and Ruby reacting to something she found in a book. Totally unrelated events. But the damage is done, as I panic and manage to break the bronze needle off the award.

"Lacy, come look at this. Let me know if it means anything to you."

I put the award back where I found it and set the broken needle next to it.

"You didn't happen to find any super glue, did you?" I ask foolishly.

Ruby is holding a little black notebook and pondering a card she found inside.

"This is Gretchen's day planner," she observes as she hands me a business card. "Everything in here relates to her work for the travel agency, except this."

I look at the card. It is white and embossed in gold lettering that reads 'The Survival List, How to Survive in a Post-Doomsday World'. Rather morbid, I think. I wonder where she came by obtaining this card when I notice the website address and phone number. Something about those digits hits home with me. I reach for my cell phone and get to scrolling. Sure enough.

"That's Gretchen's number," I hear myself say. I am shocked. I do not know this girl at all.

Ruby takes the card from my hand. "You don't mind if take this, do you?"

Perhaps I am being too judgey, but there is something creepy about the card. I hand it to Ruby who pockets it and takes me by the arm. "I think it's time we leave," she says. "That broken window changes things quite a bit if we should happen to be seen here."

She doesn't need to tell me twice. We slip out the way we came in, back into the dark alleys and to the back of Stax's bookstore where my car is waiting. It is a fast, quiet walk for the two of us. We don't speak about it, but we both keep our eyes focused on our surroundings. There is somebody out there with a sharp pair of scissors and the ability to make people disappear into thin air. We have no intention of allowing them to practice their skills further on us.

I let Ruby off at her house with the promise we'd see each other tomorrow evening at Run For It for the Tuesday night group run. While driving home I realize 'tomorrow evening' is actually tonight, as it is now after 2am. I didn't think I'd be able to fall asleep after our rather harrowing adventure, but I am out as soon as my head hits the pillow.

I wake to the sound of Meatball's meows. I failed to set my alarm the night before and am fifteen minutes late getting up, but thanks to my furry friend, I won't be late to work.

I drink a LIT when I get to my desk and decide it won't be my only caffeine infusion today. I am grateful for a slow day at work. Bill and Caroline are doing a financial seminar this evening in the banquet room of a steak restaurant, so they remain locked in Bill's office most of the day preparing their PowerPoint. I have plenty of time to ponder the mystery surrounding my little running group.

Ruby is convinced that Marlene's been murdered by some ghoul who must be in possession of her corpse. As gruesome as this is, I've no grounds on which to argue against it. Given the evidence, it's a more likely scenario than her having run away from home. Somehow, this all ties in with an unsolved murder from eighteen years ago and a break-in to the Petrick Travel Agency. It would be enough to make my head spin if not for the crick I still have in my neck from crouching under Marlene's desk.

I've had enough of small, homey offices for the time being and decide I'll take my lunch out of doors. Cedar Mill is flush with beautiful parks, some as monuments to the founders, or those from the town who served their country in war. Others are for enjoyment and celebration, two things I could use a little bit of right now, even if I receive it vicariously.

I have a second packet of my precious LIT but decide to save it for later. I rarely break my 'no caffeine after 2pm' rule, but I am willing to make an exception today as I barely got any sleep and I have a three-mile run after work. Skipping the run isn't an option as we are 'on the case' and the running group is a great opportunity for gossip.

I think about grabbing lunch from Larry at the Read It or Eat It café and catching up with Stax in the process, but sandwich and chips sounds a little too heavy for how my stomach is feeling. I settle instead on a grilled chicken salad from the grocer and a stone bench in front of a rose garden in Tranquility Park.

The park's name is no misnomer as one cannot help but feel their burdens lift as they inhale the pure aromatics of nature at its best. Watching a boy chase his dog, then vice versa, and back again, I almost manage to forget tonight's run will be led by Carly, who in Marlene's absence will now be run leader.

A young mother and her daughter, no older than five, mosey up to the bench across from me and appear to be looking for something in the grass around it. The little girl's blonde locks and the way her smile pushes up her cherubic cheeks makes me smile in return. For a moment I am in her world and not my own.

Then my phone rings.

"You on lunch?" says Stax.

"Yep, I'm in the park."

"My food not good enough for you?"

"It's Larry's food and I felt like a salad today. Don't worry, I'll get my Stax time in this evening."

"You're getting your Stax time right now. I got the lowdown from Carly about her time at the trail run."

"You spoke to her?"

"Yes. I made a bunch of calls last night while you and Ruby were off playing hide-and-go-seek in Marlene's place of business."

I take another bite of salad and watch the little girl play with her mother while they look in the grass. I try to listen to the girl's laughter with one ear and Stax with the other, but it seems tranquility is not on the menu this day in Tranquility Park.

"I take it you've spoken to Ruby?" I ask.

"Yep, called her earlier and gave her the lowdown. She told me all about your little adventure. Must say, I'm kind of jealous."

"Good, then next time there's a choice between felony and phone calls, I'll make the calls. What did you learn?"

"Carly said the rocks had given her blisters and somewhere in the final quarter she got a bad charley horse. She's apparently never heard of potassium. Anyway, she says she lost time rubbing out her calf and that's why she had a bad run."

"You believe her?"

"I don't know, I guess so. Let me tell you, it was an awkward call. It's not like the two of us have a lot to say to each other, but I used her friendship with Marlene as an excuse for the questions. You know, 'I'm sorry your friend went poof' and all that. But if what happened to Marlene fazed her, she didn't show it a bit."

"Then why do you believe her?"

"It's not her I believe, it's the other runners. I got ahold of a few of the other top finishers and they all remembered seeing Carly off to the side of the trail, rubbing her calf and acting like a baby. She couldn't be doing that and killing Marlene at the same time."

"What did Ruby make of it when you told her?"

"She called it 'interesting'. To tell you the truth, I think that old lady would find a loaf of bread interesting if you stabbed it with a knife. She did tell me not to talk to anyone else about our 'inquiry' as she called it. She does know she's not British, right?"

I watch as the little girl leaps from the grass with one hand over her head. She jumps up and down, calling out 'I found it! I found it!'

"Anyway," continued Stax, "I told her for the tenth time you're the only one in the running group I communicate with aside from the occasional finger gesture. I think it's starting to sink in. But hey, that goes for you, too."

"Got it. I'll keep your lowdown on the down low."

"Hey, you made a funny! I think I'm starting to rub off on you."

The little girl catches me staring at her and bounces towards me.

"Stax, I've got to get back to work. I'll see you at six."

I feel a little hand on my knee as I end the phone call.

"Look, I found it!" exclaims the little girl. She holds up a piece of cheap jewelry: a little silver locket with chips in the paint. "I lost it Saturday when I was playing. It's got my daddy's picture inside. He's overseas fighting bad guys, but he'll come back to me, too. Just like this locket did."

She is so cute I want to pick her up and kiss her, but her mother comes over and kneels beside her.

"I'm sorry she bothered you," the mother says. "She's just excited she found her locket."

"No bother at all," I say, and I mean it. Her precious little face and more caffeine is all I need to get me through the rest of the day.

"Mommy said I'd find it and she was right!" effuses the little darling.

"Mothers usually are," I say in return. Mom kisses her daughter on the top of her head and smiles at me. They have the same smile. Daddy is one lucky man.

"I told Lacy here not to worry," said the mother. "Nothing stays lost forever, isn't that right?"

I agree with the woman and don't bother to tell her my name is also Lacy. The moment is fine as it is. They leave with the girl hopping along beside her mother, sharing a song. I stare at my unfinished salad and think about what the woman said.

Nothing stays lost forever. Hadn't Ruby said something similar? If I were superstitious, I'd say this was something like an omen—a girl with my name pointing me towards something I'm supposed to know or understand. But I'm not superstitious. I know it is just coincidence.

That doesn't mean it isn't true. Perhaps some things do stay lost forever.

But not most things.

Not Marlene.

FIFTEEN

F or those enrolled in Run For It's training program, Saturday is the official training run day, but on Tuesday and Thursday evenings free supplementary social runs are also offered. Although not mandatory, it's an unspoken directive that if you're serious about running, you'll do your best to attend one or both of these runs. This goes for all the levels and groups.

Walking into the store this evening I sense something has changed in the more than 48 hours since the trail run. There is an electricity in the air that isn't usually present. People enjoy the group and use it as a way to let go of the tension of their daily lives, but not this evening. The usual relaxed conversation one hears walking through the store has been replaced by hushed whispers in corners and private huddles outside. This in spite of the fact that there are half as many people as are usually present for a Tuesday run.

Carly stands staring at her cell phone by an armless mannequin whose job is to display the latest official Run For It gear. She looks naked not sandwiched between Marlene and Gretchen, though I'm sure if given time Carly could turn even a mannequin mean.

Hmmm, where is Gretchen?

I make my way around the different groups and say my hellos, catching murmurs and snippets of conversation here and there, all of it gossipy theorizing about Marlene's fate. Most of it is to the effect that she is a no-good cheat who cuckolded poor Anderson and made good her escape with her lover. Other theories reflect a different view of Anderson Petrick and cast him as some sort of serial killer. In short, none of us are safe.

I find Ruby surrounded by her fellow walkers, nodding and smiling and enduring talk I know she considers baseless nonsense. But our job tonight is to keep our ears open and our mouths closed and that's what we're both doing. Stax has not shown up yet but it is typical of her to arrive at the last minute if a customer keeps her through her 6pm closing time.

Ruby spots me milling about and pulls me aside for a private chat. "I see you've been mixing. As much mixing as one can do with a crowd this small."

"I was just thinking the same thing. I wonder where everybody is?"

"It's controversy, dear. It either repels or attracts. When something happens that's not supposed to, you can expect fewer people to want to be around it. But those who come always get there early."

The little bell above the north door jingles and in comes Stax. It is obvious she changed her clothes in a hurry as she's holding her GPS watch in her hand and her water bottles are upside down in their belt slots. She impatiently smiles her greetings in passing to the others and makes her way directly to us.

"Hey there, cat burglars. So, what's the scoop?"

"Keep your voice down," I say. "Everyone's in gossip mode right now and I'd like to keep my name out of it."

"Gossip, ey? So, what's the word on the street?"

"That Marlene ran off with some mysterious lover. Nothing useful."

"I wouldn't say it's useless," offers Ruby. "Gossip is a lot like folk lore. It's embellished and not to be taken at face value, but there's usually a kernel of truth in it."

I can't think of Marlene and her 'secret lover' without thinking of Chase. I glance over to the counter where he stands with Marti, looking out solemnly on their dwindling group. The store depends on the support they get from their running group, as these runners are their most active customers.

"Are you saying you think there's something to it?" I ask.

"No, not at all. As I've said, Marlene has not run off. But that's not to say there isn't a lover mixed up in this somewhere. After all, where there's a murder, there must be a motive. And unrequited love is as good as any."

An older gentleman I recognize as belonging to Ruby's walking group taps her on the shoulder and whispers they are about to head out. Ruby thanks him and turns back to us. "I'll catch up with you two after the run. Or, in my case, walk. If only I were twenty or thirty years younger you'd be eating my dust. But one does what one can."

The smirk as she turns away and the little gleam in her eye gives me a warm sense of comfort. She is much more in her element with all this mystery and intrigue than I am. Stax, too, seems to be thriving. I am glad I'm not alone in this.

"I suppose Carly's in charge tonight," says Stax. "Are you ready to run like a hamster on a wheel?"

I roll my eyes. It is true. As vain as Marlene is, always running us past her billboards and advertisements, she would at least put effort into blocking out new and different routes for us to take. As deputy run leader, Carly is occasionally in charge and her route is always the same—a boring trip in a square around the block we would repeat *ad nauseam* until we completed the prescribed number of miles. It is all sidewalk except for a detour down an old graveled back alley I'm convinced exists solely to torture my blisters. Fortunately, tonight is only a three-mile run, which means I only have to suffer that blasted alley three times.

Carly's monotone voice rises above the lull. I can't hear what she's saying but other members of our group are collecting in front of her, so she must be summoning the troops. Stax and I move to the back of the group. Carly stands apart and stares out at us with her usual blank expression. She steps a few paces away to grab her water bottle and I notice she is being careful not to put too much pressure on her right leg.

Carly is taller than all the women present and many of the men. It is always obvious when she is about to speak because she arches her arms and grabs her hips in a classic Amazonian pose. "Okay, Marlene is not here. I know you all know that because it's all you seem to be discussing. We're here to run and I don't think it's helpful to spread gossip and rumors, but whatever.

I'll be taking over as run leader and so I'll need a new deputy for the time being. Lacy, I'm going with you."

Me? There isn't another Lacy in the group, is there?

"Um, okay, sure."

Carly acknowledges my assent with a blink. "I've got a blister in the most terrible place and a shin splint from hell, so I'll be running caboose. You don't mind taking the front, do you?"

"I guess not, but—"

"Great, well, let's head out then, shall we? We're late as it is. You take off and we'll follow."

I don't want to lead the run group, but I'm not comfortable participating in yet another confrontation in Marti's store, so I say 'okay'. I exit the store and when the others follow I start off in a trot down the sidewalk, following Carly's usual route. I'm not looking forward to the gravel. It is a short alley, but not short enough when your blisters are still healing. I can feel my blood boil and this makes me run faster. It didn't occur to Carly to ask if I felt up to leading the group. She saw me at Chicken Hill. She knows I ran the same trail as herself. Some people!

And why me? It should be Gretchen, but she's not here. Or Stax, who has been with the group longer and is a faster runner than myself. Perhaps Carly is extending an olive branch. Nah, not Carly. Gretchen hangs out with them because Marlene's her boss and she feels a sense of obligation. But with Carly it is birds of a feather. She and Marlene are two sides of the same bad penny.

As I turn into the alley I find myself trying to remember the last time Gretchen missed a run. I can't say whether it was out of genuine concern or residual guilt for having pilfered through her desk, but I committed myself to checking in on her this evening before I went home. It is the least I could do.

Ouch! These jagged old rocks are wrecking my shoes and my feet along with them. And what's that up ahead?

Oh great, somebody's laundry fell off the back of their truck, and now we must either jump over it or run through it. I get a little closer and decide it isn't so bad, just a small pile spread out across the narrow alley.

Then I see a hand.

As I said before, I'm not a superstitious person. I don't believe in premonitions. Marlene had to turn up sometime and she (or whoever) chose today and this alley to make her reappearance. And, of course, I had to be the one to find her.

Her face is turned away from me but she is wearing the same clothes I'd seen her in at the start of the Chicken Hill run. I won't go into detail about her injuries, but the right side of her head did *not* look as it had the last time I'd seen her.

I am grateful I was not alone when I found her. Grateful, that is, until a few of the ladies who caught up with me decide to start screaming their heads off. This creates a general panic and residents of the houses on either side of the alley pop their heads out to see what the matter is. I wouldn't be surprised if 911 received at least a dozen calls all at once.

The neighbors aren't the only people in the area attracted by the screams. Ruby's walking group was passing along the road on the opposite side of the alley and turned our direction. Ruby pushes her way to the front and there we stood, facing each other, with Marlene's corpse between us.

Ruby points out the scissors and more screams follow. They are lodged by a single shear blade into a pitted old utility pole directly above the head of the corpse. I watch Ruby lean in close to get a good look at the blades. I motion to her to chill out with the sleuthiness as it might be misinterpreted by some of the frantic souls circling around us. But I can't help noticing the scissors are quite large, a good two sizes up from the pair I'd seen sticking out of Marlene's tire. Ruby ignores my signals and kneels down to get a closer look at the body.

A few minutes later the police are on the scene with an ambulance and everything moves fast from that point forward. Officer Diebold is first on the scene and blushes red when he sees faces familiar to him from Chicken Hill. We tell him the corpse belongs to the missing lady from two days earlier (who, he assured us, was just fine) and for a moment I worry I might have to call for a second ambulance.

Diebold gathers himself and, with the aid of two fellow officers, pushes us out of the alley and 'clears the scene' pending the arrival of a superior. Said superior turns out to be a tall, slender man with tired shoulders under a nice suit worn out at the elbows. I can hear Diebold, who ran to him like a dog finding his master, call him 'Detective'.

The body is taken away and the detective, who tells us his name is Luke Bentley, asks us to congregate back at Run For It and wait until our statements can be taken.

The store looks small with all the people crammed into it. It makes one think of a hospital waiting room after a tragedy, with stressed people pacing back and forth past women crying their eyes out, surrounded by a group of consolers patting shoulders and saying 'There, there'. Some of those crying the loudest and wettest are the ones who, an hour earlier, were condemning Marlene for her sin and debauchery. A few of the men stand, arms crossed, outside the front door, as though to protect the people inside from some invisible entity.

Stax, Ruby, and I hang by ourselves. It occurs to me Stax hasn't spoken a word since we started the run. I am sure this is the longest she's gone in her life without speaking. I couldn't say firsthand, but I'd bet she even talks in her sleep.

"Hey, you all right down there?" I say, trying to ease the tension in the room with a little height humor.

"No, not really," is the deadpan answer.

"What's wrong?"

There is a long pause, and then: "I've never seen a dead body before."

I put my arm around her shoulder. "Never been to a funeral?"

She looked up at me. "Well, yeah, but that's different. It's old people all dressed up and laid out like they're sleeping. Not…"

"Not laying out abandoned in an alley? No, you're right. But Marlene will be pretty and laid out like she's sleeping in a few days. We just saw her too early."

I didn't know if what I said was true, but I saw Stax's shoulders loosen and drop, so it had its desired effect. That is the moment Detective Bentley joined us in the store.

Diebold is back to his puffy-chested best and loiters with two other uniforms behind Bentley as the detective attracts everyone's attention. He informs us we will be split into groups so our statements can be collected as quickly and efficiently as possible. After which, he says, we'll be released. The news is welcome as I pictured us camping down in rows of bodies as the police plodded about their work. Bentley said he is separating us into four groups, from which I gather the three uniformed men would each take a group aside while Bentley handles the fourth.

I end up in the detective's group. And not by accident.

SIXTEEN

Detective Bentley asks Marti, Chase, Jessica, and Billy—the employees on duty at Run For It—to meet with him individually. The other two names he calls are Carly's and my own. This didn't hold any particular significance to me until I realized the three much larger groups were to remain in the main lobby, while my own little hand-picked collective is escorted to the same back rooms I couldn't get out of fast enough the day before.

We are placed together in one of the bigger rooms with frosted windows and a flimsy door. Bentley asks Chase to remain in the hall with him and directs us to remain seated and not to discuss Marlene or the murder. He will talk with us one at a time after which, he assures us, we can leave the store if we choose. I am all for leaving and hope I'll be interrogated after Chase so I can make good my escape. Naturally, I am to be the last one sitting.

I resist the urge to look at my phone once I am alone. I could use the distraction, but I don't want to appear too relaxed when Detective Bentley comes for me. I also don't want to appear too nervous, so I monitor the palms of my hands for sweat, wiping them periodically on my shirt for good measure. This leads to incessant lint-picking and I am mid-pick at some mysterious something or other (probably a Meatball hair) over my breast when the door swings open and Detective Bentley sticks his head in.

"Ms. Purdy, I'm sorry to keep you waiting so long. If you'll follow me I'll have you out of here in a few minutes."

I remember to smile when he meets my eye. I think he smiled back, but he may have already been smiling. I was too busy poking at my boob to notice. Now I am blushing, but too late to do anything about that.

I follow him further down the cramped hall to an office that looks like the one I just left, except this one has a small desk crammed sideways into a corner. I assume this is why the detective chose this office. Sitting behind a desk makes him look more officious and lends him an air of authority. As if the badge and title aren't enough for the likes of us.

I take a seat in the chair provided and wait while the detective flips some pages in his notebook and hurriedly scribbles some notes. What could he possibly be writing? I haven't even opened my mouth yet.

"Your name is Lacy Purdy, is that correct?"

"It is."

"And your middle name?"

"Annette. Should I spell it?"

"That's not a bad idea."

I spell it out as he dutifully takes note. I am surprised we aren't all ushered 'downtown' and put into a small room with cameras recording our every word and motion. I don't mention it for fear of giving him ideas.

Something about the detective tells me he is no small-town gumshoe. It is the easy way he carries himself in spite of the fact he is circling a murder, and yet when he speaks, he sounds genuine. I feel like a child called to the principal's office, but I also feel comforted and assured in his presence. It is an almost immediate sensation, before we even really begin to talk, and I imagine such a gift is invaluable to a man in his profession.

"Lacy, I promise not to keep you too long today. At this point I just have some perfunctory questions. I assume you understand this is a homicide investigation, correct?"

"Yes, of course," is my answer. It is an obvious if not stupid question, but perhaps in his line of work he has suffered his share of stupid witnesses.

"During the course of the investigation, I may need to return to you with further questions. Is that all right with you? This is something I let everyone I speak with know."

"Sure, if there's anything I can do to help, just let me know."

"And you promise to be frank and honest with me?"

He tilts his face up from where it hovered over the paper. His eyes match his blue shirt.

"Of course; why wouldn't I be?" I say with more protest than necessary. This because I'm not entirely sure I will be completely frank and honest with him. After all, unbeknownst to the good detective, I am immersed in my own independent investigation. If I attempted to explain this I would also have to explain my reason is because I make one helluva good prime suspect. I don't think that would fly.

"I can't think of any reason," he says, waving away any suggestion of impropriety on my part. I'm not sold by this and wonder what the previous interviewees might have told him about me. In particular, Carly. But true to his word, after collecting my contact information and taking a brief statement outlining my discovery of the body, I am set loose.

When I reenter the store area I find Stax and Ruby still held hostage by their uniformed interrogator, so I slip out the side door. The store is now a crime scene, at least by proxy, and there is no way I am going to hang out here and wait for my friends. Besides, there is something I need to do. Something that has been niggling at me since I arrived for the run.

Where is Gretchen? She never missed a run and, with all that has happened recently, I am more than a little concerned about her. I call her cell phone on the way to my car and feel a wave of relief the moment I hear her answer. But my relief doesn't last long.

"Hello, who is this?" she demands. She sounds frightened. It's not lost on me that she had not saved my number into her phone as I had hers. Or she deleted it along the way. I tell her who I am. "Oh, Lacy, I'm sorry. I didn't recognize the number and wasn't sure if I should answer, you know, with all that's going on. But at the same time, I was afraid not to."

I think I know what she's talking about, but I'm not sure. "So, you've heard about Marlene?"

"Oh, did she turn up?"

So, maybe I don't know what she's rambling on about.

I don't want to give her bad news over the phone, and certainly not when she's so obviously wound up, so I ask if I can come by. To my surprise, she says yes and gives me her address.

Gretchen lives on the old side of town in a small garage apartment above a mid-century mechanic's garage converted into private storage, probably for her father's company. She hears me coming up the rickety wooden stairs and is waiting for me at the open door.

"Excuse the mess," she says over her shoulder as she turns her back to me to head further into the room. "I'm trying to get out of here and can't seem to find anything I'm looking for."

She is moving around frantically and with her back to me. She tries to hide her face, but I don't need to see her eyes to know she's been crying. I can hear it in her voice. Also, there is a pile of used tissues on the coffee table. Two half-filled suitcases sit open on the couch.

"You're moving?" is the best I can muster. A more appropriate word, based on the scene in front of me, would be 'fleeing'.

"More like running home to daddy. It took everything I had to break away from him. I wanted to prove I'm a grown up and can stand on my own two feet. Now look at me, crawling back on my hands and knees."

She is buzzing back and forth, throwing shirts and sweaters and shelf trinkets across the room and onto the couch. I stick close to the far wall to stay out of the line of fire.

"I don't get it, Gretchen. What's going on?"

"My life is in danger, that's what's going on. I'm not about to let whatever happened to Marlene happen to me. By the way, you said you found out something about Marlene?"

I'll say I found something…her corpse.

"You might want to sit down." I try not to sound too morose. As it turns out, you can't say that line and not sound morose.

"If I don't sit down, will you refuse to tell me?"

"Well, no, I wouldn't do that."

"Okay, then. Let 'er rip. At this point I'd find a piece of *good* news more shocking than anything you could tell me."

I close my eyes and let it spill out: how and where I found Marlene, the large pair of scissors, the mass interrogation at Run For It. By the time I finish, she's taken a seat on the couch.

"Oh, wow, Marlene's dead," she says to herself. Her skin begins to take on a sickly pallor.

"You were pretty close, weren't you?" I speak as soothingly as possible. I know Gretchen wasn't close to Marlene, but death hits us all differently, particularly when we're young.

It takes a moment for it to register with Gretchen that I am speaking to her, but when it does she turns to me with large, bloodshot eyes. Her ginger hair is flat and oily. "No, you don't get it. This confirms my worst fear."

"And what's that?"

153

"I'm next to be murdered."

I didn't expect this revelation. How on earth could she know that?

"I can see you don't believe me," she continues. "But did you know the office where I work—where Marlene worked—was broken into last night?"

Gulp.

"I hadn't heard that," is my lame response. It was true enough, though. I had seen it, participated in it, but I had not *heard* about it.

Gretchen jumps from the couch, her animated arms taking swings at the air. "It was horrible, Lacy! I went to work like any other morning, but the window in front was all smashed in. There was glass everywhere. I was terrified."

Terrified? You should have been there last night!

"Oh my, I didn't know about that. I'm so sorry!"

I hate lying, but I see no way around it under the circumstances. Gretchen stares at the floor, nodding mindlessly, and I can tell she has no suspicions where I am concerned.

"I don't think the word has gotten out, but the police know, of course. And Anderson."

"Poor Anderson. He loses his wife and now this, and on the same day."

"And that's not all. He also lost his only employee."

"You quit your job?"

"You bet I did. It isn't worth dying for."

I remember her off-the-wall comment about being the next to die and ask about it.

"Oh, there's no doubt I'm in danger. Whoever broke into the office didn't even steal anything. The computers and everything are still there. And I know he saw it because he was at my desk."

"Your desk? Why do you say that?" It didn't seem like there'd been enough time for the intruder to riffle Gretchen's desk before making his way into Marlene's office, where I'd been hiding. I wonder if there was something we'd missed.

"Look what he did to this award I won." She holds up the base of her 'Sew What?' award in one hand and the needle I'd broken off in the other. "If this isn't a message, I don't know what is. Are you all right, Lacy? You look like you're about to have a stroke or something."

I become dizzy when it hits me that all the frantic activity in this little apartment is on account of my clumsiness with the award.

"Is that why you're so scared?" I ask, though it is obvious.

"I'm not just scared, I'm freaking out. And I'm moving back in with my father. I said nothing could ever get me to do that, but I guess everything has its price."

"You don't get along with your father?"

"Given enough space we do okay, but I can't stand living under his roof. Working with him is bad enough. He's a total control freak. I suppose I am as well, but hey, it's his genes, his fault, right?"

She manages a smile and I force one back. I feel horrible for this poor girl. Not only for her personal plight but for the fact that my own actions have led her to make some pretty significant life decisions. My mature way of handling it is to make an impulsive offer.

"Would you like to come stay with me?"

Gretchen stiffens and looks me in the eye. I can see her wheels spinning, considering the pros and cons of staying with me. If she knew I made the offer more out of guilt than altruism, I suspect her choice would be much easier. And different.

"With you? Are you serious?"

"Well, yes. I suppose so. Why not? I live alone, except for my cat. Do you like cats?" I force my lips closed at this point, lest I start babbling.

"I love cats. But I don't want to put you out. My father isn't the most easy-going guy, but he is old fashioned and sees it as his responsibility to take care of me. I hate living with him, but I wouldn't feel bad about it. If I thought I was putting you out, I'd hate myself."

"Well, you're not putting me out at all, Gretchen. And I wouldn't be taking care of you. You're a grown woman. But you are in need and I'd like to think we are something like friends."

"Of course, we are! I swear, it would only be temporary. Until they catch this madman and I can find another job. You're sure you won't mind?"

I'm not sure at all, but I can't tell her that. "Not another word about it. Just get what you need and you can follow me over to my place. Oh, please excuse me."

My ringtone blared out from inside my purse. It's Ruby calling. I don't want to speak to her in front of Gretchen lest something be said that she shouldn't hear.

"If you don't mind, I'm going to step outside and return this call."

"Go ahead." The haze lifted from her eyes and her voice went an octave higher. "I'll just need a few more minutes to finish up here. I'm not bringing everything, you know. I need a place to lie low until they find this maniac. I'm sure that won't take long, right? Oh my gosh, I'm so excited we're going to be roomies, Lacy. It'll be like college."

I take myself outside, feeling glad that someone is profiting from my impetuous sense of guilt. I ring up Ruby.

"There you are, Lacy," Ruby says. She sounds as grumpy and impatient as usual, but I find it strangely comforting. "I was concerned when you didn't answer."

"I'm with Gretchen. I excused myself so we could talk."

"Gretchen? I didn't realize you two were social."

"We're not. But she's going to be staying with me for a while."

"So, you're bypassing 'social' and going right to 'domestic'?"

"It's not exactly like that."

"Isn't it? You recall her name is on our suspect list?"

"Yes, but I really don't think she's a murderer."

"I suppose letting her in where you sleep is one way of finding out. Perhaps we should alternate with the suspects—each will get a week in your home. When you show up dead, we'll just check the sleeping schedule and we'll have our killer."

"Do you have a reason for calling, Ruby?"

"Yes, I do. I wanted to ask you not to make any plans for after work tomorrow. We need to pay a return visit to the scene of the crime."

"The alley by Run For It?"

"That's the dump site, dearie. We're going to Chicken Hill."

The prospect of going back to the woods with only a little old lady for protection doesn't strike me as at all appealing, but I am once again prepared to trust Ruby's judgment.

"I'll swing by your place once I'm off. Do I need to bring anything?"

"Just yourself. And only yourself, please. Gretchen and any other would-be murderer you manage to court today can stay put, if it's all the same with you."

SEVENTEEN

Gretchen follows me home in her car, a little red
bug, and we quickly get her settled into a guest
bedroom. The bed has not been used in ages and the
comforter is a bit musty, so I toss it in the washer while
she unpacks and takes in the lay of the land. Meatball
watches her from his perch atop the guest room dresser
while I pound my head against my hand (in lieu of a
wall) for having guilted myself into a roommate.

After a short while we gather in the living room
with a tray of tea and sandwiches. Neither of us feel like
a heavy dinner but we are too wired for sleep, so instead
we nibble and chat. We start with life stories. Or, more
to the point, life disappointments. I talk about my
failed marriage and Gretchen opens up about her
difficult relationship with her father and her reticence
to stay working at his construction company.

I'd forgotten she quit her job today. How is she
supposed to pay her own way without a job? I'm always
one to lend a helping hand, but I don't have the spare
money to support another person. But I digress. After
our little pity party, we get around to addressing the
white elephant in the room.

I get the ball rolling by stating I didn't like Marlene at all. This isn't my way of being disrespectful of the dead, or of venting (well, maybe a little). It is my clumsy attempt to make Gretchen feel enough at ease to share with me her experiences with Marlene that she otherwise might not feel comfortable sharing. After all, I'm investigating a murder, and if I'm to be playing host to someone who knew the victim professionally I should take full advantage of it.

It worked. Gretchen became a fount of stories and anecdotes, each casting Marlene as a villain of varying degrees, from indifferent to outright thoughtless, from cold to vindictive. I cautiously inquire about Anderson, recalling the sighting of him with a younger redheaded woman, and monitor Gretchen's reactions for any signs of suspicious discomfort.

There are none, but she does recount a recent event whereby she was at the office, making her way from her desk and along the hall. As she passed Marlene's office the door swung open and a noticeably disenchanted Anderson exited. Before the door could close she caught sight of Marlene at her desk, her cheeks red and tear-streaked. Gretchen said it was about this time Marlene started avoiding her everywhere but at Run For It and runs they participated in together.

She says Marlene also became increasingly competitive, pushing herself hard to run faster and for longer stretches. Gretchen got the impression she was somehow the reason for her boss's new obsession. Marlene was intent on not only beating her own best times, but also Gretchen's. And Marlene picked the single toughest run—Chicken Hill—to prove her point.

"How do you know this?"

"She told me. More than once. Oh, she said it with a smile, tried to sell it to me as a friendly rivalry, but there was nothing friendly in her tone. And I have no interest in competing with her or anyone else. That's not why I run."

"Was she jealous of you?" I brace myself as I ask this, not sure how it will be received. I'm not getting the impression Gretchen is the mysterious ginger seen on Anderson's arm, but I can't rule it out based on what she's given me thus far.

"Jealous? You mean of my speed?"

"Sure, that. Or jealous of you in other ways?"

Her eyes bob up and I perceive a slight head nod. She is about to open her mouth to answer when her cell phone screams and pulls her away from her thoughts.

"Please excuse me." She glances at her phone screen. "It's my dad, I guess I need to take it."

I nod my consent and she disappears into her room where she remains for the next thirty minutes. She emerges perturbed at her father for being perturbed by her last-minute decision not to come back home. After that, the mojo of the evening had gone. We never settle back into our cozy spots in the living room, but instead retire to our respective bedrooms. In recompense for all the confusion he suffered with Gretchen coming in, Meatball finds himself plied with a second helping of treats and a copious amount of cuddles.

The next day at work is delightfully uneventful and I am surprised as the day progresses to find myself anticipating more and more the evening's exploits with Ruby. Only a couple of hours of good daylight remain, not near enough for two people to do a proper search of Chicken Hill, but Ruby doesn't strike me as the frivolous type. She must have a specific objective in mind. Or object, maybe. My body might be at my desk in my little front office, but my mind is off on a fantastic treasure hunt in the hills above Cedar Mill.

This morning I tossed some hiking clothes in the car to avoid having to go home to change. Gretchen is there and I don't need her tagging along. I told her I'd already made plans with a friend for that evening, which is completely true. The knowing grin she flashed my way said she believed my 'friend' is of the male variety and I make no attempt to contradict the notion. Perhaps if enough people think I have an honest-to-goodness social life the universe will come around to the same way of thinking and provide me with one.

When 5 o'clock comes I take my bag of hiking clothes into the cramped office bathroom for a quick stand-and-change. I bid Caroline adieu and hightail it to Ruby's, where she, as expected, is keeping watch for me.

Mine is the only car in the parking lot when we arrive at Chicken Hill. I am relieved by this as my mounting paranoia makes me sensitive to the fact I am a potential murder suspect returning to the scene of the crime. When Ruby and I make it up the first path and behind the cover of the tree line I feel my chest loosen and my lungs expand.

"We've got a bit of a walk ahead of us," Ruby says over her shoulder.

"Should I keep my eyes open?"

"I would advise it, dear. The time to nap is not when one is traversing a wood."

I'm still unsure if she is being literal or ironical when she responds like this, but I play along. "I mean should I be looking out for anything in particular?"

"Feel free to relax your eyes, dear. We're headed to a particular spot in the path. The spot where I believe poor Miss Marlene disappeared herself."

"I see. Wait—disappeared herself? Don't you mean was *made* to disappear?"

Ruby slows her pace and turns my way. She touches my hand. "It's true her killer would eventually disappear her, and very much against her will. But before that, she disappeared herself. And I believe I know where she did so."

For a woman of a certain age who has only recently resumed good perambulating habits, Ruby keeps up a surprisingly consistent pace. Over rocky turns and up slippery slopes we pad, around sharp turns and under shadowy foliage we trek, until finally Ruby comes to a stop. We stand just ahead of a turn in the trail that is about two-thirds of the way along the one we'd taken days earlier for the run. To our left is the short railing that marks the drop off of the 'canyon'. To our right is the woods. This is what holds Ruby's attention. She is staring into the grass and walking slowly forward.

"Right here," she finally says. I can't tell what is different about this patch of green from the thousands of others we passed. Until I look closer. "People have been walking here."

Ruby takes a deep swig of her water bottle as though to celebrate the discovery. Coming up for air, she says, "Good eyes, Lacy. But it was created by only one person, and right in the vicinity of the final big turn in the run. That's what I was looking for."

"Why were you looking for that?"

"We're losing light. Follow me along the path and I'll tell you."

The path is faint, but there is no mistaking the depressed grass leading in a line from the dirt trail into the forest beyond. Ruby continues her explanation. "You mentioned how Marlene pledged to beat Gretchen's time in the run. Do you recall that?"

"Yes, and Gretchen brought it up again last night."

"Doesn't it strike you as odd that Marlene would say such a thing? She was a good enough runner, but Gretchen is better. And for beating one's personal best, a trail run is nothing if not a series of disadvantages. Except under one circumstance."

Having experienced firsthand how grueling a trail run is, I can't imagine what advantage it could offer to one's personal speed. "And under what circumstance could that be?"

Ruby giggled, pleased with herself for knowing something I don't. "The only reason she could expect to overtake a runner like Gretchen is if she planned to cheat. And the only way she could cheat and expect not to get caught is if she cut across the woods at a particular point where there'd be few if any potential witnesses and ample opportunity to separate from the trail and run unencumbered in a straight line while Gretchen is slowed by the wide turn. That's why it had to be in this vicinity."

"When did you figure all this out?" I was impressed not so much that Ruby figured out Marlene cheated on her run as that she figured out where, how, and why it happened.

"Oh, in bits and pieces over the last couple of days. Last night I sat up with an overhead view of Chicken Hill—you know, those satellite images they have now are something else!—and the running statistics Stax was good enough to provide. Gretchen averaged a three-minute lead over Marlene the past several runs. Marlene would have been aware of this and sought a point in the run where she could gain on her by at least a minute. And that could only be at a roundabout."

"But there are a number of roundabouts on Chicken Hill."

"Yes, but this is the last of them. Any earlier there would have been too many risks, not the least of which being that Gretchen would have plenty of time to retake her lead. No, it had to be here. Ah! I believe I've found what I was looking for."

Ruby stops in the middle of the slight trail we are following and motions to an almost non-existent veering-off to our right. Only because the grass is so tall here is it obvious that someone has been here.

I am confused by the new trail. "I don't get it. Why would Marlene turn off that way? It's the opposite direction."

"She wouldn't, at least not by her own choice. That's precisely why it's a clue."

"You think there was someone waiting here to grab her? How could anyone know she would run through here?"

165

"To your first question—maybe she was abducted, but I don't think so. We'll find out more about that soon enough. As for the second, do you notice how well-tread this primary path is? That means Marlene had been coming out here for some time before the run and training. Can you fathom someone training to cheat? Outrageous! But that's what she did."

I see where Ruby is going with this. "If she was sneaking out here regularly to plan for the run, then that gave someone an opportunity to follow her and—"

"Concoct their own devilish plan. Yes, indeed. And that plan brings us to this very point in Marlene's secret trail. Shall we?"

Ruby steps away from Marlene's trail and follows alongside the mystery path, careful not to disturb it in any way. I follow. I spot nothing out of place in the grass and weeds surrounding us and apparently neither does Ruby.

A thought occurs to me. "Couldn't these prints belong to the search parties that looked for Marlene?"

Ruby conceded the possibility but pointed out the lack of additional footprints in the general vicinity. Whoever these prints belong to had made a beeline for this spot.

The mini-trail ran several yards and concluded at the base of a large tree. I thought it odd that the steps did not then turn and go back to the primary trail.

"What do you think happened here?"

Ruby knelt down and studied the base of the tree. I thought she hadn't heard me, but then she spoke. "I'd say we're standing on a crime scene."

The hairs on my neck stand up. My third crime scene of the week. I'll figure out how to process that reality later. Right now, Ruby wants my attention.

"See these loose pieces of grass?" She plucks pieces of grass and weeds one by one. "They didn't grow loose. Something happened here to pull them out of the ground. The remaining grass has clearly been trampled on. Can you see it?"

I can see it from standing position but join Ruby in a kneel for the sake of appearance. "Yes, I can. You think there was a struggle here?"

"I should say that much is obvious. The question is—why here?"

I thought the same thing. If Marlene was burning through the woods intent on getting ahead of Gretchen, then why did she veer off her worn path to come to this tree?

"Do you think she was grabbed and dragged here?"

Ruby crinkles her brow and stands up straight. "That might be the case, but for the life of me, I can't see how someone could stand here in wait without Marlene seeing him from yards back."

"If it was someone she knew, she wouldn't have felt threatened."

"Perhaps. But if she was grabbed back at the trail then why isn't there evidence of a struggle there? And where are the other party's footprints?"

She had me there. I look off into the trees for inspiration and am instead distracted by some tree-hopping birds silhouetted by the burnt orange hue of the falling sun. I ponder what Ruby is saying and find I have no response. If Marlene was accosted on her trail, there should be some evidence of it. There isn't. So, where does that leave us?

And then the inspiration came. "The killer had to approach somehow, didn't he? And if we're not seeing any sign of him at the trail, it must have been from another direction."

Ruby is holding her eyes so close to the bark of the old tree that she might as well be kissing it. "Good thought, dear. Why don't you poke around and see what you can find. I might be here a few moments."

Invigorated by my own deducing, I do as she suggests and examine the ground around the big tree coming from directions other than Marlene's trail. If Ruby is correct in her supposition that Marlene was assaulted at this spot, I should expect to find clear signs of activity through the brush. Knowing this made it nonetheless startling when I did, in fact, discover a line of flattened grass and broken twigs zig-zagging away from the big tree and back in the direction of the primary walking path. I barely inhaled air enough to convey this information to Ruby when she flung herself away from the tree and cut me off.

She held her hands out excitedly. "Do you have a hair pin?"

I caught myself reaching for my hair, even though I'm pretty sure I've never once in my life worn a hair pin. "Sorry, Ruby. I don't. Does anybody use hairpins nowadays?"

"Do you have anything small and sharp on you?"

I reach into my pocket and find some stray safety pins. One thing any runner is never in short supply of is safety pins. Any time you enter a run, you're provided a packet that includes a bib and a handful of pins with which to affix it to your clothes. I can't speak for other runners, but I just can't bring myself to throw any out, so I keep a jar filled with them at my house and always seem to have a few on my person. I now hand one to Ruby.

"Ah, perfect!" she exclaims, opening the pin and returning her attention to the tree, where she sets about performing a delicate operation between two pieces of old bark. "You can't see it from where you're at, Lacy. In fact, I don't think it's visible to anyone not looking for it, but I've found a hole!"

"A hole? And why were you looking for a hole in a tree?"

"I had an idea I'd find one. And it looks as though there's something in the hole."

Ruby extracts this something. A piece of paper so small a slight breeze could blow it away.

"Do you notice there's a fold in it?" asks Ruby, excited at the discovery. I do see it and ask what it means. "I suppose it means someone folded it," was the answer.

"Ah! Now there's something! Take a look at that." She's no longer looking at the paper but towards the sky. I follow her finger and my eyes land on a branch overhead. Or, what is left of one. It has been sawed most of the way through, evident by the smoothed grain. But below a certain point it is jagged and splintered, as though someone got impatient with the sawing and tore the branch loose from the tree.

"I don't know what to make of a broken branch, Ruby."

"Me, either. Not yet, anyway."

I show Ruby the second trail leading away from the big oak and am elated when she confirms this must be the approach and escape trail used by Marlene's killer. We follow it to its end (or, more probably, its beginning) and are surprised to find it terminates at a rather open and public location on the main path. Ruby is holding her thoughts close to her chest but remarks in astonishment that if the killer abandoned the run to beat Marlene to the big oak, he would have been spotted doing so by any number of runners. She considers such a course unlikely and says there must be another explanation.

It seems that the mounting clues should now be pointing to the killer, or at least a viable suspect. But, in fact, we know little more now than when we started. But it is early days yet and our adventure on Chicken Hill gave me a new boost of optimism that soon we'd have a suspect in our sights.

I return home and Gretchen informs me I received a call. Yes, I'm a dinosaur with a landline and a voicemail machine. I rarely use either, but keep both out of tradition and an irrational fear that the world will lose all power and once the batteries on all cell phones have died I'll be the last person on earth with a working phone.

I hit play on my machine and immediately recognize Detective Bentley's voice: 'Hello, Ms. Purdy, this is Detective Bentley. If it's not too much trouble, I'd appreciate it if you could come by the station tomorrow. I have some questions I would like to ask you face to face. Please call me after 8am to schedule a time...'

Oh boy, I thought. *This doesn't sound promising.* And Gretchen heard the whole thing. No telling what ideas she has about me. I briefly consider discussing the case with her but decide to stick to the pact of confidentiality that Stax, Ruby, and myself loosely made. After all, Gretchen's name is on our short list of suspects.

And I surmise from the detective's brief message that my name is on a similar list at police headquarters.

EIGHTEEN

"I'm going to grab a water from the fridge. You want one?"

I say 'no, thanks' and Detective Bentley whisks out of the room. I remain sitting in his office at the station in one of a couple of tumbledown chairs in front of his desk. At least I'm not in some cramped interrogation room.

Last night, after I heard the voicemail from Bentley, I called Stax to get her take on the situation (and because something about her reminds me the world doesn't totally suck). She assured me I shouldn't worry unless he started asking me a lot of personal questions in order to find common ground between us. This would mean he was attempting to establish a rapport, and the only reason he'd want to do that is to keep me from suspecting him of suspecting me of murder.

"I hope you don't think me too forward," Detective Bentley says upon reentering the room. "But I got you one any way. To save me another trip if you get thirsty."

He sets a small bottle of water in front of me and pops the cap off an identical one of his own, plopping down in his chair like it was a favorite nook.

"Are you planning to talk me dry, detective?"

He smiles. Not too big and with just a little teeth.

He isn't un*handsome.*

"That's up to you, Ms. Purdy. I should mention you're not obligated to say a word to me. Although I appreciate any help you can give me, I can't compel your help."

"Fair enough. I'm happy to help any way I can."

He stands and slips out of his suit jacket, tossing it in the air and landing it squarely on a wall hook four-feet away. It was an impressive sight.

"Good," he says, resuming a relaxed posture in his chair. "We'll get started on the heavy stuff in a minute. First, let's talk about you. I understand you're relatively new to Cedar Mill?"

"Correct. I've been here about six months."

"From?"

"Missouri. Kansas City."

"Great town. What's the song say? 'They got some mighty pretty women there and I'm gonna get me one."

"I think it says 'crazy little women'."

"No, I'm sure it says pretty. Why would a guy travel for a crazy woman?"

I laugh. I can't help myself. "I'm telling you, it says 'crazy'. My mom used to play oldies all the time."

He reaches into his pocket. "We're going to settle this right now." He pulls out his phone and begins doing a search.

"Bah! It looks like we're both right. Fats Domino sang it 'crazy little women' and Willie Nelson, which is the version I know, sang it 'pretty little women'. I guess it's a tie?"

"Not exactly." I am now immersed in his funny game. "Fats Domino sang it first, didn't he?"

"Yes, I suppose he did."

"That makes it official. Crazy little women it is."

"Can I quote you on record?"

"Quote me how?"

"That women from Kansas City are crazy?"

He stares at me. I stare back at him. We both laugh.

"Sometimes it doesn't pay to be right," I say.

His smile disappears and his eyes narrow. "Would you like to make a confession?"

His question first confuses, then concerns, me. My hand curls into a death grip on my purse when I recall I'm talking to a cop investigating a murder. "Confess? No, not at all. Why do you ask?" I am proud of myself for not stuttering.

"Because I *do* have a confession. You know the cool jacket throw I did earlier, where it landed on the hook? Blind luck. I maybe pull that off one out of every ten times. That's why my jackets are always crinkled."

This guy is something else. I let go of my purse and grab my forehead. I can feel my shoulders quake and realize I am laughing. For the next several minutes we chitchat as though it's something we've done countless times before. He tells me he, too, is a recent transplant to Cedar Mill, having transferred from Boston PD in search of a quieter town with a less demanding crime rate. He is divorced and childless, further compounding our similarities, and fancies himself an amateur chef.

I get so involved in our conversation I forget my purpose for being here. He, too, seems to be enjoying himself. Eventually, the time comes to get down to business.

Bentley picks up an ink pen and sets a legal pad in front of himself. "About Marlene Petrick," he asks. "How did you know her?"

"Through the running store. I ran in her group."

"You didn't know her socially outside the group?"

"Not at all. I don't think I've ever seen her outside the store, except on those billboards."

He taps the back of his pen against the pad three times. "Yes, I've seen those. How can you miss them? Have you ever done business with her travel agency?"

"No. Like I said, I've never seen her outside of the running group."

"And would you say you were close?"

I don't like the pointed nature of his questions. He has spoken to others and knows Marlene and I were the opposite of 'close'. "No, we were not close."

"I'd heard that," he concedes, "but I also learned from a store owner in the area that after she was reported missing, you were in their store with photographs asking if they'd seen her."

Gulp.

"Yes, that's true. I was just doing my part."

"Was there some sort of concerted effort I'm not aware of? Because Anderson, her husband, wasn't aware of any such grassroots campaign to find his wife."

"Maybe he should have been. If I were him I'd be knocking on every door in this town."

"Fair enough, but you didn't answer my question."

"I don't know what to tell you. I don't see anything wrong in helping find someone who is missing. If I were missing, I'd hope others would do the same."

"I also learned you and Marlene were not on particularly friendly terms."

"That's correct. Should I have been indifferent about her being in possible danger?"

"No, no. I don't mean that. But based on what I've heard, and you're welcome to correct the record, if you'd like, but—"

"Let me guess, you heard I've said things to the effect that I'd like to kill Marlene. Is that it?"

"In a nutshell, yes. Is it true?"

"It's true I said it. I did not mean I'd actually kill her or would want to see harm come to her."

"I get that. But since she was, in fact, murdered, you can see how this might look."

"Not really. She wasn't a nice person. I'm sorry to say it, but it's true, at least as far as I was concerned."

"Lacy, please understand I have to ask these questions."

"If I didn't understand that, Detective Bentley, I wouldn't be here. As long as you have questions for me and not accusations, you can count on my help."

"Got it. But I have my bosses, and they'll want an explanation as to how the woman who threatened the victim's life and subsequently found her body shouldn't be looked at as a suspect."

There it is. I knew the fact I found the body would be an issue. He wouldn't be much of a detective if it weren't. But still.

"Yes, I found the body. But that just means whoever put it in the alley knew we'd be running that route."

"How could they have known that?"

"That's the same route we always run when Carly's run leader. It's common knowledge."

"Not too common. And from what I've learned, you chose the route that evening, not Carly."

"Did Carly tell you that?"

He grins slyly. "I can't tell you that. But you're welcome to deny it if it's not true."

Does he smile that way at everyone he interrogates?

"No, it's true. Carly injured herself running Chicken Hill and asked me to take lead. But she was still run leader, so naturally I took off on her preferred route. I had no way of knowing she'd ask me to take lead."

"True, but you also had no way of knowing she'd be too sore to take lead herself, and therefore would be taking your group down that alley."

"That's right. But as I mentioned, anyone familiar with our group and Carly's habits would expect we'd take the route we always take when she leads."

"We're going around in circles."

"Funny, that's what I always say when Carly leads our run."

Bentley turns his face away, but I can see the edge of his lips turning up into a smile. "It would be entirely inappropriate for me to laugh at that, so I won't. What I *will* do is let you get out of here and get some lunch."

"So, I'm free to go?"

"You've been free to go the whole time. You know, you're not obligated to answer my questions."

Truth be told, I'm rather enjoying the experience and a little disappointed to be leaving. Realizing this makes me feel weird, but for me, feeling weird is nothing new.

"No worries, Detective, you made it painless."

"Thank you. In that case, I do have one more question if you feel up to it."

"Shoot."

The detective's eyes narrow. In that moment he looks the part. "Who do you think murdered Marlene?"

Wow. As soon as he asks the question a few faces popped into my mind—Anderson, Carly, Chase, even Gretchen. There are reasons to suspect all of them, but is there anything solid on any one of them?

"I honestly don't have a clue."

"What does your gut tell you?"

"If my gut has any suspicions, it's keeping them to itself."

"Well, I can't compel your gut to answer my questions any more than I can compel the rest of you."

I laugh. I can't imagine how my expression reads right now. Something about the thought of this man 'compelling the rest of me' makes me go flush.

"I'll walk you out," he says, standing from his chair. I follow him out into the hall and to the front door of the police station. He opens the door leading outside. "Thank you again for your time, Mrs. Purdy. I may have more questions for you yet. We'll have to see what kind of turns the investigation takes. But there's one thing I'm sure of."

"What's that, detective?"

"The song, 'Kansas City'? I'm sticking with the Willie Nelson version. I've yet to see any evidence that women from there are crazy."

Before I can reply he disappears back into the building. It was just as well as I'm not sure what I might have said to that, particularly when it dawns on me he more or less called me pretty.

Whether he is buttering me up as Stax suggested he might do, or whether he is genuinely flirting with me, it doesn't matter. As far as police interrogations go, I'm pretty sure they don't get much smoother than this, and for that I am grateful.

I am able to finish out my workday without sparing another thought to the murder of Marlene or the threat of suspicion falling upon me. Ruby is more imaginative than perceptive. Poor, sweet, old lady. Maybe she is just bored with life and got caught up in the excitement of a real-world mystery so similar to the fictional ones she used to concoct for her books. It is nothing I can hold against her, since I, too, found myself caught up in the intrigue of it all. But I am glad to see the cloud lift and I look forward to returning to the humdrum of my uneventful, but peaceful, existence.

On my way home, I call Stax and give her a quick rundown of my talk with Detective Bentley. I make the mistake of telling her I think he called me pretty and she teases me for being such an inveterate flirt.

I call Ruby and tell her the same story. Unlike Stax, she doesn't have any opinion on the matter. In fact, she appears distracted, saying she has some firm ideas of her own, but won't know more until she receives some deliveries she is expecting. I ask what sort of deliveries, but in typical Ruby fashion, she doesn't want to say.

No matter, I think. Let the lady have her fun. As long as she doesn't get herself hurt, there's no harm in it. And who knows, maybe she'll catch Marlene's killer yet. As for myself, if I'm not the detective's suspect, there is little reason for me to play sleuth. That's why we pay professionals like Bentley.

I am cruising the streets behind Main Street to avoid traffic. The wheels crunch on gravel but I feel as though my feet are floating above ground, liberated as they now are from the metaphorical gumshoes I've been wearing since the trail run. In my present state, I am not prepared for what awaits me as I come upon Marlene's office.

I train my eyes on the little building as I approach. After all, this is sacred ground, being the location of my first (and hopefully last) breaking and entering. The broken window in front has been replaced and there is no sign anything untoward recently took place here. More interestingly, there are cars parked outside. Marlene is dead and Gretchen quit, so Anderson Petrick must be doing his grieving at the office.

As I am about to drive past the front of the office, the door opens and out steps Chase Reynolds. I almost lose control of the steering wheel and wipe out the rustic wooden 'Petrick Travel Agency' signpost embedded at the curbside. I break hard and come to a sudden stop but Chase doesn't notice me. He's in a rage, spewing obscenities at the ground as he storms towards his car. I notice a white shirt appear in the doorway of the office. It is wrapped around Anderson

Petrick, who, unlike Chase, appears at home in the midst of discontent.

"Get ahold of yourself," Anderson says, his deep voice resonating without effort.

"You're lucky I don't get ahold of you," replies Chase, the spit flying from his mouth. "What if Marlene were here? What then?"

Anderson grips the knob of the outside screen door. "But she's not here, Chase. I am." He slams the door closed and disappears. Chase throws himself into his car and I get while the getting is good.

I spend the drive home trying to imagine why Chase, of all people, would be paying Anderson a visit. Does Anderson know about Marlene's affair with Chase? Was there even an affair? And what did Chase mean by 'what if Marlene were here?' Is he accusing Anderson of the murder? If so, Anderson isn't denying it.

By the time I reach my driveway I decide, suspect or not, I am too close to the case to let it go. I resign myself to continue investigating as long as Ruby and Stax want to, but I am equally determined not to lose any more sleep letting my mind run wild with speculation. My plan is to continue collecting facts and putting them together until they form a picture.

I enjoy a relaxing evening at home, chatting with Gretchen over a delicious dinner prepared by her of steak marsala and grilled asparagus. She makes multiple attempts to befriend Meatball, but for some reason, he is not having it. Gretchen, too, is less of a wreck than the day before and I find a lot of pleasure in sharing the company of a younger, hipper woman. She sparks like an ember as she discusses her dream of making a living out of her love of sewing, embroidery, and similar disciplines. She says her own small business is gaining momentum. I think of the business card I saw in her office and wish I could ask about it, but of course I cannot. Nevertheless, having a conversation about something other than Marlene and murder is refreshing.

I have to admit the day has gone my way, and when my head hits the pillow I feel altogether lighter.

The next morning starts as mornings tend to start, with a cat to be fed, a lunch to be prepared, and a beauty regimen necessary to make myself presentable to the world.

There's nothing exceptional about it—with one exception. I exit my door and walk into the shiny, metallic handle of a pair of barber scissors protruding from one of my wooden porch posts.

Marlene's killer has paid me a visit.

NINETEEN

Detective Bentley's groggy rasp told me I'd woken him. But he lodged no complaint and said he'd be right over. Gretchen, who is no longer gainfully employed outside of her Internet business, is still asleep. She will have to be up and about before the police get here, but before waking her I use my phone to take pictures of the scissors. I thought about texting the pics to Stax, but decide to wait until the police left, lest Stax should barrel over here and put her foot in my mouth. But I sent them to Ruby.

The gravity of the situation doesn't hit me until after I wake Gretchen and escort her out to the front porch. Seeing the look on her face reminds me that as I slept a blade-wielding killer stood mere yards from me on my own porch and struck out. Sure, it's only wood, but it just as well could have been my throat.

I sit down on the porch steps to keep from hyper-ventilating and call Caroline at the insurance agency to once again ask for time off. I feel obligated to explain what is going on and brace myself for her cries of anguish. When she putters down to a mere whimper she assures me I can have whatever time off I need. If not for the ominous threat hovering over my head like a halo, I'd have taken that moment on the steps to consider how blessed I am.

Detective Bentley arrives in short order with Officer Diebold towing in moments later like a lazy, blue caboose. In spite of my frantic state I manage to notice how the light blue button-down shirt the detective is wearing accentuates his eyes.

Man alive, I've been single too long.

Bentley smiles as he comes up the walk to where Gretchen and I are sitting on the porch.

"We really must stop meeting like this," he says, his voice sounding tired. "Oh, that's quite a pair you've got there."

"Ahem."

"I mean the scissors, of course!"

Yes, he's definitely tired.

Bentley leaves Diebold to guard the scissors and escorts Gretchen and myself back into the house to talk. We take seats in the living room and talk about the events of the night. I say there isn't much to tell, as it was a night like any other. I awoke only once when I heard Gretchen come out and use the restroom. In response to Bentley's question, I tell him I know this occurred at 2:03am because I looked at my phone for the time. I went promptly back to sleep and remained so until my alarm went off. Gretchen confirms getting up in the middle of the night to use the restroom and states she returned to bed right after. Neither of us heard anything else.

Bentley turns to me. "Lacy, when we first spoke, you told me you live alone. Is this (he motions to Gretchen) a new development?"

"Yes, quite new. I assume you know she worked for Marlene and Anderson's travel agency?"

"Correct."

"Well, after Marlene was murdered and the office broken into, Gretchen didn't want to be alone. I told her she could stay with me a while."

"Very altruistic of you."

I'm not sure whether I should be offended or impressed by the detective's use of 'altruistic'.

"Altruistic? Is that sarcasm, detective?"

"If opening one's home to someone in need isn't altruism, then what is?"

"I don't know, crazy?"

"I thought we covered that. Kansas City women are *not* inherently insane."

Is that a wink? Did he just wink at me?

"Um, excuse me," interjects Gretchen. "First the needle is broken off my plaque in the office, and now these scissors get stuck in the porch not two days after I come here to stay. Am I missing something or am I the one being targeted here?"

Gretchen's voice cracks as she speaks. I reach my arm in her direction for comfort and she melts into me.

"Now, we don't know what this is all about," Bentley says, attempting to sound reassuring. "It might be a stupid hoax, or it might be something else."

I give Gretchen a squeeze as she clings to me. "You mean I might be the target."

"Could be."

I came to that obvious conclusion myself, but hearing the detective give voice to it drops a lead weight in my belly.

Bentley stands from the chair, signaling the end of our discussion. "We're going to be in the area today asking questions and seeing what we can find out. I'll ask that you not speak to anyone. If curious neighbors come by asking questions, tell 'em I say mum's the word. I'd also advise both of you to take extra precautions to protect yourselves."

Gretchen jumps from the couch and gets in his face. "Isn't that your job? Can't you provide us with protection?"

Bentley looks warmly upon Gretchen but shrugs his shoulders helplessly. "I wish I could, but we don't have the resources. Of course, if anything happens, you call and we'll be here within minutes."

The detective leaves and I spend the next half hour comforting Gretchen. I remind myself she is a suspect in this case. She was close to Marlene, whose husband was seen in the company of a mysterious redheaded woman. And now, within days of moving into my house, the same scissors haunting Marlene prior to her murder have found me. I feel terrible having these thoughts as she soaks the shoulder of my blouse with her tears, but the reality here is someone murdered Marlene, and this someone knows who I am. It therefore stands to reason I know them.

I need to get out of the house for a bit. Since I'm not expected at work, I decide to bug Stax at Read It or Eat It. Besides, if the killer is hip to my snooping around, Stax and Ruby might also be in danger. I call

Ruby on the way to the bookstore but get her voicemail. I leave a message cryptic enough to assure she'll call me but nothing too revealing in the event she isn't the only one listening.

• • •

"How old is he? Is he single?" I join Stax among the stacks in her shop, pulling copies sold through her online store. She is all ears until I mention the detective, and then she is all gossip.

"Did you not hear the part where my life was threatened?"

"Oh, please. If they wanted to kill you, they would have marched those scissors into your house and put them in your head."

"That's a pleasant thought. Thanks."

"You were given a warning. That's all."

"That's all?!"

"Sssshhh, use your library voice."

"Stax, a real-life murderer visited my house. There can only be one reason."

"I'll bet Ruby would say there's never only *one* reason."

I ignore her attempt at diversion. "Be that as it may, the killer knows I'm onto them. And if they know that, they know about you and Ruby as well."

"Then why are there no scissors stuck to my porch?"

"I don't know. Maybe because I found the body?"

"It doesn't make sense. The police were looking at you for the murder, right? Or, at least, they should be."

"Stax!"

"Ssssh, library voice, remember? I mean on the surface you make a pretty good suspect. You hated Marlene, you were at the run, and you were the one who found the body. So, why take a perfectly good prime suspect and turn her into a potential victim? Doesn't make sense. Unless…"

"Unless…what?"

"I don't trust Gretchen. Hey Stretch, grab me that Carolyn Wells from the top shelf, 'The Maxwell Mystery'."

Gretchen? That's random. I hand her the old hardcover. "What does Gretchen have to do with it?"

"Either nothing or everything. If it's nothing, then my bad. But it seems odd to me that she moved into your house and—Kablam!—you get scissored. And you said you heard her moving around late at night?"

"I heard her using the restroom. That's hardly evidence. Who doesn't get up at night sometimes?"

"But what did you really hear, Lacy?"

I hadn't thought of it that way before. My instinct is to argue against what Stax is saying, but when I take a second to think about it I see her point.

"Well, I heard feet moving. Some of those old boards are loose and you can hear someone walking. And I know the squeak on her door. I used the room for storage and it always jarred me when I had to go in there."

"So, there's no doubt it was Gretchen you heard. But how long between the first squeak and the second?" I shake my head, not understanding her meaning. "I mean, if the door squeaked when she left the room, it would also squeak when she went back in, right? So, how much time between squeaks?"

"I only remember one squeak."

"That's odd, isn't it?"

"Not if I nodded back off after the first squeak."

"Or the second."

I nod in agreement. "I wasn't awake for long. It's hard to tell time when you're half-asleep, but it might have been seconds. No longer than a couple of minutes."

Stax is holding a copy of an old romance paperback with a shirtless, dark-haired Fabio-type pulling a young vixen from—or pushing her into—the water. She smacks it down on an exposed shelf space and straightens her posture. When I see her lips purse and her eyes narrow, I know the finger isn't far behind.

"So, it's like I said." She jabs the air in front of my face with her finger. "You don't know she was up to use the bathroom. You assume it." Like a champion sword fighter, she goes in for the kill with a final poke to my arm.

"I didn't 'assume', you goof. It's what she told the detective. Should I assume she's lying?"

"I've been in your house, have I not?"

"I dare say you have been."

"And I know that for her to go to the bathroom, she'd have to take a left turn and go down the hall. The bathroom is on the right. But a couple skips past the bathroom is your back door."

"Your point?" I already know her point, because the same thought crossed my mind. But my heels are in too deep by now.

"My point is she could have slipped out the back, made her way around to the front of the house, did her thing with the scissors, and returned back the same way to her room."

"That's pretty risky," I counter. "What if I'd caught her?"

Stax looks at dark-Fabio for inspiration. It doesn't take her long to find it. "If you caught her in the act of actually jabbing the scissors in, the jig would be up. But if you caught her coming out, she'd just say she was using the bathroom. And if you caught her coming back in she'd say she heard a noise and went to investigate."

I am out of juice. I'm not about to agree with Stax that Gretchen is a mad killer, but I also can't argue her points. What she suggests is a real possibility. I'm about to concede the point to Stax when my cell phone goes off.

"Sssshhh, airplane mode!" jokes Stax.

It is Ruby.

"Hi, dear. I've just returned home and heard your voicemail. It sounded rather urgent."

I told her about the scissors in my porch. Her response is instant. "My house, tonight. Eight o'clock. Tell Stax. In the meantime, be safe."

"I can't avoid going home. Meatball is there."

"Home is the very place you should be. With all the dust the good detective and his men are stirring up, I'm certain eyes will be in every window up and down your street. Neighbors make the best police, mark my words. Whoever visited you last night would know better than to strike again so soon."

Stax heard the conversation and said she'd pick me up later at my house. I head home to find Gretchen and a large, older man loading her things into the back of a dirty pick-up truck. The man, stacked like a tree trunk, has the darkened skin of a life spent in the sun, but his shirt appears clean, pressed, and ill-suited for labor. An awkward introduction confirms he is Gretchen's father.

"I'm sorry to be bugging out on you this way," Gretchen says. "I appreciate what you did for me, but after last night I feel like a sitting duck staying here."

Gretchen's father is off messing around with some items in the back of the truck, so I speak freely and frankly. "But you said the last thing you wanted to do is move back in with your dad."

"That was true, until I started getting stalked by a murderer. Now, being murdered is number one on my list of things to avoid. I'm so sorry, Lacy. I hope you know this has nothing to do with you."

I am disappointed, but I understand. I am stuck living here, she isn't. And whatever issues there are between her and her family, she'd at least be protected. And for all I know, she is right—it may be her and not me the killer is after.

I help Gretchen load the last of her things and see her off with a sad wave and a smile. She says she will not be at the run tomorrow but might return once Marlene's killer is caught.

I linger on my porch for a while, touching the scarred wood left by the removal of the scissor blade. I hear the hollow echo of knuckles on wood nearby and look out to see two uniformed police officers—one on each side of the road—knocking on doors at the top of my street. I think of what Ruby said about all eyes being on me and suddenly feel very exposed.

I spend the next few hours behind closed curtains, cleaning what doesn't need cleaned and reorganizing what is already in its place. Eventually, I allow myself entry into the spare room that for two nights served as Gretchen's bedroom. I can still smell the fruity scent of her lotion. I decide I might as well wash the sheets and pillowcases and put them away. Goodness knows when I'll need them again. As I strip the bed I tinker with the notion of inviting Stax to room with me temporarily. But why put her in danger? No, I just need to suck it up and ride it out. And learn to sleep with one eye open.

I crawl across the bed to pull out the far edge of the fitted sheet and feel something poke my knuckle. It's a lime-green notebook folder stuffed with about a half-inch of papers. It isn't mine, so it must have been left by Gretchen. I flip through it and find mostly unused paper, except the first couple of pages which are covered with numbers and random words. I set it aside with the intent of returning it to her later. Her nerves are too raw right now to warrant bothering her with such a trivial matter.

I don't feel like eating anything, but Stax will be here in an hour to go to Ruby's, so I warm up some tomato soup on the stove and make a cold ham and cheese sandwich. I am eating at the kitchen counter when my phone starts vibrating and dancing about.

It's Detective Bentley. I drop my sandwich and nearly cause a tomato tornado in my rush for the phone.

"Hi Lacy, it's Detective Bentley. Did I catch you at a good time?"

"That depends on what you have to tell me."

"I'm at the station. Would you be able to leave now to come here?"

Am I about to be arrested? "Is it necessary?"

"I believe it is. Lacy, a woman's been murdered."

"Not by me!" My own response surprises me and I wish I could rewind and hit erase.

The detective laughs on the other end of the phone. "Is that what you think this is? You think I'm having you come down to arrest you?"

"You're not?"

"No, Lacy. We make house calls for that sort of thing."

Whew! "Okay, then, sure, I'm free to come down. What do you need me for?"

"I need your eyes."

"My eyes?"

"Yes. I have an image of the person I believe planted those scissors in your porch. I need you to tell me who it is."

TWENTY

I call Stax to let her know I'll meet her later at Ruby's and make my way to the police station. I get the VIP treatment at the front desk as I am once again led to Detective Bentley's office. He receives me warmly (are we becoming friends or am I hopelessly naïve?) and escorts me down the hall to a small audio/video room replete with TV monitors, a soundboard, and other equipment I don't pretend to understand.

Bentley settles into a rolling chair in front of the command board. "A couple of your neighbors happened to see a figure strolling along the street last night at about 2am. One is a woman who let her dog out to do his business and the other a man with insomnia who stepped out for a smoke. Both describe the same figure—a tall woman in a black coat with either brown or red hair, walking in the direction of your house."

A chill went through me. "Red hair? Are you thinking Gretchen?"

"I was, at first. But it didn't make sense to me why Gretchen would be seen coming from the top of your street towards your house. It wouldn't serve any purpose except to put her at risk of being seen. Then I got on idea."

"You mentioned a photograph?"

"Not a photograph, *per se*. Something better. I got the idea that unless this person lived in your neighborhood, they would have to drive to get there. And yet they were seen walking. So, where did they park their car? I supposed they could have parked it anywhere on the street, but I took a shot and pulled surveillance footage from the businesses nearest the turning onto your street—a convenience store and a bank. I hit pay dirt with the store."

Bruce's Pit Stop is a regular stop of mine for gas, coffee, and conversation. They're a great bunch of people and I'm sure the manager, Kevin (who graciously answers to the name of 'Bruce', though no Bruce has been associated with the business for decades) was more than happy to help the police.

"What did you find?" I ask.

"That's what I called you down here to see." His expression and voice betray a mounting excitement. "I already showed this footage to the two witnesses on your street and they positively identified this as the woman they saw walking. I need to know if you recognize her or the vehicle she's driving. Give me a moment."

He whirls around the room, turning out lights and cuing up the monitor in front of me. Frozen on the screen is the image of a dark minivan. I don't know enough about cars to identify the make and model, but I know I don't recognize the vehicle.

"All right, here we go," announces the detective as he returns to his seat next to me and hits 'Play'. Under other circumstances, what happened on screen would be commonplace and nondescript. But I am riveted as I watch a woman in a fashionable, black raincoat step from the driver's side of a black vehicle, close the door, and walk away. Visible in the left corner of frame is the familiar air pump machine Kevin keeps free for anyone needing to air their tires. The direction in which the woman walked is not towards the store (which would have closed hours earlier) but towards my street.

The detective wants to know if I recognize her. The problem is, I do not. He explains the spot where the woman parked is a good distance from the camera, which is mounted on the side of the store. He zooms in to make the scene more visible and in doing so pixelates the image to such an extent the woman's features are obscured. But I can see her hair is something like a bob cut reaching past the ears but terminating above the shoulders. The color is obviously red, but a deeper, less natural shade than Gretchen's.

"It's too hard to tell. Can you show me the original footage, without the zoom-in?"

Bentley obliges and although the pixels are gone, the action is too far away to give me great detail about the woman's face. But I can see she is tall and shapely. Whoever that is, she is definitely not Gretchen, and that gives me a sense of relief. But as I watch the image of the woman walk away from the vehicle, I have an epiphany.

"Rewind that, please. Let me see it again." He does so without hesitation and what I see all but confirms my identification of the woman.

"I know who that is," I blurt out.

"Are you sure?"

"I think so. I mean I *feel* sure."

Distracted by the woman's image, I don't look at the detective, but I sense he is smiling.

"I don't know what that means. I think 'feeling sure' falls a bit short of certainty. But at this point, I'll take it. So, tell me, who is this woman?"

"It's Carly," I say with confidence.

"Carly? You got a last name?"

It never occurred to me before that I don't know Carly's surname. "No, I don't. I'm not sure she even has one."

"Everyone has a last name."

"Not Madonna," I retort, a little miffed at what I take to be condescension.

"Even Madonna, I'm afraid. I believe hers is Ciccone."

Now I look at him. He is wearing a smug grin and I realize I find him more adorable than infuriating.

"Is that something everyone knows but me?"

He laughs. "I don't know. But I'm pretty sure that every guy who grew up in the eighties with pre-teen sisters knows far more about Madonna than they want to."

I am doing it again, falling into an easy rhythm with Luke. Then I remember he's not 'Luke', he's 'Detective Bentley', and I'm telling him who the vandal of my house is.

"Now, back to business," I say, clearing my throat. "The woman in the video is Carly from the running group. You took her statement."

"Yes, I knew who you were talking about, but it's always good to confirm. Her name is Carlita Van Duson. I'll be honest, Lacy, when I look at this video it doesn't scream 'Carly' to me. As I remember, she has long, dark hair."

"That's true, so she must be wearing a wig here. But I'm telling you, that's her. I can tell by her shape and the way she moves."

"The way she moves?"

"You'll remember the reason she gave you for letting me lead the run group the other night."

"Because she hurt her leg at the trail run and needed to go slow?"

"She walked stiff on one leg that day. The woman in the video is walking the same way. When you had it blown up to show just her face, I couldn't see that. But here in the long shot it's visible."

"Hmmm, you're right, at least about this particular woman. I can't speak as to Carly herself. But I will take what you're telling me under advisement."

"Under advisement? Aren't you going to arrest her?"

"For what? Parking her car and taking a walk? And that's supposing you're correct in your identification."

"I know I'm right!"

"A minute ago, you merely 'felt' sure. I can't make an arrest based on a feeling."

I am frustrated, but I can't argue. He is right. What evidence do I actually have against Carly? I am certain it is her in the video, but I have no way to prove it. I opt not to press the point until I can get with the girls and see what else we can cook up.

"I see your point, detective."

"Hey, don't look so dejected. Believe it or not, I do trust you. If you say that's Carly on there, I don't disbelieve you. And if that is Carly, then she's the one who put the scissors in your porch post."

"And the one who killed Marlene?"

"Ah, I wouldn't quite go that far just yet. But I am anxious to talk to her if a solid reason to do so should present itself."

"Do you need a reason? Can't you call her in like you did with me?"

"Yes, I could. But if she's guilty and feels we're onto her, she'll lawyer up and shut me down. I'd rather have more to put in front of her when I do sit down with her."

I leave the police station with my head spinning and call Stax to let her know I am on the way. I wish I could take them the video, but they'll have to settle for the revelation that Carly is a scissor-wielding vandal, if not worse.

I arrive at Ruby's house to find her enjoying tea with Stax in the parlor. We retire to the study, which has become our *de facto* war room. Flanked by ancient oil lamps casting their cozy orange glow, I give the news about Carly appearing in the surveillance video near my house. I'm not embarrassed to admit I relayed the story with exhilaration and an air of suspense. And why not? I felt I had helped solve the case.

Ruby's response is not at all what I expected. "That is very interesting, Lacy. What else do you have for us?"

Is she kidding? "What do you mean 'what else'? I think we've just solved the whole case. Don't you?"

"Sure sounds like it to me," offers Stax. And I am glad for it in light of Ruby's seeming apathy towards my revelation.

"Don't misunderstand me," Ruby says, standing from her chair as though addressing a boardroom. "I'm intrigued by this Carly business and fully intend to return to discussing its implications shortly. But we shouldn't be too hasty on our trek down a single path lest we get lost in the weeds. Let's put Carly out of our minds for the moment and discuss that last. Does anyone have anything new on our other suspects?"

I can't believe what I am hearing. "Excuse me, I don't mean to be rude, but I feel like the first real evidence we've had is being dismissed."

Ruby stretches her arm over and pats my knee. "Don't sound so dejected, dear. I've got my own set of leads I'm following and they may not lead in the same direction as yours."

"You sound like Luke."

Stax perked up. "Luke?"

"I mean Detective Bentley."

"Awww, look who's getting comfy with the first names. How sweet! By the time this case is solved you'll be calling him Lukey-poo!"

"Gross! Anyway, I saw the video. I know what I saw. That was Carly parked in my neighborhood, wearing all black, right before someone jabbed a sharp pair of scissors into the front of my house. If you have a better set of leads to follow, I'd love to see them."

"Whoa," Stax says. "Passive-aggressive much?"

"Nobody's taking anything away from you, Lacy," Ruby says in a placating fashion. "I have every faith that what you say is true. I'm just not sure how to interpret it yet."

"Interpret?" I am less combative now. My curiosity is genuine.

"Yes. I'm reminded of a time when I visited this quaint little New England village, to learn what I could of how the wheels of justice turn in such an environment. I had just finished a late breakfast in a diner off the main square and was headed back to my nearby lodgings when I saw a young man sitting on a bench, crying uncontrollably. Because of some loud road construction, I could not hear what he was saying, but I noticed he was holding a newspaper. The scene was quite unbearable and I imagined him coming across an unexpected obituary, perhaps a former lover. My heart went out to the man, so much so that before I knew it I found myself moving towards him, longing to offer some kind of comfort.

"I approached his bench and opened my mouth to mutter some half-formed condolence when he held the newspaper up to me and said 'Lady, you've got to read this Blondie strip. Funniest thing I've ever seen'. He wasn't crying at all. He was laughing at the funnies. I'll admit I felt foolish for a moment, but only a moment. And in reflection I should not have felt foolish at all."

"Why not? I'd have felt like an idiot," remarks Stax.

"And quite right, too," replies Ruby with impressive alacrity before continuing, "but I realized I'd reached the conclusion I had—that what I was witnessing was a man in the throes of emotional agony—because of insufficient data. The eyes don't lie, but the way we interpret the data we receive can be misleading if we're denied a key piece of information. In my case, it was an audio deficiency. I'm quite certain that had I been able to hear the sounds emanating from the man I would have been aware he was laughing. But because of the road crew, I had only what I saw to work from. Now, why I would suppose tears over laughter perhaps speaks to some underlying darkness in my own conscience and is of little use to our enquiry, but the moral of the story most certainly applies."

She has me perplexed. "The moral?"

"Yes, we remain aware that until our theory is proved, the next discovery may cause it to blow up in our face, to point us in a completely different direction. We should be prepared for such an eventuality to the extent that we welcome it."

"We should welcome being proved wrong?" asks Stax. "Seems self-defeating."

"Quite the opposite. It teaches us humility, and humility keeps us honest, at least to ourselves. If we want to find the truth, we must *be* the truth."

Stax grips her forearms as though overtaken by a chill. "Whoa, that's deep. Okay, I'm sold. Sorry, Lacy, but she's a lot better at this than either of us. I say we roll with it."

My gut reaction is to fight it and yell *'Nonsense! Of course, Carly is the killer. She* has *to be!'* But I can't deny what Ruby said is true. I don't have proof enough to accuse Carly or anyone else of murder. I also can't deny the suspicious behavior of other individuals.

"There is something I saw yesterday I can't make sense of," I say, both in the spirit of what Ruby is trying to achieve and because I want their insight. "I was driving past the Petrick Travel Agency and who do I see coming out but Chase Reynolds."

I tell them about the angry exchange between the two men and this leads to a discussion of what it all might mean.

Both Anderson and Chase are on our suspect list but have never been known to associate with each other. If Chase was having an affair with Marlene, what is he doing talking with her widower? And if either Chase or Anderson is the murderer, why would one be conferring with the other so soon after the deed? Ruby and Stax have no real insight to offer, other than the intangible feeling we share that there is something we're missing lying just out of reach.

"I have some interesting developments of my own to discuss," Ruby says, looking quite pleased with herself. Stax and I lean in close. "Do you recall the material Marti found in the woods on the day of Marlene's disappearance? The police were not interested in it, but I was, and I sent it off to be analyzed. It's a substance called jute. Are you familiar?" Neither of us is. "Well, it's not exactly a household word, is it? But it's not altogether uncommon. What I found most interesting is the odd pattern in which the jute thread is woven. It sparked an idea and I sent off for some materials I expect to receive in the morning. I believe it could lead to something."

"But you're prepared for the eventuality that it won't?" I wink at Ruby to let her know I am being facetious.

"Me? Not so much, dear. I say all that mostly for your benefit. I suspect an arrest will be eminent once I have the final pieces to present to police."

I am so frustrated I can feel the blood swell in my cheeks. What a hypocrite! "And I suppose you'll tell us this arrest will be someone other than Carly?"

"Yes and no. You'll be at the store run tomorrow, will you not?"

"Yes, I will. But what do you mean by—"

"Do you happen to know who else will be there? Gretchen, for instance?"

"No, I think she says she's laying low until all this is over. Wow, that reminds me. I meant to get her papers back to her. I guess I'll have to track her down at her dad's house tomorrow. I'm not looking forward to that."

Ruby stiffens in her chair as though struck by an electric current. "What's this about papers?"

I tell her about the binder left behind in my spare room.

"I must have that!" I'd never seen her so intense.

"I don't think so, Ruby. It belongs to Gretchen. It's just blank paper with some random notes. I promise you it has no bearing on the case."

"I need to see it. I couldn't be more serious, Lacy."

"Are you telling me you think Gretchen killed Marlene?"

"I'm not ready to point fingers at anyone, but we're supposed to be working as a team to gather evidence."

"I get that, but come on… Gretchen? She's the only one of the 'sneerleaders', as they're called, who's remotely human. If not for her I wouldn't have known half the things Marlene was saying about me. And what about her times on Chicken Hill? She crushed it! Unlike Carly, she had no chance to stalk Marlene through the woods and kill her. And finally, I'm the one who stood in her apartment and watched her freak out over the break-in at her office—"

"Oh, and the award of hers you fat-fingered and broke," Stax stays. "That's what really freaked her out, right?"

"Yes, thanks for mentioning that, Stax. My point is I saw the fear in her eyes, the uncertainty, and I may not be an Inspector Butterwell, but I know real terror when I see it. And I don't think she would have uprooted her life to move in with me just to throw us off her scent. Do you?"

"Yeah, I thought that was kind of weird, myself," offers Stax. "I just didn't want to say anything."

"You *did* say something."

"I did? Oh, my bad."

"Lacy, I know you consider Gretchen your friend," Ruby says, her usual calm manner restored, "and far be it from me to cast aspersions. But I believe we are becoming friends as well, are we not?"

Her words take me by surprise. "Yes, of course we are, or at least I think so."

"I'm asking you to trust me. That's all. I know that's a lot to ask, given how new our acquaintance is, but I'm asking it nonetheless. Do you feel you can trust me?"

I feel somewhat stupid for having reacted as I did, though I still believe she is barking up the wrong tree with Gretchen. But I do trust Ruby. For better or worse, I believe she possesses some sort of instinct I don't. So, I acquiesce. "Yes, I trust you, Ruby. And yes, I'll show you Gretchen's papers. But I can't let you keep them."

Ruby puts her hands together in a silent clap. "Oh goody! And I don't believe it will be necessary for me to take possession of the entire contents of the folder. Do you have it in your car?"

"No, it's at home. I can drop it by some time tomorrow."

Ruby closes her eyes and wobbles her head back and forth. Not for the first time, I feel like a second-grader trying to sneak in late to class. "No, no, that will not do. I'll need to see it tonight, as soon as possible. Could I trouble you for a quick ride to your place and back?"

I have zero interest in playing taxi for Ruby so she can look at a stack of blank paper, but I know I will give in, so I cut to the chase. "Sure, let's go. You can meet Meatball."

Stax throws a hand in the air. "Ooh, can I come?"

"What, you want to look at Gretchen's folder, too?"

"No, I'm out of coffee creamer and I know you always keep plenty of the good stuff."

TWENTY-ONE

The sun is gone and the moon is playing peek-a-boo behind clouds as we travel the few miles to my home. Ruby sits shotgun and Stax makes herself comfortably horizontal in the back seat.

Stax stares up at the car roof with her arms folded behind her head. "Rubes, I got a question for ya."

"Rubes?" replies Ruby. "Sure, Juanita, I'll answer if I can."

I snicker out loud. Stax hates to be called by her Christian name.

"Ahem. My question is about Carly. Do you really think she's innocent or were you just busting Lacy's chops back there?"

"I do not think she's innocent. No, not at all."

"So, you think she killed Marlene?"

"I said I don't think she's innocent. That's not to say I think she's a murderer."

"You get how that's confusing, right?"

"I do, and I don't mean to be so evasive. but I prefer to possess all the pieces before I offer my solution to the puzzle. It's a habit I picked up when I was writing mysteries—never talk about your book until it's written."

"Stax isn't the only one confused," I point out. "You were pretty hot on Carly for a while. At least lukewarm. When did you go cold?"

"Are you asking when it occurred to me she might not be our killer?"

"Erm… Yes."

"That would have been when you woke to find the scissors embedded in your front porch."

"What, you don't believe Carly was the one who did it? You don't believe me?"

"No, I *do* believe you. And that's why I don't believe she is our murderer. So, this is your house? It's so charming! Say, what's that stuck to your front door? You're not being evicted, are you?"

I want Ruby to expound on how Carly managed to clear herself of a scissor murder by creeping around in the middle of the night with scissors, but her comment about eviction and the big piece of pink paper taped to my door now has my full attention.

I bolt for the porch and am relieved to see it is a handwritten note and not any sort of notice. It reads 'Meet me at the store—Marti'.

"It's kind of late for a store run, isn't it?" says Stax, who, along with Ruby, followed me up the steps without my hearing.

"I don't think it's a run."

"Then what is it?"

"I have no idea. But I don't like it."

"Peculiar," observes Ruby. "I recognize that paper and can just make out the lettering on the other side, bleeding through. It's one of the flyers for the Valentine Run that Run For It sponsored last February."

I leave the note in place and open my front door. "Let me show you Gretchen's folder and then I'll run you two back to Ruby's and go see what Marti wants."

Stax steps in front of me. "Huh uh, no way. You are not leaving us out of this. Where you go, we go."

I look to Ruby. "There's at least one villain on the loose, dear. And I don't know about you, but I'm in no position to vouch for this handwriting actually being Marti's."

Neither am I, so I agree we'll all go together. Inside, I show Ruby the folder Gretchen left while Stax pilfers my coffee creamers.

I look over Ruby's shoulder. "Does any of her scribbling hold a particular significance for you?"

"None whatsoever. It's more the paper I'm interested in. I'm sure she won't mind if a sheet is missing, wouldn't you agree?"

"A blank sheet? I suppose that won't hurt."

Ruby thanks me with a smile, removes a sheet and daintily folds it into fourths before securing it in her slacks pocket. "This will be another project for me before the run tomorrow."

Stax slips a handful of my creamer cups into her pocket and joins Ruby and myself in the living room. "Projects? Why don't I have any projects?"

"Do you need projects?" I ask. "You have a store to run."

"Meh, Larry can handle it. That's what brothers are for."

"I have the perfect project for you, Stax," says a cheerful Ruby, quite happy since she got the paper sample. "We can discuss it on our way to the store."

"Lacy, you'll be happy to hear I have not abandoned investigations into Carly," says Ruby as we make our way to Run For It. I normally find the dark sky and quiet streets calming on a late evening drive, but Marti's note left me unnerved. I half-listen to Ruby as she gives Stax her marching orders. "Stax, I'd like you to work your photoshop wonders. Do you have some photographs of Carly?"

"Maybe if I had a dart board. But yeah, I can pull some off the Internet. Why?"

"I'd like you to photoshop a wig similar to the one Lacy described onto Carly's face, maybe from a couple of different angles. Make it as clean as you can and then print out a copy on sturdy paper stock."

"Are we pounding the pavement again? I can make some free time but even my pushover brother has his limits."

"No, nothing like that. I have a very short list of shops I'd like to personally visit."

"Okay, no problem. I'll get to it tonight before I hit the sack. Hey, is that Marti's car?"

I'm relieved to see Marti's car in the parking lot of Run For It. There is something not right about the note on my door. Marti has my cell number, so why not call or text me? It occurs to me I may be walking into a trap.

"What do you suppose she wants with you?" Ruby asks.

I park next to Marti's car. Ours are the only vehicles in the lot. "I really don't know. If I had to guess I'd say it's about Marlene, or maybe she needs an extra run leader. You guys stay here. I'm sure I won't be long."

"Have you flipped your wig?" says Stax, hoisting herself up and opening the door. "I'm not about to let you have all the fun yourself."

This is Stax's way of looking out for me without admitting what she is doing. "Come on, then."

Ruby stays put. "I'll be your eyes on the outside."

I can see she is serious. She is still suspicious about the evening summons to the closed store. "All right. Feel free to come in at any time if we're running long."

Although the store has a street entrance, out of habit we walk around to the side entrance that faces the main parking lot. It's as though a black filter is lowered over my eyes as we step under the overhang and lose the moonlight. My foot comes into contact with something and I feel it give and roll away. I ask what it is and Stax bends to grab it.

"It's one of those massage balls." She hands it to me. "It looks like there's a couple more of them down here." I know what it is as soon as I feel it. The store makes a good profit selling various massage tools for runners to use to combat their tight, aching muscles. Although I prefer the sticks with multiple edged rollers, some people like buying the deep tissue massage balls, which are about the size of a baseball, only smooth, and made of hard rubber with something denser in the center, which makes them heavy and balanced.

"I don't like this," I say. The store's inventory should be *inside* the store.

She retrieves two more balls from the concrete walkway in front of the door. "Me either. But these might come in handy."

"Marti? Hi, it's Lacy," I say upon opening the door. It is dark inside so I hesitate to enter, hoping to hear her cheerful voice ring out from somewhere in the shadows. I am met with dead silence. And there is something wrong about the shadows, something unfamiliar.

"I think we should leave and call the police," I whisper.

"And tell them what? That the closed store on Main Street has its lights off? Let's at least check it out first."

So, we enter. We step a few paces into the store and stop. The counter and registers are to our right and the door leading into the offices where I had my meetings with both Chase and Luke are to our left.

"What the heck happened here?" asks Stax. The moonlight comes through the front windows across the storeroom from us, silhouetting the racks and shelves. As my eyes adjust to the new light I can see what's concerning Stax. Many of the clothing racks and central shoe shelves are toppled over. "Lace, do you see this?"

I know we are not alone. It is a knowledge, not a sense, and I know whatever is in here with us is not friendly. I hear a commotion behind me, a door swinging open. The air around me is disturbed. I feel the pressure of impact, of someone running into me, and then pain. There is someone breathing down my neck and they hold a threatening pair of sharp, shiny scissors. I hear someone yelling 'I've been stabbed! I've been stabbed!'

It's me.

A figure in a dark hoodie flies by me and darts behind the sales counter, the little gate swinging in its wake. I drop the massage ball and grab for my left arm. I've been stabbed.

I am preoccupied by my injury when I hear Stax yell out 'Hey!' and I notice her make a sudden move. My ears shake with the unmistakable sound of glass shattering. Lots of it. The figure goes down out of sight at the far end of the counter.

"Got him!" yells Stax.

"You got him? With what?"

She holds up a massage ball. "With one of these! Hey, are you hurt?"

"Yeah, I think so. My arm—"

"Let me turn on a light."

She reaches over the counter rail and flips on the overhead lights. The darkness around me turns to bright yellow and I see my injury for the first time. My shirt sleeve is torn and bloody, but assuming the scissors weren't dipped in flesh-eating bacteria, it's little more than a superficial cut.

Stax inspects my wound. "Bah, it's nothing. Won't even scar. And here I thought you were getting disemboweled or something."

"Stax, I was just stabbed! I'm sorry if I'm not bloody enough for you, but that was terrifying. And it hurts!"

"You're right, I take it back. Better you than me. We'll need to get you looked at, but first…"

She tugs at the sleeve of my uninjured arm and motions forward with her head. I'm clueless as to what she is getting at. "What?"

"What do you think?"

"You mean the hoodie guy? Yeah, I think we should get out of here before he wakes up."

"No chance. I've still got this ball and as you've seen I'm not afraid to use it. I'm going in for a look-see."

"No, you're not."

"Yes, I am!"

Before I can protest further Stax is pushing open the gate allowing access to the area behind the sales counter. I suppose I could have grabbed her by the shoulder and pulled her out the door we came in, but something in me had to know—craved to know—who was behind the nightmare we'd all be living lately. So, I follow her behind the counter.

As we creep closer to where the dark figure is lying face down and motionless, I take note of how different the store looks now. Nearest me, there is broken glass all over the floor from a display case behind the counter. This must have been what I heard after Stax threw her massage ball. I can see we are dealing with a madman as only someone out of their mind would wreak this kind of havoc, pilfering the store and piling the shelves and racks into some sort of a barricade.

The street side front door is propped half open for some reason. I hear the glass crunching under my feet. We are standing next to the intruder who, as far as we can tell, is knocked unconscious. Scissors lay where they landed, about a foot in front of the person's right hand. Whoever it is, he or she is not a large person.

Stax puts her finger to her mouth, motioning to remain quiet, then bends into a kneeling position. I mirror her motions until we are kneeling on either side of the prostrate figure. I let Stax know the next move is all hers.

For all her bravado, Stax is white as a sheet and for a moment I worry I'll soon be kneeling over two unconscious bodies. But she keeps it together and reaches her hand forward, slowly, as though the Phantom might jump and bite her. Once she has a two-fingered grip on the rim of the hood, she pulls back a little, and then—

"Well, butter my butt and call me a biscuit," she says. The look of surprise on her face sends shivers down my spine.

"What? Who is it?" I ask.

"Take a look for yourself." Stax pulls the hoodie back and I lean forward. I hear the side door open behind us and Ruby's voice call out, asking if everything is all right. But I don't answer her. I can't look away. I am transfixed on the face of the person who stalked Marlene, who murdered her, and who vandalized my home. It is a face I've looked on fondly so many times before.

The face of Marti Reynolds.

TWENTY-TWO

My legs dangle off the back of the ambulance as the EMT dresses my injury. The steel bed is cold through my jeans, but I am grateful for the distraction from the pain in my arm. I'm also grateful for the news that the stab was not deep or long enough to necessitate stitches. Now, if only I could turn back time and make It Carly's face and not Marti's I saw when Stax lifted that hood.

"You all done with her?" Luke...err...Detective Bentley materialized from behind the ambulance and addressed the tech who had just finished wrapping my arm.

"All done, detective. As long as she keeps an eye out for infection and sees her primary care doctor in a few days, she'll be right as rain."

Yeah, I almost got murdered less than an hour ago. I'll be fine.

"Lacy, are you good to talk?" Bentley says, his eyes warm and comforting. I'm glad he's here.

"Let's see. Yes, it appears neither my tongue nor my vocal cords were injured in the kerfuffle this evening. What do you want to know?"

"Are you sure it's 'kerfuffle' and not 'kerfluffle', with an 'L' in the middle?"

"Not according to spell check."

"Wow, so that's a word you use on a regular basis."

"Only when a good friend attacks me with a sharp object."

"About that. I've talked with Ms. Best and Ms. Maplethorpe."

"And now you need my statement?"

He has a great smile. "You know me so well," he says.

"You know me *too* well."

"If I weren't on the clock, I'd beg to differ."

"The chief doesn't allow begging whilst on the clock?"

"No, he much prefers we grovel."

Then I start crying. "I can't believe it was Marti." Yep, volleys of tears burst forth right there, in front of this tough yet sensitive man. I am living the cliché of the shattered victim. I feel the detective's hand grip my shoulder. It is warm and firm and for a moment my eyes close and I imagine him massaging my neck. I must sound as bad as I look because Stax and Ruby, both of whom were giving the detective a wide berth with me, came over to offer comfort.

He quickly removes his hand from my shoulder.

"Is she gonna live?" asks Stax.

Bentley is smiling. "As long as she stops chasing criminals."

"What's Marti's status?" asks Ruby. I feel selfish for not having thought to ask that myself.

"Still unconscious, pulse faint, but now that she's got medical attention they say she'll be fine."

Ruby nods but betrays no emotion. "Is she under arrest?"

"Not until I can read her her rights, but that'll be soon enough."

"Good. Would it be possible for us to have a conversation inside?"

Bentley scratches his head and looks perplexed. "It's not kosher for a detective to let civilians walk around a crime scene. Do you have a particular reason for wanting to go back in the store?"

"Yes, I think it might jog something loose."

"From what?"

"From my rattled skull."

"But you said you weren't in the store when it all went down?"

"I think it's a good idea," I find myself saying. "Stax and I might benefit from seeing it with the lights on."

I don't think I'd see anything I hadn't seen before, but Ruby is anxious to get in the store and I want her to know I've got her back. I am surprised when Detective Bentley relents. Stax rolls her eyes at me as though to say it is more my charms than my logic that persuaded Bentley. And what's wrong with that?

"Okay, I'll give you guys a few minutes. My men are still digging around in the back." Bentley escorts us back into the crime scene that, up until an hour ago, was our favorite hangout.

Ruby walks into the middle of the store and stares intently at the pile of shelving stacked up between the counter and the street door. "What do you make of this, detective?"

"I'm not sure, Miss Maplethorpe. It's on my list of questions to ask Mrs. Reynolds when she wakes up. It didn't make the top five, though."

"But what's your gut tell you?"

"My gut, huh? Well, when I first saw it I thought of a dugout or barricade. Criminals will build those if they're anticipating a shootout."

"Did Marti have a gun on her?"

"No. No, she didn't."

"A barricade was my first thought, too. So why wasn't she behind it when Lacy and Stax came in? They said she was waiting behind the door into the offices."

"I'm sure I couldn't say. Maybe she had a change of mind."

"After all this work? And did you notice the street door was ajar?"

"Of course, I noticed it."

"Do have an idea as to why? It's the furthest entrance from where she parked."

"Well, she might have anticipated Lacy entering that way. That must be why the barricade is in front of that door. And when she saw through the window that the women would be entering by the side, she ran into the back room. This way, her bases are covered."

"I can see why you're a detective," says Stax, visibly impressed.

Bentley sidles up to Ruby. "Talking out a problem is often how I'm able to reach the correct conclusions, although it's not very common I talk out the evidence with witnesses."

"Yes, that's the purpose. But I don't think you're arriving at the correct conclusions."

"Oh, is that right?"

Gulp.

I feel embarrassed for Ruby and offended on behalf of Detective Bentley.

"Ruby, you can't say that," I whisper into her ear.

Bentley waves it off in a good-humored manner. "No, it's fine. I don't claim to be infallible and a detective's best asset is always an extra set of eyes. What did I miss, Ruby?"

"The barricade, for lack of a better word, was built with the supports on the inside. As you can see, the high part or 'wall' is on the side facing the street door, and not on the inside as you'd expect if she were planning to conceal herself from someone entering through this door."

"Score one for the old lady."

"Stax!"

"What? When she's right, she's right!"

"I wasn't reacting to that, you called her an... oh, never mind."

"It's all right, Lacy," Ruby says. "I've been called worse by better. But we're not trying to score points here. Detective Bentley, do you see the point I'm trying to make? If this is intended to be a barricade of any sort, it's in the wrong location."

"Yes, Miss Maplethorpe, I do see."

"Please, call me Ruby."

"Ruby, I do see. And if you have an idea what Marti's purpose was, I'm all ears."

"That's just it, I don't. Not yet. Let me have a look back here." Ruby moseys back in our direction and walks past all three of us as though we are invisible. We are standing in front of the side entrance door and watch as Ruby pushes the swing gate and creeps inside the associates area behind the sales counter.

"Watch out for the glass," I caution.

"That's precisely what I'm looking at," is her response. "How many of those strange balls did you girls throw?"

"Just one."

"My aim is true," Stax says, hoisting her chin into the air.

"Then can anyone explain how the glass case became broken? Look, the ball is still in the case."

"Don't touch that!" orders Bentley. "It'll need to be printed.

Ruby heads back towards us. She looks me in the eye and I can see the wheels of her brain spinning and fuming. "How was it you came to be holding those balls?"

"I thought I'd mentioned it to you. There were a few of them sitting outside the entrance here when we walked up. Stax thought they might come in useful, and I'm glad she did."

"Almost as though it were preordained, don't you think?"

"I don't follow your meaning."

"And what did you see when Miss Stax threw the ball?"

"Well, Marti ran past me, stabbing me in the arm, and she ran behind the counter, right where you just were. I saw Stax's arm go through the air and watched Marti hit the ground."

"And the glass broke at the same time?"

"Yes, I imagine it bounced off her and hit the case. Or else her arm went through the glass as she fell."

"No, that couldn't be it. The ball is in the back of the case. But you're sure you saw all of what you just described? You weren't preoccupied with your arm?"

"I grabbed my arm when I felt the pain, but I'm telling you, my eyes were locked on that black hood. I saw the whole thing."

"And you?" she says to Stax.

"Ditto to all the above. It was dark, but not so dark I couldn't see what happened."

"Did either of you happen to go behind the counter before Lacy was stabbed? Or take a look back there?"

We had not.

Ruby is pacing holes in the carpet. "It doesn't make sense." She twists her wedding ring back and forth on her finger so hard I fear her frail little finger will pop right off. "The broken glass, the pile of shelving facing the wrong way, the open door. Nothing is as it should be."

"You're right, Ruby," I say. "Nothing is as it should be. Marlene shouldn't be dead and Marti shouldn't be in a hospital on her way to prison. But that's how it is and we're going to have to come to terms with it."

Stax walks over to the edge of the counter, running her hand along the rim as though for the last time. "It shouldn't have been Marti, though. I like Marti."

On that we can all agree. I feel the emotions in me starting to swell and I pray they won't bubble over until I am back home in my robe and slippers.

"I hate to ask right now," says Bentley, "but I don't think there'll be a better time. Can any of you tell me why you think Marti would do all this?"

My mind is a blank. Although we tentatively put Marti's name on our suspect list, it had been for the sake of objectivity more than anything. She was never a real contender for the mantle of murderer.

"That's just it," whispers Ruby. "I don't believe she did."

The door behind us bursts open and I jump. Officer Diebold barrels into the room, waving something in the air. "Detective, I've got something here."

"What's that, officer?"

"It's a motive, is what it is."

Diebold looks full of his own steam and is bursting to share his news, but he sees us standing there and halts in his tracks, gripping his item close to his chest. I can see it is a thin, cardboard envelope, such as you use to ship documents. "Maybe I should show you this in private."

"Just hand it over," says Bentley, extending his hand. Diebold relinquishes the envelope and waits like a dog for a treat as his superior fishes out its contents.

I can't see what Bentley is holding, but from the way he handles the items I imagine they are photographs.

"Is that—"

"Yep. Found this on her desk."

Bentley sighs and excuses the uniform, with the directive to 'keep looking'. When Diebold doesn't leave, Bentley says "Good work" and this pleases the young man enough that he again disappears beyond the door to the bowels of the store, a big square smile on his big square face.

"Ladies, I'm going to show you these in confidence, because you are material witnesses."

Bentley hands me the small stack of photographs and before I can glance at them, Ruby and Stax attach themselves to my side. The photos are of Chase Reynolds and Marlene Petrick walking together, all smiles, along Main Street and its side roads. Two more are of them standing outside Chase's car in front of what appears to be her and Anderson's office. My stomach knots when I recognize in a couple of photos the same scene Hilda witnessed in her chocolate shop and told me about.

Bentley reaches for the photographs and I gladly let them go. "Were any of you aware Chase and Marlene were seeing each other? Or that Marti had suspicions?"

I tell him of what I'd heard from Hilda and added that I never noticed any chemistry between Marlene and Chase when I'd see them at the store or at runs. I never picked up on any friction between Marti and Chase as you might expect when one thinks the other is cheating. Ruby and Stax say the same.

"I'll be talking to Chase about this," Bentley says, returning the photographs to the envelope. "But I think we just found our motive."

Stax is shaking her head, looking as gobsmacked as I feel. But Ruby looks crestfallen. "No, no, no, that can't be right," she says, her voice cracking. I put my arm around her more to keep her from falling than for mere comfort. "I couldn't have missed it by that much. I need sleep, Lacy. I need sleep and time to think."

My heart breaks for Ruby. She tried her best. I know it is important to her that she help her friend—me—but the case means something more for her. It is a puzzle. A chance to pit her wits against a master criminal, just as she fantasized so many times when concocting her Inspector Butterwell tales.

I see Ruby to her house but I don't stay. Neither of us is in the mood for company. I go home, take a long bath replete with jasmine and frankincense to help calm my nerves, and decide some peppermint chamomile tea to slow my racing mind isn't such a bad idea, either. I stand in the kitchen in my beloved slippers and robe, waiting for my tea water to boil, and in my mind I replay all the events from the past several days.

I remember the Chicken Hill Run and how upon my arrival I saw Marlene and Chase talking together. How did I not remember that until now? Oh yeah, because there's nothing special about seeing Chase talking with a regular customer of his. It might as well have been me as Marlene. Except it wasn't me. It was the woman photographed in public with him. A woman now dead.

I recall how odd Chase behaved when I was alone with him in the back of the store. Was it the stress of running a business or the stress of trying to manage a love triangle? Marti never showed any outward signs of being unhappy with Chase, but what happens behind closed doors often stays behind picket fences, so who knows? Evidently there was a lot going on inside of Marti that none of us could see.

The tea does little to calm me. I lay in bed squeezing Meatball a little harder than he's used to, resulting in his choosing the throw rug on the floor over me. I go over the Bruce's Pit Stop surveillance video footage again and again in my head and try to imagine the figure in it as Marti. I couldn't see the woman's face and she was clearly wearing a wig, but she appeared taller than Marti. Could that have been a trick of the angle? And what about the limp? Marti didn't run at Chicken Hill so she wouldn't have a limp. But how certain of that could I really be? It's not like I have spent much time with her since that day, and committing murder, hauling bodies around, and whatever else goes along with such nefarious pastimes, could presumably be quite taxing on one's extremities.

I sympathize with Ruby's self-doubt, because, try as I might, I cannot associate Marti with the cold-blooded killer who stalked the forest of Chicken Hill for her prey. The bandage on my arm and the sore, mangled flesh underneath reminds me Marlene is not the only victim here. Had Stax not insisted on coming along, Detective Bentley might now be investigating my homicide. I felt so sure that Carly was the killer. To find out how wrong I was—humbling is not the right word so I'll go with soul crushing.

Shortly after I accept that I won't get a wink of shuteye tonight, I fall into a deep sleep and don't wake up until it is too late to call it morning. A hungry Meatball is nibble-kissing my cheek and chin. When that fails, I catch a fuzzy mitt in my open maw. Time to get up.

I don't have to work today so I didn't bother to set an alarm. I can't imagine anything other than a natural disaster getting me to leave my house today. Then my phone rings.

"Crimes of nature, you sound like death warmed over. You go on another bender, you hapless one-armed lush, you?" It's Stax.

"Another bender? Where do you get this stuff? No, I was up half the night crying. And you?"

"Slept like a baby. But hey, I'm calling to let you know to be at the store tonight at six o'clock."

"What store?"

"Run For It, duh. Geez, drink some coffee or something before you drive."

"You've got to be kidding. What could possibly be going on at the store?"

"It's Thursday run night, isn't it? It's what we do, girl."

"Yeah, but… I mean… how?"

"I can't go into details, but it's happening."

"Will Chase be there? And what are these details you can't go into?"

"Yes, he will be there. And ixnay on the etailsday."

"Are you and Ruby up to something?"

"Let's say there's more to the story and we're going to hear it tonight. Honestly, I don't know what's going to happen. She just called me with her usual cryptic talk where she hints a lot but tells you nothing."

I know what she means. Ruby's a sweetheart, but a frustrating sweetheart.

"Come on, I know you know something," I say.

"Well, I know she has me running errands."

"Regarding the case? But Marti is as good as convicted."

"That's what I thought, but who knows? I guess we'll find out tonight. Anyway, I've got books to sell. See you at six!"

Not for the first time in recent days I find myself befuddled. It doesn't surprise me that Ruby is still holding to her delusions. I don't know the woman well enough to be surprised by it. But I've come to know Stax pretty well and I can't see her wasting her time just to appease an old lady. I certainly cannot understand why Chase would be opening his store to people with his wife unconscious in the hospital and facing murder charges. Talk about capitalism at any cost!

I need to clear my head and the way I do that is to run. There's something about the rapid inhalation of fresh air, feeling my blood pump faster, hearing the rhythm of my heartbeat in my ears, that clears the muddy waters and lets me see what I need to. Whatever is being planned at the store this evening is not a run, so I slip into my exercise garb, fill my water bottle, and head out to my favorite walking trail.

The clear sky and bright sunshine are just what I need. I've been so involved with group running that I almost forgot how refreshing a solitary jaunt can be. Seeing children playing, dogs running, and families enjoying picnics are just the distractions I need. I'm not tracking my pace but it feels strong. The sweat comes a mile in and with it I can feel the stresses of the week melt away and fall off my shoulders.

Two miles in I am fighting harder for my air, the drum in my chest beating harder, pounding away the self-doubt and uncertainty that has hounded me since I became a murder suspect. It is in my third and final mile that I have my epiphany as to why Ruby is summoning us all to the store tonight.

She's going to tell us *how* the murder was committed.

I've been so preoccupied with who the murderer might be and proving it is someone other than myself that I'd lost all sight of the mystery within the mystery—how the murder was accomplished at Chicken Hill.

I recall my trek through the woods with Ruby and the confusing clues we found. She alluded at that time to having worked out how Marlene was made to disappear in a public place in front of dozens of runners, but she never revealed the secret. Understanding how Marti could have pulled this off right under his nose would explain why Chase would be willing to host a private meeting.

I grab some Chinese food on the way home. My body needs the salt and my brain craves the indulgence. Lo Mein in place of rice is my idea of treating myself. I eat my meal on the couch while watching the five o'clock news and am surprised not to see a mention of Marti's arrest. It occurs to me I also haven't seen any on my social media feeds, though I subscribe to all the local news outlets. A satisfied Meatball purrs next to me, having begged his way into a piece of bourbon chicken. As I pull out the fortune cookie, my phone sounds off.

"Good afternoon, Lacy. This is Ruby." She must not be aware that cell phones tell you who's calling.

"Hi Ruby, how are you holding up?"

"If I were doing any better, dear, there'd be two of me. Did Miss Juanita deliver my message?"

"If you mean to come to the store at the usual time tonight, yes, she did. And I suspect I know why you want us there."

"If you've guessed 'vindication', you've guessed correctly."

Then I'm not even close. "Vindication? What are you vindicating?"

"My good self, dear! And the truth! Oh, and you, as well."

"Me?" I wasn't aware I required vindication.

"To an extent, yes. Remember what I said about reading the signs? They're there, you just have to recognize them when you see them. Well, I was a bit slow on the uptake, but I got there some time after the witching hour this morning and I've been on it ever since."

"You haven't slept?"

"I'll sleep the sleep of the dead, but not until all the loose ends are tied up."

"So, you *will* be telling us how the murder was committed? Is that what tonight is about?"

"Tonight, all skeletons will be aired. All questions will be answered. But how Marlene was murdered is the least interesting of my revelations. Oh goodness, look at the time. So much to do before tonight. I'll see you there!"

The phone goes dead. I stare at it in my hand for a moment as though willing it to give me more of the answers I seek. With none forthcoming, I set it aside and realize I hold something else in my hand. A small slip of white paper. The fortune from the cookie I cracked open as Ruby called. I turn it over and am reminded of Ruby's maxim that the signs are there if only you can recognize them.

The fortune reads 'Time reveals all'.

TWENTY-THREE

When I arrive at Run For It I find a nearly empty parking lot. Whatever is happening tonight is obviously a private affair. From the cars I can tell Chase, Gretchen, Carly, and Ruby are already inside. Stax either walked over from the bookstore or hasn't made it yet.

I enter the store and about fall on my keister when I see Ruby talking with Gretchen at the back near a rack of visors and hats. Yesterday, she all but accused the young woman of murder and here they are chatting like old friends.

Jessica and Billy, the store employees, are also here helping Chase straighten up the racks and shelves thrown about the night before. They must have been at it for some time as the store is all but returned to its normal appearance.

The area behind the sales counter is still sectioned off with yellow police tape, forcing Carly to rubberneck over the cash register to see what evidence of criminality might still be on display. A quick glance tells me there is nothing more than a broken display case to show anything untoward happened.

Upon seeing me, Ruby abandons Gretchen and Chase sets down his broom to come over and greet me. Chase reaches me first and wraps me in a tight hug. I'm pretty sure my feet left the floor for a moment.

"Thank you for coming," he says in my ear as Ruby appears over his shoulder.

"How's Marti?" I ask Chase. He makes a sound, like a little laugh, and it strikes me as inappropriate.

"She's fine. Quite good, in fact. She took a heavy blow to the head, but I've always said she has a thick skull."

And it gets weirder. Chase puts me down and I waste no time in moving myself to another side of the store, closer to the street entrance and window displays. Maybe if I mingle in with the mannequins, everyone else will forget I'm here. Ruby follows me.

"Is your little friend on her way?" she asks.

"If you mean Stax, I haven't talked to her. I assume she'll walk up here from the bookstore like she usually does."

"No rush, I suppose. I have another guest I'm expecting and although I'll be doing much of the speaking this evening, you might say he is the master of ceremonies."

The door behind me opens and in comes Stax. She wears a soft pink chiffon blouse with puffy sleeves, her arms adorned with a random assortment of bracelets. I manage not to laugh.

"Did I miss anything good?" she asks.

"Are you expecting something good to happen?" Because I certainly am not.

"I don't know what the heck to expect. Why do you think I wore my good blouse?"

That's Stax. It doesn't have to make sense as long as it makes sense to her. I find it adorable she fancies herself gussied up even though she is still wearing her usual pair of old jeans.

Carly saunters up a little closer. "You have a lot of nerve to show your faces here." Her brown locks are as shiny and as coiffed as usual, but the thicker foundation applied under her eyes does little to hide the baggage. Something has kept her up at night. I don't know what Carly is talking about and I doubt Stax does, either, but that doesn't stop her from firing back.

"Is there a mirror behind me? Because when I saw you I thought the exact same thing." Stax's bracelets rattle like a jar of screws as she swings her arms in exaggerated motions.

"You can make jokes, but if you ask me, the cops have the wrong person. I think your friend, Lacy, is the one who should be behind bars."

How audacious can she be? Sure, I accused her of the same murder, but not to her face and in public! "Carly, I don't appreciate your accusations. You know I haven't done anything."

"I know you threatened to kill my friend, and now she's dead. I know you've been sticking your nose in people's business. And I know Marti wouldn't hurt a fly."

I couldn't deny anything she said, but I had plenty of my own ammo on her if she wanted to play war. "Oh yeah? I know a few things about you, too, Carly. Should we air it all out right here?"

"Ladies, that is enough for now," Ruby says, putting her hands in the air and stepping between us like a boxing referee. "We have a lot of business to attend to. Chase was good enough to set out chairs for us all, so if everyone would, please take one. I'm still awaiting the arrival of one very special guest, but I suppose now would be a good time for the preliminaries."

Everyone is dumbstruck to see this little old lady bossing them around. Everyone except Stax and myself, that is, and Chase, for some inexplicable reason.

"Come on, folks, grab a chair," Chase says as he takes one of the armless plastic chairs and turns it to face Ruby. He sits down in an obvious fashion, as though to encourage the others to follow suit. And indeed, they do. I choose to remain standing, not to be obstinate, but simply because I am too high strung for a chair right now. If I sit down now I'll fidget everyone to death.

Ruby begins her slow pacing again, warming her engines. "Some of you are aware, and some are not, that the recent crime is not the first murder mystery in which Marlene Petrick found herself entangled. It was eighteen years ago now and only six months into the new century that a young lady by the name of Kayleigh Cook lost her life amidst circumstances no less gruesome and mysterious than Marlene herself. Although a great many of the details of the original investigation are now known to me, I'll discuss only those pertinent to our present situation. Because, make no mistake about it, the two murders are very much connected."

Ruby makes the sales floor her stage and sets about delivering a mini-lecture on Marlene's previous life as a salon owner. She doesn't shy from scandalizing the more sensitive souls present by addressing the rumor that the girls in Marlene's employ were encouraged to offer other, more illicit, services. Her grand finish is a spine-chilling recounting of the tragic murder Kayleigh Cook.

Ruby paces. "She was stabbed to death with a pair of barber scissors. Scissors identical to those left around town for Marlene to find as of late. Whoever was doing this to Marlene knew what they were doing. Did the police have a suspect in mind for the Cook murder? They looked at some individuals but found nothing solid against any of them. However, a friend of mine who happens to be a retired-police-detective-turned-private-investigator has recently discovered something in the file overlooked by the original investigators. Can I tell you about it? I could, but I won't. At least not yet. Am I being coy on purpose? You bet your sweet bippy, as the kids used to say!

"I must be careful about the words I choose, when I use them, and who is within earshot, because in this quaint little running shop we all love so much, there are more secrets behind every door, around every corner, and in every nook than in any of my Inspector Butterwell novels. My stock in trade for many years was inventing the most dastardly villain I could imagine and cloaking them in the image of an angel. I would then devise for them a plot so cunning the sharpest minds could not see it for what it was until it was too late. I can attest to the fact that this was no easy task. I did all my work at a desk and was held accountable only to my publisher should I go astray.

"The villain we seek is an entirely different breed. This is a person who committed their crimes in the real world, out in the open, and not holed up in a study. And to achieve their wicked aims they risked everything precious to them. No, indeed, this is not someone I'm eager to have against me without taking precaution!"

"Ruby, dear, are you feeling all right?" It was Jessica who spoke from the back of the room, seated in a chair between two racks of shiny black windbreakers that threatened to swallow her. "You invite us all here for—whatever this is—and now you're saying all this about wickedness and dastardly this and villain that while Chase is not ten feet from you. It was just last night that he found out his wife…well, you know. It's in poor taste what you're doing."

Gretchen lets out a sound like 'Pffft' and says under her breath "From what I hear, Chase isn't so innocent himself." All eyes turn to her, shocked that someone so sweet and quiet would be so forward. "Oh my gosh, did I say that out loud? I'm so sorry! Chase, please forgive me." Her cheeks blossom and her eyes tear up.

Chase laughs—yes, laughs—and waves it away. "It's perfectly all right. And Jessica, thank you for what you said, but what Ruby is doing here tonight is with my full blessing."

"Boss, well, I don't…" Jessica is unable to comprehend why a grieving man appears so lighthearted as he listens to a near stranger denigrating his duplicitous wife. Jessica holds a hand up in truce and forces a smile as she swallows whatever unfinished thoughts are still in her head. I confess I am right there with her.

"You'll have to excuse me," continues Ruby in her usual congenial fashion, as though nothing had been said against her, "but I'm trying to kill a little time until my final guest can arrive. Once he does we can begin in earnest."

I wince as the dark sky outside suddenly goes bright, like a giant flashlight pointed in my eyes. The source is the headlights of multiple cars pulling into the parking lot.

Carly rises and lurches over to the floor-to-ceiling display window that runs the length of the store's front. "Cops? What are the cops doing here?"

"Oh good, my guest has arrived. We can begin," Ruby says excitedly.

Detective Bentley enters and nods to everyone present. Unless I'm imagining things, his eye lingers on me for a moment longer. It looks like he is to be accompanied by a uniformed officer, but instead the cop remains outside the door. I look to the side entrance and see another cop, who might be Diebold. Is something about to go down?

"I don't think I like this," Carly says. "You didn't mention anything about the police when you called me."

Ruby ignores Carly and engages in a hushed conversation with Detective Bentley.

"You got something to be worried about, Carly?" asks Stax, a snarky grin on her face.

Carly returns to her chair, smiling smugly. "No, but your friend might."

I've had enough of the insinuation. "Carly, if you'd like to accuse me of something, now is your chance to present your evidence. Otherwise, please keep your mouth shut."

"Ladies, don't make me put you in the corner," Ruby says. "The detective is here for the same reason as the rest of us. He's here for the truth."

Gretchen raises her hand and clears her throat to draw attention her way. She appears tepid, almost mousy. "I don't want to fight with anyone, but I must say I'm curious about the police as well. They arrested Marti, right? If the case is solved, why are they here?"

I am wondering the same thing. I know Ruby is up to something, that she can't accept Marti as a murderess. While I could *maybe* see her convincing a desperate Chase that someone other than Marti is behind the grim business of late, I cannot fathom Ruby succeeding in convincing Detective Bentley of anything with charm and persuasion alone. She would need to bring the hard evidence. So, what is he doing here?

I look to Ruby for a sign. After her silent pleasantries with Bentley she glances over to Chase, who is again smiling oddly. He nods to Ruby, as though giving approval for something, and she nods back. What is going on here? Chase stands and walks away from the sales counter and over to the door leading back to the catacombs of the building. He raps his knuckles three times on the door and steps away. Chase, Ruby, and Bentley all stare towards the door. So, naturally, do the rest of us.

It is like watching paint dry for a moment until the knob of the catacomb's door turns. Someone is coming out, but the door opens outward and from my vantage point I can't see who. They are taking their time emerging. Is it another cop? A ghoul in a black hoodie? I am about to rush over and pull open the door myself when the figure steps out of the shadows and saves me the trouble.

It is Marti Reynolds. She is dressed in her street clothes and waves sheepishly at us with her uncuffed hand. "Hi," is all she says.

I decide I could use that chair now.

TWENTY-FOUR

"You'll have to pardon the dramatic entrance," Ruby says, her words all but lost in the eruption of gasps and murmurs, "but I thought it prudent that Marti not be standing behind the counter greeting everyone as they came in this evening, lest you all turn and run in fright."

I wouldn't have thought so few people could make so much noise, but in its previous life the store was a bank, so there's something to be said for thick walls. At least one person (I believe it was Jessica) yelled out 'Marti!' as though she were a celebrity on the red carpet.

Chase walks over and hugs his wife. As she falls into his embrace I see the bandage on the back of her head.

Stax is scratching her chin. She stands from her chair as though she is going to approach Marti, then sits back down. It is relieving to know she is as lost as myself.

"It's cool to see you, Marti, but… shouldn't you be in jail, or something? Maybe the hospital? Or, you know, jail," asks Stax incredulously.

Marti laughs. It is hard not to. "The doctor cleared me," she answers. "I've got a bruised bean, but that's all. As the for the other thing, would you like to answer, Detective Bentley?"

Bentley looks perfectly at home surrounded by all our madness. He says in his usual chill manner, "You can trust me, if Mrs. Reynolds had broken any laws, she'd be in jail right now."

Stax claps. "So, it's legal in Cedar Mill to stab Lacy Purdy? Anyone got a pair of scissors I can borrow?"

"Enough, Stax," I say.

"A knife? A machete? Heck, I'll settle for paper cuts."

Marti laughs and hugs Stax. "I love you, too."

Stax, as is her way, goes rigid in Marti's grip before loosening into a hug. "I gotta bust your chops, right? But seriously, you have some explaining to do, and I mean good explanations, like with annotations, references, the works. Some signed affidavits wouldn't hurt you, come to think of it."

"Really, affidavits?" I say.

Stax puckers her lips and nods sharply. "That's a fun word to say."

"I'll say she has explaining to do," says a salty Carly.

"I'll be the one doing the explaining this evening." Ruby steps in front of Carly as though expecting she and I might resume our war of words. "As soon as everyone has settled back down."

Marti is not yet ready to settle. After letting go of Stax, she looks my way. I don't mean to, but I wince, and I can tell she notices. I swear it was an involuntary reaction on my part; I am happy to see my friend free and healthy, but a part of my subconscious is screaming at me that this 'friend' stabbed me last night. What do you believe, your heart or your eyes?

"Oh, Lacy, what you must think," Marti says, her eyes tearing up as she pulls me into a deep hug of the long-lost-sibling variety.

"I don't know what to think, Marti. But I'm glad you're okay."

"I swear, I'd never hurt you."

"See, this is where I get confused," Stax interjects. "Far be it from me to put a damper on this lovefest, but Lacy wasn't alone last night. I was here. I'm the one who threw the ball that put that lump on your head. I saw your face. I mean, I *saw* your face!"

Marti starts to plead but Ruby manages to shut her down with the simple wave of a finger. Shutting Stax down isn't likely to be quite as easy.

"Illusions, Miss Stax. What you saw and what actually occurred are not, in this instance, one and the same. All will be explained shortly."

"Hey, if you say so, I'm cool," Stax replies nonchalantly.

Say what? A simple word from Ruby and Stax is willing to believe what she saw—what *we* saw—wasn't real? What's more frustrating is I find myself willing to accept it as well. But not solely based on Ruby's word. The presence of Detective Bentley makes me think they have something up their sleeves.

Ruby puts her two skinny arms in the air and says "If everybody will settle back down I can continue with the narrative. Where were we before the arrival of the good detective and his merry band of lawmen? Ah, yes, the scissors! Let us talk about the scissors."

Everybody grabs a seat, anxious for an explanation as to why Marti is a free woman. Ruby resumes her public speaker stance and digs in.

"The scissors. Calypso Cut Scissors model nine. A very specific brand of barber scissor. They stopped manufacturing them in 2010, and yet Marlene's stalker must have had several in his or her possession. This, to my mind, was an important clue. Either the individual is themselves a hair stylist and maintained a collection of instruments from yesteryear, or else we are dealing with a diabolical mind with an eye for detail. I see no reason for a hair stylist to want to murder Marlene, except, perhaps, for the way in which she'd occasionally curl just the bangs on one side, but I digress.

"Whoever murdered Marlene moves within her sphere and possesses intimate details regarding the murder of Kayleigh Cook. You see, information about the weapon used to kill Miss Cook was never released to the press. That knowledge was possessed only by those closest to the case: the investigators, Marlene—"

"And the girl's killer, of course," observes young Billy, who rarely speaks unless forced.

"Yes, the killer would certainly have known."

"And the killer of this Cook girl, that's who you think murdered Marlene?"

"No, young man. The diabolical mind I'm describing had no involvement with the murder eighteen years ago."

"How can you be sure?"

"Because I know who killed Kayleigh Cook."

This statement brings forth a collective gasp from a group quickly growing tired of gasping.

"Or at least who the one eye witness believes killed Miss Cook. But we're getting ahead of ourselves again," continues Ruby. "I must finish with the scissors business so I can get on with answering the many burning questions you have. And believe me, I wouldn't waste your time if I did not already possess the answers to the most salient questions posed by these mysteries.

"But the scissors! Whoever had been leaving these terrifying tools for Marlene to discover must also be the same individual who visited Lacy's home in the middle of the night to do the same. It's hard to conceive of yet another individual learning the make and model of these scissors, hunting a pair down at last minute, and deciding the thing to do with them was to leave them embedded in Lacy's porch."

There is a smattering of nods and concurring murmurs. This pleases Ruby and she pushes on. "So, this individual, the stalker, must have scoured the Internet, the auction sites, and whatever brick and mortar stores exist that sell old and used barber implements. This shows a decided focus and no lack of patience. As I said before, a very diabolical mind. But even the most patient mind can panic, and that is what happened to our stalker a few nights ago as Lacy and Gretchen lay innocently sleeping in their beds.

"Our stalker, anticipating the potential for cameras and witnesses, thought she could evade identification if she used a vehicle other than her own and an expensive wig to disguise her appearance. You know, it's a funny thing, but Inspector Butterwell—he's the fictional detective I used to write about—was fond of observing that the clever criminal seldom subscribes to the maxim of 'less is more' when working to conceal their skullduggery. In being so clever in their methods of concealment they inadvertently provide the keen-eyed investigator with the means to catch them. Such is the case with our midnight stalker."

Ruby pauses either for effect or to refill her lungs and you could have heard a safety pin drop. Everyone is glued to their chairs, with one exception. Someone in the room is shuffling and fidgeting, uncomfortable with the things Ruby is saying.

"Some of you might not be aware," Ruby goes on to say, "that the person who deposited the scissors into Lacy's front porch was witnessed not only by two of her neighbors but also the camera lens of the neighborhood convenience market where she parked. All spoke of a quality hairpiece of a deep red color. Now, had she purchased a cheap wig of the Halloween store variety, it would have proved impossible to trace. But I happen to know—and don't ask me how I know!—that there are only three shops in the metropolitan area specializing in realistic wigs of supreme quality. So, I set about visiting each of them.

"I never had the pleasure of making the acquaintance of the proprietor of the third, as upon my visit to the second shop—a lovely boutique with the unfortunate moniker of Gettin' Wiggy—I encountered a clerk with a keen eye and clear memory, to say nothing of receipts, who was able to assure me the wig in question could only have come from her store and was purchased by its owner some months ago. No expense was spared in having it tailored to fit her client's head. The apocryphal glass slipper, wouldn't you say?

"In any event, I now possess a witness with documentation who can prove who purchased the wig in question and when. Furthermore, while I was busy with this exercise, our good Detective Bentley was following up his own lead. It seems our *faux* ginger was the only person within a forty-eight-hour period to rent a vehicle of the make, model and color that appears in the convenience store video. You've guessed by now the renter of this vehicle and the purchaser of the hair piece are identical and proving as much will be a simple matter as soon as—Detective! Stop her, she's getting away!"

I hear a frantic commotion behind me and see both Jessica and Billy fly from their chairs. Detective Bentley makes a dash for the street door, followed by Chase, but both are a split-second late and their target makes it outside.

"Got her!" I hear a voice yell from outside. It is the uniformed police officer that Bentley posted on door duty. So *that* is why he brought the backup!

The culprit is brought back inside the store, her arms twisted behind her back, her hair flying at all angles, her face contorted into a mask of guilt and antipathy. The porch post poker, the midnight stalker, the sneerleader supreme herself—Carly Van Duson.

"You're caught, Carly," Ruby says, her voice suffused with resolution.

"Hah!" Carly snarls, "you can't prove a thing."

"I believe I already have. If I'm mistaken in my evidence, you've done little to help your case by bolting for it as you've just done."

"I know a frame-up when I see one."

"Once the police have access to your electronic gadgets, I'm sure they'll uncover a wealth of data, not the least of which will be your purchase of the many scissors used in your campaign of terror. That should be more than enough to make a firm believer of even the most open-minded of jurors, don't you think?"

The uniformed officer, whose name is not known to me but who possesses an impeccable sense of timing, pulls Carly's cell phone from her purse. Carly looks upon it as one would a spurning lover. Her cheeks quiver, her jaw melts, and her resolve gives way.

"What's the point of lying? I did it."

The atmosphere is suddenly electric and I expect Ruby to jump for joy, but she remains unmoved. Here is the vindication she celebrated. I'm not too proud to say I feel a small sense of vindication myself, as I had been screaming from the rooftops (metaphorically speaking only, as I'm not a nut case) that Carly had to be the murderer. It was Ruby who fought against me on the idea. But to her credit, she's the one who uncovered the proof it was Carly and not Marti, in spite of what my own eyes told me last night.

Carly looked beaten a moment before, when she uttered her confession, but when I turn my eyes back to her I see her body stiffen. It's as though she's grown two inches in as many seconds. The muscles in her neck swell and her jaw juts forward. There is a ferocity in her eye now.

"I did it and for good reason. Anderson loves me; he doesn't love Marlene. But he wouldn't leave her. I tried to accept that, but I can't. And when I realized there is no way I could make him leave her, my only option was to make *her* leave *him*. And it was working! You could see that, right?"

Bentley motions with his finger for the officer to take custody of her again. "That's about enough from you. Why don't you go with this gentleman to the station where you and I can have us a nice little chat."

Ruby steps forward, waving a white, slender finger at Bentley. "Wait! I have one more question for Carly, if she doesn't mind."

Bentley shrugs his consent. I imagine he's thinking that if she is willing to talk without a lawyer present, let her talk. Ruby dives in, not waiting for Carly's consent.

"Before the Chicken Hill Run, we were all present to witness Marlene finding the scissors embedded in her car tire. Would I be correct in surmising this was the last pair of barber scissors you had in your possession?"

"Yes, but—"

"You realized a pair of scissors you planted in Marlene's office had gone undiscovered, but would be found once her disappearance was investigated, so you broke into the office to retrieve them. And these were the scissors you left in Lacy's porch. Would that be correct?"

"It's correct, yes, but…how? Are you psychic, or a witch, or something?"

It was like my stomach ate my heart for lunch. Is Ruby about to tell Carly—in front of Detective Bentley—that we broke into Marlene's office and were present when the 'real' break-in took place? I wonder if the food in jail is as bad as they say. Will an orange jumpsuit wash out my skin?

Ruby laughs. "My dear, I'm no more psychic than you are rational. I expected the break-in of the Petrick Travel Agency would somehow be related to the other events in the case. You couldn't have an inexhaustible supply of Calypso Cut scissors at your disposal, so I deduced you perpetrated the burglary with the objective of removing something that might implicate you. Given your *modus operandi*, what else could it have been but scissors?"

Carly gapes and backs up into the officer holding her arms. "Get me out of here. This woman is creeping me out."

Bentley taps the officer's shoulder. "You go ahead. I'm not done here yet."

The officer escorts Carly out the door. We all shuffle to the display window to rubberneck her final walk in the open air. With a first-degree murder charge, Carly will never be a free woman again.

As the officer ushers her around the corner and out of sight I realize someone in the store is crying. It's Gretchen. She has wadded herself into a ball and is crying into her hands.

I kneel down to offer comfort. "Gretchen, hun, what's wrong?"

I know what's wrong, of course. She's been terrorized by an unknown killer who is no longer unknown but revealed as her good friend. And she'd been there to see her confess and get hauled off.

"I just can't believe it," Gretchen says, her voice high and raspy. "How could I not have known it was Carly? All this time…"

I feel bad for the girl, but my cynical side recognizes that she is young. Perhaps it isn't such a bad thing she learned now that sometimes people aren't who you take them to be.

Gretchen recovers her composure and now it's everyone else's turn to react and blurt their feelings. Billy is shocked but Jessica says she saw it coming. Marti sort of feels bad for Carly but Chase wants to wring her neck. Stax ponders becoming mayor of Cedar Mill and bringing back public hangings in the town square, with Carly first on the list to take the long walk. I'm pretty sure there have never been public hangings in Cedar Mill, but Stax doesn't care. As for me, I still have questions. A lot of them.

"How long have you known about Carly?" I ask Ruby.

"Known? Not for long."

"Suspected?"

"Oh, for quite some time."

I could have used one of those massage balls now as a stress ball. I would have squeezed it flat. "I don't get it. If you suspected Carly, why did you give me such a hard time when I laid out my case for her being the murderer?"

Ruby reels and looks at me as though I'd accused *her* of murder. "Being the mur—oh my, there's been a grave misunderstanding."

"I'll say there has, but I don't know. I think I was pretty clear about my suspicions against Carly."

"No, it's *you* who has misunderstood. Carly is no more a murderer than you are!"

TWENTY-FIVE

S tax sidles up to Bentley. "Detective, did I hear you say you have more business to attend to here?"

"You did," he replies.

"Would this business happen to be asking my friend here out on a date?"

She grabs my arm and pulls me over. I was too busy emoting into a big pile of goo to beat Stax's head in with my bare fists.

"What? No, that's not... not that I wouldn't, it's just... I have—"

"It's all right, Detective," I say. "You're off the hook. I have an idea why you're sticking around."

"If it's to ask me out," Stax says, "you already know the answer. But don't take me for Italian on our first date unless you want to kiss a girl with tomato sauce all over her face."

"It's because he has another arrest to make," I say. Bentley blinks his eyes, which I guess is a cop's way of nodding.

Stax backs off. "In that case, keep me off your radar, dude. But I'm getting confused with all these arrests. First Marti was the killer, now Carly, but it wasn't Carly who jumped you last night. It wasn't Carly I raspberry'd with the massage ball. So, maybe Marti and Carly were accomplices in Marlene's murder?"

What Stax lacks in a personal filter she also lacks in volume control. Everyone who surrounds Marti, offering their support, are now stepping away from her.

"Oh, for crying out loud! Would you all stop?" Marti exclaimed, flustered. "I am not a murderer!"

"Marti is correct," Ruby says. "I thought we'd established that she is as pure as fresh snow. At least as far as current events are concerned. While not nearly as pure, Miss Carly is also free of any charge of murder."

I am beyond frustrated with my little old friend, and from the cries of consternation ringing out, I'm not alone.

Bentley motions everyone to cease. "Everyone, settle down. Ruby, should I explain?"

The room quiets. "That won't be necessary, Detective. I'm happy to elucidate matters."

"First time for everything," mutters Stax. If Ruby heard her, she offers no acknowledgement.

"Carly confessed all right, and it was an honest confession. But what she confessed to was not the murder of Marlene Petrick, or the assault upon Lacy's person. She confessed—and is indeed guilty of—the stalking of Marlene prior to her murder, the breaking and entering of Marlene's offices to remove a pair of scissors she planted, and the vandalism of Miss Lacy's house with said scissors. But not murder."

"Are you sure of this?" asks an incredulous Chase.

Ruby bobs her head. "Carly is a misguided soul with terrible taste in men, but she's no murderer."

It is Detective Bentley's turn to be incredulous. "How *can* you be so certain?"

"It's simple. Think about the scissors. Carly went to great lengths to procure the exact model of scissors used in Marlene's shop almost twenty years ago. The same scissors used in the murder of Kayleigh Cook. And yet a different kind of barber scissor was found with Marlene's body and used in the attack on Lacy right here in this store. Those scissors, I'd wager, were plucked off the racks of a local store without too much thought. Carly is too meticulous for that. Our stalker and our killer cannot be one and the same."

Marti looks up from her chair, eyes dancing. "Which means…"

"The killer is still among us."

We all look around at one another for a hint as to who conceals the darkest secret known to man—what it is like to take a fellow human's life. I see nothing except fear, wonder, and in one case, annoyance.

"Don't even be looking at me," barks Stax.

Ruby clears her throat. "First things first, I think we deal with the events last night involving these young ladies." She motions to Stax, Marti, and myself. "Miss Stax, in a nutshell, what did you see last night?"

"I saw Marti run out from the back and stab Lacy with a pair of scissors. Sorry, Marti, she asked what I saw and that's what I saw."

Ruby stares at her feet. "Now, Lacy, tell me what you saw. Only walk us through the details."

I recount the story of finding the note from Marti on my door and traveling to the store with Stax and Ruby. Ruby waits in the car as Stax and I approach the store from the side entrance, where we find three massage balls rolling around loose. We pick these up and enter. The store is dark, but because of the floor to ceiling windows on the street side there is some backlighting. We can see the shelves and racks have been upturned.

I close my eyes and recount hearing someone rush from the back rooms and felt them slam into me, then the sharp pain in my arm, and seeing the fleeing figure drop to the floor behind the sales counter as Stax rocketed one of the hard massage balls at it. We waste no time in investigating and discover the figure in the hoodie is Marti.

Ruby is still staring at the floor, still nodding, her fluffy white hair bouncing around. "I believe you did as you were expected to do. You saw what someone wanted you to see. But none of it was real."

I glance down at my left bicep, where a bandage covers a still-healing wound. *This sure feels real enough.*

"It was no hologram, I'll tell you that," Stax says, unconvinced.

Ruby smiles. "Those massage balls you found outside the entrance...they did not roll themselves outside. They were placed there in the hopes you'd pick them and throw them at the assailant. You will be pleased to know, Lacy, there was no intention of causing you serious harm. But an assault had to be made in order to frame Marti."

"About Marti," I say, recalling the moment when the hoodie was pulled back and I saw her face.

"What you haven't yet been told is that you were not the first assault victim last night. That honor falls to

Marti. As she tells it, she was locking the store up for the night when somebody accosted her from behind, hitting her over the head with goodness knows what, probably one of those balls. She remembers nothing else until the moment she was revived at the hospital, but the rest of the story can be inferred from the evidence.

"The Phantom—that's my name for this particular miscreant—used Marti's keys to gain entrance to the store, dragged Marti inside, and pulled matching hoodies off the racks so they'd be dressed identically. I can't speak as to what pants the Phantom wore, but I presume it was banking on you not getting too good a look with the lights off. I asked Billy to check the inventory of the black hoodies and, as expected, two are unaccounted for. Once Marti was dressed, she was dragged behind the counter and placed where you would later find her."

"So, you're saying when this person—the Phantom—stabbed me and ran behind the counter, he or she expected us to throw the ball?"

"Indeed! Now you're getting it. When Stax threw the ball and shattered the glass case, the Phantom dropped down. You thought you hit a bullseye, but I'm sorry to inform you, Miss Stax, your aim is not as true as you think. The pitch went wild and hit nothing but the glass of the case. Only a direct hit could shatter glass that thick, and the ball was to be found resting inside the case. But none of this mattered in the moment. The Phantom took the fall, abandoned the scissors near Marti's right hand, and scurried out the front entrance."

I am beginning to get the picture. "So that's why the front entrance door was left ajar."

Stax thrust her stubby finger in front of my face. "And why that big pile of shelves was put where it was! That way, nobody could see him—her—it—escape!"

"Precisely!" Ruby says, excited to see us finally catching on. "Other areas of the room were tossed around a bit to give the impression that Marti lost her mind and ransacked her own store. But all real effort was put into the barricade of sorts that ran from the far counter exit to the front door. Once the significance of the construction occurred to me, the rest fell into place. From where you stood, you would not be able to see the Phantom creep across the floor and out the door."

"But wait," I say. "What if Stax had not thrown the ball?"

"Oh, that's easy. He or she was going to take the dive regardless. You would have assumed Marti slipped in the escape and hit her head."

She seems to have an answer for everything. Well, almost everything...

"Wait again. You just said 'he or she'. But don't you know who the killer is?"

"Oh yes, I know perfectly well who it is. But I'm not playing that card just yet."

"Building suspense, right? Like in your books," Stax says.

"That might be a tiny part of it," Ruby admits, pinching two pruned fingers together. "I'm hoping the guilty party will choose to step forward themselves."

"Do you know what the purpose was?" I ask.

"You mean why Marlene was murdered? Yes, I have an idea."

"No, not that. I meant why the charade last night with Marti and myself. Why the note on the door? And the photographs…"

I'd almost forgotten about the photos. Whatever else might be an illusion, those are not. Chase might not be a killer, but he's certainly a letch.

"The Phantom realized the good detective here is no slouch, and it was only a matter of time before things started to get hot. The purpose of last night was to cast suspicion on Marti, and therefore away from themselves. Similar to Carly's motive for stabbing your porch."

"Well, if anyone else is looking to commit a crime, please find yourself another fall guy. My dance card is full."

Marti clears her throat. "About those photos the police found on my desk. I suppose you all saw them? You should know they aren't mine. I've never seen them before."

"Oh, honey. You poor thing," Stax says, pulling Marti in for a hug. Glaring at Chase, she says "Looks like there's no shortage of villains around here."

"Villain?" says a confused Marti. "No, Chase explained everything."

"Oh, I'm sure he did."

"Easy, Stax," Chase says. "I'm standing right here."

"So I see. If you were my husband, standing wouldn't be an option."

Ruby giggles. "Chase, would you like to explain the photographs?"

Chase bristles. "I hate that it has to be explained at all. It was supposed to be a surprise."

"Oh, honey, it was a surprise," Marti says, grabbing his arm. To the rest of us, she says "He was doing it for me."

"You wanted him to have an affair with Marlene?" asks Stax. "If that's modern marriage, I think I'll stay single."

I did the only thing a person can do when they have a friend like Stax. I pounded my head on the counter.

Chase looks scandalized. "Affair? No! I was going behind Marti's back, all right, but it was to plan a vacation in January when things slow down at the store. Get her out of Oklahoma for the winter and someplace warm. I was seeing Marlene to discuss travel options."

"Is that true?" asks Stax.

Bentley nods. "It's true. I confirmed it with Anderson Petrick today. Even saw the paperwork they'd started."

I recall what I'd witnessed driving past the agency and couldn't keep my mouth shut. "I happened to be driving past the travel agency when I saw you leaving, Chase. You and Anderson were having words. It looked pretty heated."

Chase goes pale and I regret the question. But there are too many loose ends in this case that still needed tying up.

"It was heated. *I* was heated. And I'm sorry you had to witness that. After Marlene's murder and the press surrounding it, I knew there'd be negative impact to the store. Marti and I wouldn't be able to afford the vacation if that happened, so I went to cancel the trip and get my deposit back. Anderson refused to relinquish my deposit money. That's what the argument was about."

"Sorry, Chase. My bad. You're not the big heel I thought," Stax says with genuine sincerity.

He throws a big, muscled arm around her. "It's not your fault. Someone was obviously trying to set us up."

"Enough about the photographs," I say. "Tell us who the killer is!"

"Funny thing about that," Bentley says. "Those photos of Chase and Marlene are going to go a long way in proving the case against our suspect."

Stax squints her eyes suspiciously at Bentley. "You'd better not tell me Chase is the killer after I just apologized to him."

"No, your apology is valid. The photos are important because we know exactly when and where they were taken, and with the help of the surveillance cameras along Main Street, it won't be a thing at all to identify the photographer. My guys are working on it as we speak."

"Because whoever took those pictures is the one who planted them and therefore—"

"The one who attacked Lacy and murdered Marlene, yep."

"Are you ever going to tell us who it is?" Gretchen asks. "I don't want to be rude, but I have work I've got to do before bed."

"I thought you quit your job?" asks Ruby.

"I did, but I have a small business of my own, with orders to fill."

"Yes, the Survival List, is that what it's called?"

"You're familiar?"

"I'm a customer. I purchased one of your hand-made ghillie suits. I must say, I am quite impressed with your stitching."

Gretchen looks pleased with the compliment. "Oh, is that right? I'm glad you like it. I won an award for my stitching, you know. But I don't really see you as the crawling-around-the-forest type."

"You're correct on that count. I'm more the type who wondered if your materials would match the strange fabric Marti discovered on Chicken Hill when Marlene disappeared. You won't be surprised to learn they're both a substance called jute. Oh, the sample Marti collected and gave to me wouldn't be admissible as evidence, of course. Chain of custody, and all that. But I understand the police collected their own, much larger, sample at the time. Their findings should be quite interesting, indeed."

"I use jute for some of my items. What of it? A lot of ghillie suits are made with jute and you'd expect to find them in the woods."

"Not in woods where no hunting is allowed. And how many others use your same award-winning stitching techniques?"

Gretchen is standing next to me and I can make out the corner of her eye twitch and the edges of her mouth pull down as her jaw muscles stiffen. It is like the beginning stages of a physical transformation.

"What are you trying to say?" she asks through gritted teeth.

"Nothing that can't be proved, dear."

"And what it is you think you can prove?"

Ruby inhales deeply through her nose, though what she had to say would not require much lung power.

"I can prove you murdered Marlene Petrick."

TWENTY-SIX

I sat outside atop cold concrete, under a brilliant moon, and watched as my friend was cuffed, read her rights, and loaded into a police cruiser. Diebold got the honor this time.

I don't want to believe it. When Ruby leveled her accusation, my instinct was again to jump to Gretchen's defense. But I held back. If someone accused Stax or Ruby of something so heinous, I wouldn't hesitate for a moment to speak up on their behalf. So, I take some solace in knowing (or choosing to believe) that my subconscious saw beneath Gretchen's veneer to the dark soul underneath.

When Ruby accused her of the murder, her eyes wanted to shred Ruby and the rest of us to little pieces, but her mouth pointed out she'd had the fastest run time of them all on Chicken Hill and was within everyone's sight the entire time. I'd observed the same thing before and said as much. Her alibi was perfect. There's no way she could have murdered Marlene and made her disappear without losing a step in her run.

But Ruby clearly didn't think it was impossible. All she said in response to Gretchen was 'The detective has warrants. We'll find the saw, the wheelbarrow, and everything else.' The words were Greek to me, but they hit home to Gretchen and her entire face transformed. She went from being my young, freckled ginger-haired running buddy to the nightmarish Phantom Ruby so loved to describe.

I knew then it was true. Gretchen attacked me. She lied to me. I'm not sure which is worse. But nothing she did to Marti or myself trumps the fact that she murdered Marlene. And came to stay with me after, which means I harbored a murderer. I should drywall over the door to the spare room and forget it's there.

I am sitting on the curb edge of the parking lot and hear a voice behind me say something. I am too lost in my own thoughts to hear it. Something about a friend. I turn. It's Ruby. She steps off the curb and stands next to me.

"What's that?" I ask.

"I said she never was your friend."

"Were you reading my mind?"

"Why does everyone think I'm psychic?"

"Bless you for asking that. Yes, I know she's not— never was—my friend. I should have seen it sooner."

"There's no way you could have. Unless you think like she does. And you don't."

"And you do?"

"Darling, I made a good living for many years thinking like a criminal. I'm not proud of it, *per se*, nor am I ashamed. You shouldn't feel shame over not thinking like a criminal. If you're not a writer, or a detective, it's more a liability than an asset."

"How did she do it, Ruby?" I sound more pleading than I intended, but I need to know how the guilty party is the person with the best alibi.

Ruby exhales deeply and I see her in the moonlight, not as some superhuman crime fighter with almost paranormal instinct, but for what she is—an elderly woman who's been on her feet all day sleuthing around town and all evening bringing criminals to justice. She looks exhausted. I decide my curiosity will still be there in the morning.

"On second thought, Ruby, I'm too tired to think any more tonight. Maybe we could all reconvene tomorrow?"

Ruby lays a hand on my shoulder. "That sounds like an evening well spent. But how about we make it just Stax and ourselves. Chase and Marti know all they need to know, and whatever Jessica and Billy would like to learn they're welcome to learn from their employers."

I reach a hand up and put it across Ruby's, which is still resting on my shoulder. We stay like that for a good minute. It was a good minute.

The next day is uneventful. I had to explain to both Caroline and Bill (as well as half the people who called in about their policies) that yes, a young lady was arrested for the murder and yes, I was present, and no, I wasn't complicit. A photograph of the Run For It parking lot made it into the paper and there I was, sitting on the curb, facing the camera. Chase and Marti won't be happy about the negative publicity, but with their spirit and work ethic I have complete confidence they'll rebound stronger than before. And I intend to stick with them and the store.

After work and a light supper, I head over to Ruby's for the prearranged rap session in her war room. I allow the combined smells of mahogany and old paper to calm me as I sink into one of the big leather chairs. I choose the same one I sat in the previous time. Stax does the same. We've staked our territory. I hope it's a sign we're forming a tradition of spending more time here.

Stax is so relaxed in her chair that I suspect she's fallen asleep waiting for Ruby and her tray of *hors d'oeuvres*. Then she speaks.

"Did that detective ask you out yet? Because he should."

"No, Stax. He hasn't."

"Stupid."

"Maybe."

"Have you asked him out?"

"No."

"Stupid."

"Maybe."

The door swings open and in floats Ruby, humming a song and bouncing at the knees. It is as though all the weight of the world has been lifted from her shoulders. In some ways, I suppose it has.

She offers us a tray of shrimp remoulade deviled eggs, which, in spite of their name, are to die for. We establish a pattern of not talking 'business' while we eat, but the eggs are so good they don't hold us up for long.

"I understand you have some questions for me?" asks Ruby.

"Understate much?" Stax says with a mouthful of remoulade.

Ruby looks perplexed. "I don't follow."

I touch her arm. "She means yes, we have a bunch of questions for you."

Ruby pours us each a cup of hot caffeine-free cinnamon tea. "I suppose you want to know why Gretchen did it?"

I am most curious about how she pulled it off, but if Ruby wants to start at why, I am fine with that.

"Gretchen Herring came into this world as Gretchen Ross," Ruby begins. "Ross was her absentee father's name. A crook who spent more time in jail than out. Her mother, an orphan, did all she could for young Gretchen, including take her to work with her when need be. That's precisely what happened on the evening of June 23rd in the year two-thousand Anno Domini. Kayleigh Cook had to work the 1pm to closing shift at the hair salon and brought young Gretchen with her."

"Gretchen was Kayleigh's daughter," I heard myself say.

"Oh snap," Stax says. "You mean she saw—"

"Her mother murdered?" continues Ruby. "Yes, I'm afraid she did."

"How tragic," I say. In spite of what she's done, I can't help but feel sorry for what she experienced. Nobody should have to see their mother murdered. "But wait a minute. If she saw her mom, then—"

Stax snaps her fingers. "She must have seen the murderer as well."

Ruby put her hands together over her heart. "You girls make me proud. Such fast learners! Yes, Gretchen believed her mission was to avenge the death of her mother... by killing her murderer."

"Marlene?" I shout. In the name of decency, I won't mention Stax's choice of words in this moment. Suffice it to say she was more surprised than myself. "Are you sure?"

Ruby slowly shakes her head. "No, I'm not. I'm not sure about anything other than Gretchen was present that night. My private investigator turned up this little nugget. She told investigators at the time she'd seen nothing. I'm inclined to believe that was the truth and what Gretchen believes now is a product of her malignant mind. But who knows? She may, even at the age of four, have been plotting her eventual revenge.

"In any event, vengeance for her mother's death is only a part of Gretchen's motive. There's the man she calls her father, who is actually her uncle, and I daresay he falls short of both distinctions. Detective Bentley told me he has quite the reputation at the police station."

"He's a criminal?" I ask.

"Yes, more or less. But he could have learned a thing or two from Gretchen. She's one of the most calculating criminals I'm aware of. Gretchen hated living with the man and blamed her poor fortune on Marlene."

"Gretchen?" Stax says. "I always thought she was all foam, no beer."

"Is that a reference to her intelligence?" asks Ruby. "I can't speak to that, but as to her cunning, I hope we never meet her equal. It's no coincidence she ended up working for the Petricks. She finagled her way in there. She's been driving a wedge between Marlene and anyone who came into her sphere ever since. And nobody was any the wiser."

"How can you know that?" I ask.

"Remember how you told me you knew all the nasty things Marlene and Carly were saying behind your back?"

"Yes, Gretchen told me. But…oh."

Ruby gave me a knowing wink. "And I'd wager she was in Marlene's ear with similar tales about you."

"Why me?"

"Because people like you. Marti likes you. Alienate Marlene from you and whose side do you think everyone else will pick? I mean, geez, Marlene had two friends—one tried to drive her crazy so she could steal her husband, and the other murdered her."

"My goodness, it was Gretchen who introduced Carly to Marlene. And to—"

"Anderson," Stax says. "If this were a Shonda Rhimes show, Gretchen would be my favorite character. But as a real-world person, she totally sucks."

Ruby sips her tea. "She wanted to ruin Marlene's life, one person at a time. I believe the objective was to drive her out of her mind."

A thought occurs to me. "Do you think she put the idea in Carly's mind to do what she did with the scissors?"

"I don't believe so. Gretchen's strength is in not allowing anyone to see beneath her veneer. Carly is too much of a—how do you say?—loose cannon. No, no, far too risky."

"So, Carly stalking Marlene as Gretchen set her sights on murdering her was just a coincidence?"

"I'm not a big believer in coincidences. Not where murder is concerned. I believe killing Marlene was always to be Gretchen's final play, but I suspect Carly's stalking provided Gretchen with the inspiration to undertake the deed sooner rather than later. Working side by side with Marlene, she'd have been privy to her terror each time a new pair of scissors was discovered. Gretchen didn't know who was behind it, but she expected that if Marlene was murdered and the police tracked down the stalker, that person would be arrested for the murder as well. That is, if Gretchen could devise a method of murder so diabolical as to appear almost magical. She could worry about framing a person later if the police hadn't done as much for her. So long as the evidence didn't lead back to her."

I glance over at Stax who is looking at me with that knowing smile. She nods in Ruby's direction. I know what she means.

"No, you ask."

"Huh uh. She likes you better."

"Does not."

"Does so."

"Not. Now ask."

"Nope."

"Chicken."

"Cock-a-doodle-doo!"

Ruby's tea saucer hits the table with a rattle. "What are you two on about?"

Something about Ruby's face makes me spit it out. I ask the question that has been poking at my brain for days. However, Stax blurts out at the same time and the result of our combined enthusiasm is something akin to a banshee scream.

"Goodness, I see why you two cling to me so. You need an adult guardian."

"What we want to know," I say, "what we've been *dying* to know, is how did Gretchen make Marlene disappear from Chicken Hill?"

Ruby makes us wait as she peddles off to the kitchen to fetch more tea. I suspect she is torturing us. But once she settles herself back into her chair with a warm cup, she gives us the goods.

When Marlene started finding Carly's scissors, Ruby pointed out, Gretchen would have realized she'd been presented with both a great opportunity to murder her nemesis and the perfect fall guy in whoever was harassing her. So, Gretchen purchased her own scissors (unwittingly, the wrong size and model) and waited for her opportunity.

While stalking Marlene along the trails of Chicken Hill, she sees her boss is not merely training for a run but preparing to cheat in order to beat the times of her younger, stronger employee. This would further enrage an already vengeful Gretchen who decides Marlene's lonely trek across the wooded area would be the perfect place to strike. After all, Marlene herself would see to it she wasn't witnessed, and nobody would look for her there right away.

However, they would soon look for her, and when they did, Gretchen had to make sure they couldn't see her.

But first, the murder.

Ruby reminds me of the tiny sliver of paper she found embedded in a hole in the big tree just off Marlene's secret path. She also references the missing branch, the odd piece of jute material, and the deep impression in the grass running back towards the path in a different direction. This is the sum total of evidence that served to tell Ruby how the murder had been committed.

By following Marlene, Gretchen knew the spot in the run where Marlene would deviate into the woods to cut her run short and finish with a faster time. The night before the run, Gretchen went to this trail and followed Marlene's footsteps along the path. The big tree stood out as being perfect for her trap. And a trap it was! At this point, Ruby produced some literature emblazoned with the familiar logo of The Survival List. Apparently, Gretchen's side business is combining the skills of construction she picked up from her adoptive father with her love of sewing and stitching to create items specifically for that colorful group who believes either the world is coming to an end or coming after them.

Ruby draws our attention to an item in Gretchen's pamphlet titled the 'Dead Fall'. It's quite different from the more well-known trap of the same name where a large hole is dug in the ground and floored with spikes or spears. The description says this Dead Fall is based on traps early settlers would set to catch larger game, but thanks to The Survival List, the modern frontiersman doesn't need to collect wood or pound a hammer to develop such a trap. All he needs is his credit card.

The illustration shows a contraption both intricate and simplistic. A large wood mallet is positioned on a strong branch in a tall tree and, using a system of camouflaged ropes and pullies, it attaches to a hunk of meat on the ground. When the animal takes the meat in its mouth, it pulls a string that activates a lever that shifts the weight to the heavy mallet, causing it to fall with speed and precision, killing or stunning the animal. The hunter can then move in and finish the job.

It is gruesome to imagine such a trap used on wild game. I don't have to imagine what it can do to a person. I've seen it myself, on display in the little gravel alleyway in the old neighborhood behind Main Street.

Ruby explains how Gretchen drew Marlene into her trap. The tiny folded piece of paper gave the trick away. Gretchen left a paper note stuck to the tree with a pair of scissors, probably with Marlene's own name emblazoned on the outside. The paper was folded with the message (Marlene would presume) inside, so she had to remove the scissors to read the note. Distracted by the note, she failed to notice the string attached to the scissors, or the mechanisms overhead. It was over before she knew it.

Meanwhile, Gretchen remained in sight of the other runners, and after being an early finisher, she stayed in the open so that every moment of her time could be accounted for. She knew it was only a matter of time before Carly or someone noticed Marlene hadn't made it through and then only a short wait until someone got the idea for an impromptu search party. Failing that, she could always present the idea herself.

Once the search party was suggested, she volunteered and made sure she maneuvered herself into the area of the big tree. She allotted herself a limited amount of time to make Marlene and the crime scene disappear.

Ruby reminds me how the missing branch had been sawed only halfway through. What remained had been torn or ripped free. Gretchen must have cut the branch to a depth where it could maintain the weight of the mallet, but little else, so upon returning to the scene, she had only to climb to it and hang off, using her weight to break it free from the tree. She tossed the branch with the pullies and ropes onto Marlene's body, along with the note and scissors. From a secret place nearby, she retrieved the length of ghillie she'd created for this purpose.

The ghillie so resembled the surrounding terrain that, once placed over Marlene and the evidence, it would essentially make it disappear. If someone didn't physically walk across the ghillie, they'd have no idea of what was under it. Gretchen would have completed this entire exercise in one or two minutes and rejoined her search party before her wanderings became obvious.

Gretchen knew that with a missing person she'd have at least twenty-four hours before the police searched in earnest. So, late that night, she returned to Chicken Hill under cloak of darkness, with—according to Ruby—a pick-up truck and a wheelbarrow. The wheelbarrow is evinced by the deep line embedded in the grass leading away from the big tree and back towards the path. The truck was inferred by the presence of the wheelbarrow. Gretchen is strong enough to move Marlene's body by herself, so an accomplice wouldn't be assumed, but she must have borrowed the truck and barrow from someone. Almost certainly her father.

Gretchen must have stored Marlene someplace prior to dumping her in the alley, believing we'd find her there with Carly leading the run. The scissors left imbedded in the light pole, Ruby noted, were an afterthought on Gretchen's part, probably conceived the day we all witnessed the scissors lodged in Carly's tire.

As for the note left on my door that drew me into her trap, it was indeed in Marti's handwriting, but she says it was one she'd left for Marlene at her office the previous year when she couldn't find her at home. Gretchen most likely discovered it in or on Marlene's cluttered desk.

Ruby's detailed description of the murder of Marlene Petrick checks all the boxes. I am convinced. But I know a theory alone does not convict, so I ask where her evidence is for all this. Ruby said science would put the nail in Gretchen's coffin: There were three paper samples she was certain would match in a comparison—the paper sliver from the tree, the loose paper left at my house, and the invoice Ruby received when she ordered (under an assumed name) the ghillie material from Gretchen's business.

Her own commissioned scientist confirmed the material found by Marti in the woods matched Gretchen's ghillie suit, and more advanced tests by the police should confirm the two are one and the same, to say nothing of the hand-stitching used.

Then there's the matter of what the warrants would turn up; her father's truck, wheelbarrow, and the abandoned garage under her apartment should turn up enough DNA to force a confession or win a conviction.

"Oh dear, we're out of tea," complains Ruby, as though such a travesty is on par with the devilish doings we'd been discussing. "I could make more, if you'd like."

"Forget that," Stax says as she stands. "Let's go get tacos. On me."

"I've never seen tacos on Larry's menu," I observe, recalling how the menu of the little bookstore deli could fit on a postcard.

Stax feigns offense. "I'm not chained to my store, you know. I do venture out for cuisine from time to time."

"But you hate Mexican!"

Stax purses her lips and taps the arm of her glasses as though deep in thought. I hope I haven't talked her out of tacos, because they sound pretty amazing right now. "Can you really call tacos Mexican food? I like to think of them more as crunch burgers."

"You win," I say. I'd have agreed with anything she said if it ended in me eating tacos. "What about you, Ruby?"

Ruby grabs her purse. "Your treat, you say? Then make mine a double-decker."

EPILOGUE

Marti and Chase were convinced their days as running store proprietors were over, but Carly and Gretchen became the focus of the news stories and any connection to Run For It faded into the background. Within a few weeks, the running groups were back to near capacity and the Reynoldses are once again discussing the possibility of a much-needed vacation.

I agreed to remain run leader for our group. I initially didn't think I was up to snuff, but in time I came to enjoy the people and the freedom the position allows. I can mix up our run routes and adjust our pace according to the needs of the group members. In the course of helping others do their best, I'm not too humble to brag, I set not one, but two, personal records.

I remained dateless throughout the summer but life was good. I enjoyed time helping Stax out at the bookstore, grabbing tacos (of the regular and chocolate variety) during our downtime, and late evening talks with Ruby surrounded by her past treasures.

With the case coming to an end, I didn't see much of Detective Bentley. I thought about dropping by the station to say hi to him, but I decided that was a bit too forward and it was best to just wait for a chance meeting at the grocery store, or something. I'm still waiting.

From the press we learned everything Ruby had surmised was proved true in the investigation. Gretchen confessed to everything. The police were keen to indict her father as an accessory, but Gretchen swore up and down it had been all her from start to finish.

Anderson Petrick cleaned up on the life insurance policy he held on Marlene (I know this because the Leffertys had sold him the policy and I answered the phone when he called to collect) and left town. Nobody asked where he was going. Nobody cared. It turned out he had inadvertently provided Carly with information about the Kayleigh Cook murder by way of late night talks which led to him showing her some documents hidden away at the office. Over time she borrowed these and made copies.

Carly fared far better than did Gretchen in court. She hadn't committed any acts of violence and her primary complainant was dead. I agreed not to press charges for vandalism if she agreed to seek psychiatric help. I wish her the best, but it's not likely we'll see her around Run For It again, and for that I'm not the least bit sorry.

What had easily been one of the most eventful summers of my life tapered off into a warm, leafy fall and then a snowless Christmas; the first Christmas with my new extended Cedar Mill family.

It was a wonderful time. And then came February and Valentine's Day. Not the best time of year when you're single.

Or if you want to stay alive.

Love can kill? You bet it can.

Why do you think Cupid is always armed?

THE END

COMING JANUARY 2019

Running from Arrows

ACKNOWLEDGEMENTS

My sincere thanks to Heather Swartz for introducing me to (and, for a time, immersing me in) the world of running. Without her influence and early support this book would not have happened. And to Bronwen Llewellyn for her indispensable skills in proofreading and copyediting. Any errors (real or perceived) remaining in the text are mine alone.